OPENING NIGHT KNIVES

OPENING NIGHT KNIVES

THE FOURTH BOBBIE FLYNN MYSTERY

JACK MURRAY

Books by Jack Murray

Kit Aston Mysteries.
The Affair of the Christmas Card Killer
The Chess Board Murders.
The Phantom Metropolitan Museum
The Frisco Falcon.
The Medium Murders
The Bluebeard Club
The Tangier Tajine
The Empire Theatre Murders
The Newmarket Murders
The New Year's Eve Murders
The French Diplomat Affair (novella)
Haymaker's Last Fight (novelette)

DI Jellicoe Mysteries
A Time to Kill
The Bus Stop
Dolce Vita Murders

Agatha Aston Mysteries
Black-Eyed Nick
The Witchfinder General Murders
The Christmas Murder Mystery
The Siegfried Slayer
The Brother's Grimoire

Danny Shaw / Manfred Brehme WWII Series
The Shadow of War
Crusader
El Alamein

The Bobbie Flynn Mysteries
A Little Miss Taken
Murder on Tin Pan Alley
Murder at the Opening Night Knives

Copyright © 2024 by Jack Murray

All rights reserved. No part of this publication may be reproduced, distributed, or transmitted in any form or by any means, including photocopying, recording, or other electronic or mechanical methods, without the prior written permission of the publisher, except in the case of brief quotations embodied in critical reviews and certain other non-commercial uses permitted by copyright law. For permission requests, write to the publisher, addressed 'Attention: Permissions Coordinator,' at the address below.

Jackmurray99@hotmail.com

This is a work of fiction. Names, characters, businesses, places, events, locales, and incidents are either the products of the author's imagination or used in a fictitious manner. Any resemblance to actual persons, living or dead, or actual events is purely coincidental.

Cover by Jack Murray
ISBN: 9798337503776
Imprint: Independently published

For Monica, Lavinia, Anne, and our angel, Baby Edward.

1

Century Playhouse, New York: April 1922

She performed the part of an accomplished actress, like the accomplished actress she was. She wasn't looking for truth in the character. She was the character. The audience knew this. It's why they were there. Not to have seen her return to Broadway would have meant entering many social circles on tip toe with a Japanese fan covering your face.

With bated breath, they watched her every move, hanging on her every word, as if it were a divine decree. They laughed at her jests, wept at her sorrows and sighed at her triumphs, swept away on a tide of emotion, that only she could evoke.

For in that moment, she was not merely an actress; she was a conduit for their dreams, their desires, their failures. When the final curtain fell, they would rise as one to acclaim her. Their applause would be a thunderous ovation, a testament to the power of art to move the soul.

Middle-aged, yet resplendent, her glory and her beauty remained, undiminished, despite nearing her fifth decade. She would always be a vision of grandeur and grace. From the first moment she had taken her place upon the stage, a collective gasp had rippled through the crowd, as if they were beholding a rare and wondrous marvel.

Sharing the stage with her were five other performers. All were very capable, but they had been chosen, specifically, because they would never match the lustre of the woman stood before them. They were only satellites orbiting a star.

The world knew and adored her as Crina Colbeck. Born Joyce Alexandrescu, she was a New Yorker, through and through, but her Bronx accent had long since given way to a veritable symphony of refined vowels and aristocratic cadences. It was the sound of a crisp autumn morning in Long Island, her voice akin to the bubbling of champagne in a crystal flute. Every syllable carefully enunciated, every consonant poised like a knife, ready to strike, the vowels, drawn out with a languid grace, seemed to linger in the air like French perfume. Yet, when she spoke it was quintessentially American.

Her voice was not just warm, it had a welcoming embrace that hinted at the old money from which she most certainly had not come Beneath its polished exterior there was a hint of mischief too. But not at that moment. Just then she was a tragedian. Sadness and desolation, the twin comforts of self-pity, suffused every syllable.

She was only minutes away from being murdered.

And she knew this.

Lane Vidal watched Crina trying to hide the feeling of awe, that at times had almost overwhelmed him, as he'd acted alongside her. Throughout the rehearsals, she blended into the troupe. Her star quality treated like a well-guarded secret, hidden beneath a veil of modesty and discretion. She eschewed the flamboyance of her profession, in favour of muted tones, as if embarrassed by her status as a theatrical luminary. It was only now he realised why she had done so.

He, like the others in the cast, had been like the crew of a galleon invaded by pirates, all about to walk the plank. The prospect of appearing on stage with her had terrified them all. And yet, the run throughs over the previous weeks had gone much more easily than he could have hoped for. Crina was human: generous, vulnerable, flawed.

Confidence had grown among the players. They would not be made to seem like the cast of an amateur theatrical appearing beside a legend of the stage.

Two hours of the opening night and that feeling had ebbed away, as they realised how far above them, she was. They were merely pootling around the foothills of Mount Olympus by comparison to this Goddess.

And he hated her for it.

Polly Buckley was closest to Crina as she declaimed the final words of the play. To watch her was like having a ringside seat at a fight. She, too, was seeing the legendary actress as if for the first time. A legend and yet so human. Upon her face subtle, yet expertly applied, cosmetics worked their magic, enhanced her features, with a touch of theatrical flair, creating a delicate balance between ageless glamour and the wisdom of years.

The fortnight of rehearsals seemed to evaporate, in the heat of this star's presence. The treasures revealed by this amazing woman had been kept locked away, until the moment she had stepped on the stage this evening and revealed them to an awestruck audience, and a captivated cast. Her first major role and all the work she had put in to understanding her character, in learning her lines, seemed to be redundant because no one would be looking at her despite her youth and her undeniable prettiness.

All eyes would be reserved for Crina Colbeck.

Watching the incredible performance unfold, over two momentous hours, was one of the greatest experiences of Polly's life. She could learn so much from this extraordinary woman. In fact, the lessons she had learned, over the course of the opening night, dwarfed what she had tried to take in over the previous few weeks. Crina Colbeck had revealed a truth to her that she would use.

The monotony of rehearsals could never compare to the spontaneity and raw emotion that only live theatre could provide. Every word, every movement, was imbued by this woman with a depth of feeling that could not be delivered in the sterile confines of a rehearsal room.

Crina Colbeck had truly come alive for the first time during this opening night. And the performance Polly was witnessing could only be ended by murder.

Jason Crane, tall, debonair in his tuxedo, knew what was coming and was the least surprised, of the group on the stage, by the explosion of charisma they had borne witness to. He had stood in the shadow of this remarkable woman a thousand times, or more. He knew what the rest of the cast would be feeling as they watched Crina transform herself from an aging actress into the character of Petronella Rothschild and then into a star.

The character she portrayed was the rich widow of a man she had murdered; the only man she had ever loved. Sinclair was the lover that she had killed her husband to be with. Perhaps art could sometimes imitate life he mused as he watched Crina reveal the torment of Petronella before a family that hated her and his character.

Perhaps not just his character, either. It was difficult to endear oneself to co-workers when your greatest joy in life was mocking all around you. All except Crina. She was impervious to his waspish sense of humour or, perhaps, she simply did not listen to him. Or anyone for that matter. Once upon a time, he had been fascinated by her. But once upon a time was long, long ago.

They had faced each other in rehearsal, almost every day, for two weeks. What hurt him most was that Crina had not been angry at what had happened, all those years ago, it was that she had, plainly, ceased to care.

It would soon be time, though.

Wickham McNeill had played with Crina, more than a few times, over a long career that once had glinted with promise before the flame slowly flickered. Soon it would be snuffed out, altogether. McNeill was nearly a decade older than both the actress and Crina, but his career was already drawing, inexorably, towards an unremarkable end.

Prohibition had done little to reduce his intake of alcohol. The only thing that had declined, during this period, was the quality of the booze he drank and the amount of money he had left to spend on it.

His career, like his bank balance, tottered on, but soon there would be nothing left to draw upon. This play, such as it was, offered a last chance at, some form of financial security. The short run would be enough to remind producers that he was still relevant. Still able to carry off character roles. Still, someone the public wanted to see.

He was only sharing a stage with such a theatrical great because he posed no threat, to the attention she craved and, besides, it was a favour of sorts to the owner of the theatre, Felix 'Smiley' Stanton.

Favour?

He and Smiley both knew different.

It was debt pure and simple.

Through eyes that were misted over, for reasons that had nothing to do with emotion, he watched Crina slowly bend time and space as if inverting all the world towards her. She could do it with a gesture. With a whisper. And her voice was barely a whisper now.

He watched her without emotion. His character, a husband spurned, could hardly do anything else. It was a part that had required little by way of preparation, or research, from McNeill. Three wives had left him already. He was not looking to add to that number.

He stared at Crina, trying to remember he was performing, and not just like the rest of the audience, spellbound by this extraordinary actress.

And her moment was coming.

Bobbie Flynn had watched Crina Colbeck before. In fact, seeing her return to the stage, after a three-year layoff, was bittersweet. On the star's previous appearance on the stage, Bobbie had been with her late mother, Nancy. The first appearance of Crina had brought back all those memories for Bobbie and she had quietly wept, relieved by the fact that the auditorium was dark and few could see her emotion.

One person had though.

The man who had accompanied her, that evening: Dick Devenish.

The rich private investigator, a man who had given up a lucrative law career to take on even more lucrative private cases for an array of clients who inhabited the upper echelons of New York society.

Both had watched this mesmerising performer enthral the audience, and probably her fellow cast members, with a charismatic and sympathetic reading of a character that might have been a caricature of bitchiness in less assured hands.

Each sensed murder was in the air of the drama they were watching. The question was, who, among the cast, would be the one to do the deed? Both Bobbie and Dick had discussed the potential for such a scenario at the intermission. Yet, it was not entirely certain how the drama would play out. It was a new play, by a new playwright, a protégé of Crina and the story had been shrouded in secrecy.

Bobbie snatched a quick glance at the rapt faces around her. It was an interesting crowd to say the least. There were at least three leading mobsters in the seats just around her. She and Dick had laughed at this, just before the lights went down. The smile had left her face when she saw someone else, she knew, sitting further back in the stalls. Detective Sean Nolan was there.

In the dimly lit theatre, amidst the hushed murmurs of anticipation, she had spotted him. Her heart fluttered like a startled bird as she saw who was beside him. It was a young woman around Bobbie's age. She had long brown hair and was, without question, in Bobbie's eyes, the most beautiful woman in the theatre. She was dressed in an unshowy black dress that revealed a lot less skin, realised Bobbie unhappily, than she was. She didn't need to. The young woman had a face that could inspire Shakespearian sonnets while she, at that moment, was the green-eyed monster.

Crina finished her soliloquy in a whisper that seemed to fill the silent auditorium with the sense of desolation her character was feeling. She drew herself up and faced the four other people on the stage. Slowly she raised her arms and stretched them out in a gesture of submission, but beneath the surface raged a storm of longing, jealousy and unrequited love. The audience seemed, collectively, to draw in its breath.

Then all the theatre lights went out.

A shroud of darkness descended, like a heavy velvet curtain, enveloping the audience in an inky abyss. The, once vibrant, colours of the stage faded into nothingness, swallowed by the void. In the absence of light, the familiar contours of the room dissolved into obscurity.

Some audience members screamed. And even Bobbie nearly jumped out of her seat at the suddenness of what had happened. The blackness seemed to last for seconds. On stage someone said, 'Good Lord, what is happening.'

Nearby to Bobbie someone lit a lighter, but as quickly as it had come on, it went out.

Then a shot rang out from the stage.

The lights went up and the four cast members stood staring at the dead body of Petronella Rothschild, Crina Colbeck's character.

The audience gasped as the curtain came down. To end it like this was either a cheat or a dramatic *coup de theatre,* but such was the power of what the audience had witnessed over the previous two hours they could do nothing other than rise to their feet, in acclaim at the performance they had witnessed.

The curtain came up again and Crina Colbeck was standing with the other members of the cast basking in the admiration from the audience. They stood hand in hand looking around the at their adoring public and bowed. Then the cast members stood back to allow the undoubted star of the show to take her bow.

A little reluctantly at first and then, with a shy smile, she accepted the invitation from the spectators to step forward and receive her acclaim.

But another sound interrupted the rapture pouring forward to the stage. There were some shouts now and then a scream.

The scream came from Crina Colbeck. Her eyes were wide, terrified and anguished. She was pointing into the audience.

Bobbie glanced to her right in the direction that the actress was pointing. While many had stood up to acclaim the Crina, one man was still in his seat; slumped forward.

There was a knife sticking out from his chest.

2

Earlier that morning:

The Flynn household, New York: April 1922

Inspector Flynn stared at his daughter, across the breakfast table, a question caught on his lips. For a man who had spent a lifetime interrogating suspects, it was quite something to accept that questioning the romantic life of a twenty-two-year-old daughter presented untold challenges. How he missed the wise counsel of his late wife Nancy. She would have known how to navigate these troubled waters in a way that a man of sixty or so would never be able to fathom.

'You look like you want to ask me a question,' said Bobbie, biting into a piece of toast.

Flynn studied his daughter and, once again, had to accept that she would make a fine police detective, such was her ability to discern mind, mood and everything in between. Of course, such an outcome would be over his dead body.

'Are you seeing that Devenish again?'

Bobbie had been out dancing with Dick Devenish on several occasions since they had collaborated in stopping a major art theft and found a murderer. They'd had help, of course, which was no more comfort to Flynn.

Detective Nolan had, also, been instrumental in clearing up the crime. More troubling again was the fact that Captain Francis O'Riordan had also played his part. This was especially worrying as Flynn knew, with complete certainty, that he was in the pay of mobsters. This hardly made him unique in the New York Police Department. The question, that Flynn was wrestling with, was what to do about it. Should he call in O'Riordan and deal with him or should he wait and try and find bigger fish to fry using the captain as unwitting bait?

There was so much spinning around in Flynn's head he sometimes thought he would spontaneously combust.

'Yes, as a matter of fact, I am seeing Dick,' answered Bobbie, unashamedly. 'We have tickets to the opening of "*A Delicate Lie*" at The Century Playhouse.'

'What's that?' replied Flynn.

Bobbie sighed and shook her head.

'Sometimes, Daddy, I worry. You must be the only person in New York who does not know that Crina Colbeck is making a return to the stage.'

'I'm happy for her,' said Flynn sourly. 'I didn't know she'd left.'

Then something snapped in his mind. Crina Colbeck. A memory long forgotten.

Crina Colbeck.

His eyes met Bobbie's and he saw that she was on the verge of tears. Now he remembered the night that she and Nancy had gone out to see her. He remembered it now as if it were yesterday. It was the last time they'd gone out to the theatre together. Their excitement had been infectious.

Almost.

He'd declined to go as he couldn't abide the actress. Like Bernhardt, with added ham, he'd complained. He knew this to be an exaggeration. Crina Colbeck was an accomplished actress. His only problem with her was that she'd played one role all her life: that of Crina Colbeck. He'd seen her a few times on stage and it was the same damn part every time.

Flynn nodded to his daughter to acknowledge the shared memory.

'7th September 1919,' said Flynn.

Bobbie could no longer stop the tears trickling down her cheek. She reached out and took her father's hand and they stayed like that for a minute, both lost in the memory for one no longer with them.

The moment passed, as it had to. Then Flynn's face became sterner.

'But Devenish?' he said, conscious that he sounded like a fourteen-year-old boy reacting to a telling off.

'You like Dick. You just won't admit it. You admire him too.'

'I won't admit that. Ever,' interjected Flynn, with a rueful smile. The truth was he did, sort of, like Devenish and he certainly respected him. They'd worked together, unwillingly on Flynn's part, on a number of cases. Devenish had often played an instrumental part in clearing them up. This would have been frustrating at the best of times, but when you added into the cocktail that Devenish had an ego the size of Manhattan, then it somewhat dulled the lustre of cracking these cases.

Of course, there was nothing that a father can do. At some point you must step back and let your children make their own way; make their own memories; make their own mistakes. Was Devenish so bad as all that? Probably not, thought Flynn, but his main worry was that the biggest love of the private investigator's life was himself. Bobbie would always come second.

And how would any young man, never mind Devenish, accept the arrival of Violet into their lives. How would he, Flynn? He was not a young man anymore. To have another child in the house was going to change things for them all. Did Bobbie have any idea what she was planning to take on? He changed tack.

'What's this play about?'

'No one knows,' said Bobbie. 'There's been a few rumours, but no one has said anything about it.'

'That's unusual. Is it a new play then?'

'Yes, no one has heard of the writer.,' replied Bobbie.

'Lord preserve us from another Bonaty,' replied Flynn sourly, referring to a case that had been solved two months ago by his daughter, involving a reclusive songwriter.

'No, thankfully,' laughed Bobbie. 'The writer is called Foster Raphael. It's his first play. He's written some short stories for the New Yorker. Mystery stories. I read them. They were quite good. One of them was like a parody of Conan Doyle, from the point of view of the murderer.'

This brought a scowl from Flynn. He loved the Sherlock Holmes stories. The thought of someone making a mockery of them was a sacrilege in his eyes. Couldn't young writers find their own stories, their own style? Instead, too many just wanted to make their name by mocking what had come before.

'I'm sure it will be very good,' said Bobbie, rising from her seat. At this point, they were joined by Mrs Garcia, their old housekeeper. She stared down at Bobbie's plate and then fixed her eyes on the young woman.

'Is that all you're going to eat?'

This was probably not the first time such a question had been lobbed, like a grenade, in Bobbie's direction. It was swatted breezily away as usual.

'I didn't much like it actually. You're losing your touch,' said Bobbie.

Flynn hunkered down for the reply.

'You'll feel my touch across the back of your head *bicho,*' snapped the diminutive housekeeper back at the young woman who was like a daughter to her.

Flynn got ready to duck.

'*Eres tan fea que hiciste llorar a una cebolla,*' replied Bobbie, laughing.

A newspaper was launched in Bobbie's direction, who dodged its path easily. However, it continued over the table and Flynn had to take evasive action, to avoid decapitation by Nebular's Horoscope column.

'I'm off,' said Bobbie gaily. 'See you all later.' She departed, in the fragranced blink of an eye, through the door.

Mrs Garcia shouted after her, '*¡Vete a freír espárragos'!*

And so began another morning, in the Flynn household.

3

Offices of the New York American, Park Street, New York: April 1922

It was around eight thirty that Bobbie made it into the offices of the *New York American,* located in the Tribune Building, one of the tallest buildings in Manhattan. It was a beautiful spring day. The scent of freshly brewed coffee mingled with the sweet perfume of flowers, creating an intoxicating bouquet that enveloped the denizens of the city in a fragrant embrace. The spell was broken only by New York's own outdoor orchestra.

The shrill honking of taxicabs provided the staccato notes of a brass section, punctuating the rhythm of the city streets with their urgent melodies. Meanwhile, the screech of brakes would serve as the dissonant chords, adding a twist to the discordant composition.

Bobbie stepped through the entrance hall of the Tribune Building and walked up the stairs to the office she shared with Buckner Fanley, the head of obituaries. These days, Bobbie divided her time between the crime desk and obituaries. The two jobs had much in common, these days, as the number of gang related murders rose, thanks to the extraordinary moment of madness that saw the Volstead Act passed, which banned the sale of liquor. Overnight, criminal gangs saw both their numbers and popularity rise, as they became the sole source of supply of alcohol in the United States.

Fanley was invariably in much earlier than Bobbie. He greeted her with a thin smile that might have been a scowl in a different light. Despite a somewhat frosty relationship, Bobbie respected her boss, although she could never be quite sure if the feeling was, in any way, mutual. Praise from Fanley was rarer than silence in a subway station at rush hour. However, the lack of criticism these days, which had been a hallmark of her first year in the obituary desk, suggested satisfaction, if not actual delight, with his young assistant. Bobbie would take this any day over unwarranted acclaim.

'Any news?' asked Bobbie, as she took her seat by the typewriter. Fanley nodded by way of reply. 'You're kidding,' exclaimed Bobbie in surprise.

This was met with a raised eyebrow. Bobbie supressed a smile. The only thing that Fanley was less likely to do, other than kid someone, was dance a Charleston. Naked. At a convent.

'Mr Hearst said "yes"?' pressed Bobbie.

'Mr Kent said "yes",' replied Fanley. The Mr Kent in question was Thornton Kent the editor of the newspaper who ran this particular ship with all the collegiate affability of Torquemada, after he had caught his finger in the door.

Bobbie leapt up from her seat, immediately, and went over to a large cabinet containing two dozen drawers. In these were kept the obituaries of people who had, not yet left this mortal coil. Much of her job, over her time at the newspaper, had required her to keep this enormous file of life stories up to date and supplemented with new, potential "customers". It was sometimes a rather morbid task to do this, but Bobbie's natural curiosity about people and interest in the lives of the great and the good made the role one she enjoyed more than anyone had a right to.

She went to the drawer marked "W" and picked out a file. This was always a sad moment, when the file she selected was because someone had passed away. In this case, it was the black entertainer, Bert Williams. She had seen and enjoyed his act immensely, on several occasions, at the Ziegfeld Follies.

She looked at the cover of the brown manilla file and felt a sadness rise within her. It was as much for herself and the memory of seeing him with her mother and father, as it was for the late entertainer.

She brought the file over to the desk, put some paper into the typewriter and began to type:

```
Bert Williams, the great
```

Bobbie halted for a moment. She was aware of Fanley's eyes on her. He'd glanced up when the percussive punctuation of metal on paper had paused. Bert Williams had been a black entertainer who had made the transition into a world that was predominantly white. His popularity transcended colour. She made her decision.

```
...comedian passed away this weekend at
the age of 46. He is survived by a widow
but no children. The comedian had been
unwell for over a year now and had
recently left a stage show due to ill
health.
```

Half an hour later she had completed the obituary and handed it over to Fanley. Her boss read over the copy without expression before placing it in the in-tray which suggested that there would be no amendments to what she had written.

Bobbie wasn't sure if this relieved her, surprised or, perhaps, unsurprised. Fanley was not a man to give away much about himself. His life outside of the office was a mystery to her. She knew he was married, but, beyond this, his life was one from which he excluded most everyone. Bobbie had no idea of his politics, hence her apprehension at not making any reference to the comedian's colour. For the moment this had passed without comment.

Out of curiosity, Bobbie went over to the cabinet once more and picked out the file related to Crina Colbeck. This was not a file she had worked on previously and she was curious to find out more about the woman she was to see, later that evening, on stage. She went over to her desk, opened the file, and began to read.

```
Crina Colbeck (1876 -
Crina Colbeck was a legendary
entertainer, best known for her dramatic
talents, powerful voice and ground
breaking contributions to the worlds of
vaudeville and theater.
Born Crina Alexandrescu on October 7th,
1876, in New York City, Colbeck was the
third child of Rosa and Andrei
Alexandrescu. Growing up in the Bronx,
Colbeck displayed an early knack for
```

performing, often entertaining her family and friends with natural comedic timing and singing abilities.

Colbeck's career began to take shape in her teenage years when she joined her family in a circus with her parents, before moving on to burlesque and vaudeville, shows under the stage name Crina Colbeck. Her talent for comedy and singing quickly gained attention and she soon became a popular act in the vaudeville circuit.

Between 1899-1903 she stopped performing, and it seemed as if she had retired.

When she returned to the entertainment world it was in a completely different branch: drama. Previously she had been popular as a stage act on Vaudeville. In 1904, she found acclaim for the first time as a dramatic actress playing the role of Cordelia in "King Lear". This led to a string of roles, over the next few years, which turned the Vaudeville entertainer into a Broadway legend.

Between 1905-1919 she divided her time between Broadway and touring the country in stage productions. Her roles included: Cleopatra in "Anthony and Cleopatra" (1907), her legendary Lady Macbeth (1911), and Desdemona (1913).

Colbeck's personal life was marked by both triumphs and tragedy. She married fellow entertainer Lester Harris in 1906, but the marriage ended in divorce in 1908. In 1913, she married her second husband, Peter Shriver, a major in the US Army. He lost his life in 1918, while serving overseas in the US Army in France.

Following her husband's death, Colbeck retired from the stage.

In 1921, Colbeck married for a third time. Her new husband was businessman turned impresario Felix 'Smiley' Stanton.

Bobbie nearly choked with laughter when she read the rather euphemistic description of husband number three, 'Smiley' Stanton, as a businessman turned impresario. It was well known to everyone that 'Smiley' had been a mobster, although his interests, oddly, had not included, as far as anyone could determine, the sale of liquor.

As she already had the file in her hand, Bobbie decided to add a few lines to what was already in the public domain about the actress.

At the beginning of 1922, Colbeck made the surprise announcement that she was returning to the Broadway stage to a play to be produced by her husband at his theatre, The Century Playhouse. The play by unknown playwright, Foster Raphael, "A Delicate Lie" opened April 1922.

Bobbie extracted the paper and put it back inside the file before returning it to the cabinet. Fanley glanced up, possibly surprised at the rather short addition to the obituary and asked her, 'Who was that?'

'Crina Colbeck,' answered Bobbie. 'I'm going to see her on stage tonight and was curious about her life. I just added that she was returning to the stage after her layoff.'

'I would hardly describe mourning as a layoff,' replied Fanley. This took Bobbie by surprise, not just because Fanley was aware of Crina's story, but also, more disconcertingly, because he was probably right.

The rest of the morning was spent in a similar fashion, updating a bunch of obituaries that Fanley had deemed important. One of the benefits of having someone like Bobbie as his assistant, never admitted by the taciturn senior man of course, was that Bobbie could do this job quickly because she had a very good knowledge of who these people were without having to spend hours researching their lives.

For Bobbie, the chance to make progress on many of the obituaries offered her a rare moment of triumph over her perennial adversary. The small but satisfying reward of seeing Fanley's efforts to conceal how impressed he was by her ability to get through such a quantity of these potted histories in such a short period of time, without recourse to external references, was often a personal highlight on a dull day.

Out of curiosity, later that morning, Bobbie decided to pay a visit to the offices occupied by the rest of the journalists of the *New York American,* including the imposing figure of editor, Thornton Kent and her good friend, Damon Runyon. If anyone could give her the low down on the new owner of the Century Playhouse it would be Runyon.

4

The stale scent of yesterday's headlines filled the air of the newsroom, accompanied by the sound of typewriters clattering, like a symphony of industrious bees. The air hummed with the anxiety of deadlines a-looming. Bobbie strode through the newsroom, a vision of radiant elegance, navigating the sea of bustling newsmen, like the daughter of Trident, calming the waves with one flick of her auburn hair.

There was a noticeable drop in the clicking metal, which made Bobbie as self-conscious as a fox among a pack of hounds. Bobbie was a fragrant-fresh breath of air, in the pungent aroma of ink. Her arrival was always welcome as it gave the hard-working boys of the newsroom a lift to see such youth and beauty in their presence. Backs were straightened, ties adjusted, cigarettes stubbed out and language was mostly moderated.

Bobbie made a beeline for Damon Runyon, passing by the desk of her other boss, Ade Barton, the crime reporter. Barton bristled at being ignored. The crime reporter may have viewed himself as a hard-bitten newsman, but to Bobbie his prose and his attempts to woo her had all the nuance, and subtlety, of an alarm clock. What he lacked in journalistic repute he compensated for in boundless self-assurance.

Undeterred by the indifference of Bobbie, and the mockery of his peers, Barton continued his pursuit of the young woman hoping that, one day, he would pay back her disinterest by broadcasting his conquest to an eager newsroom.

Runyon was giving twenty-five to one against this ever happening. When news of this reached Bobbie's ears she laughed for five minutes, before suggesting to Runyon that she might put a hundred on Barton's success. Message received. Runyon duly withdrew the book, but a few in the newsroom were still prepared to have a small number of private side bets on this particular wager.

Bobbie perched herself on Runyon's desk and leaned over to the veteran sports reporter.

'When a doll leans over me like that, I think to myself this is either my lucky day or she wants something. What do you want, Red?'

The whole of the newsroom had virtually abandoned their work to listen in on the conversation.

'How could you leave me last night like that?' said Bobbie.

Runyon rolled his eyes and decided to play along.

'It's over, Red. It was good while it lasted.'

The typing began again. They'd heard this one before.

'What do you want?' asked Runyon. This time in a lower voice.

'I'm going to the Century Playhouse tonight. Mean anything?' asked Bobbie.

Runyon let out a bark of laughter and slapped the desk.

'That is funny,' he said after a minute. 'You know where I will be tonight with some friends?'

'Century Playhouse?' suggested Bobbie, a little surprised as she didn't have Runyon down as an ardent theatre goer, where the show did not have a lot of girls in various stages of undress.

'The very same.'

'I thought Follies was more your taste.'

'It is Red and don't be rude,' smiled Runyon. 'But an interest in contemporary music and dance does not stop a man of refined tastes, and a deep sensibility, having a profound appreciation for the dramatic arts.'

'I'll bet,' said Bobbie. 'Listen, tell me about 'Smiley' Stanton. How did he ever get into theatre?'

'You mean my host this evening?' replied Runyon and was rewarded with a look of surprise on Bobbie's face.

'You really do walk in some swell circles,' was her only comment.

'Smiley and I go way back. You know I have a soft spot for men who are titans of industry, who believe, as I do, that free enterprise is the bedrock of the greatest nation on this earth.'

'I thought hustlers and grifters were more your scene, Damon,' laughed Bobbie.

Runyon laughed good-naturedly and replied, 'Once in a while I like to hang with the big shots strutting around like peacocks, flashing their fancy suits and shiny cufflinks for all to see. Anyway, what is the deal with Smiley, you ask. Well, I've known him a good long time. When he was going to marry this doll Crina Colbeck, he comes to me and says "Damon, you are a stand-up man as ever I met". I said to him "Thank you my friend. Coming from you that means a lot." And..'

'Can we cut to the chase,' laughed Bobbie.

'So, he asks me what do I think of him and this doll Crina? I told him she was out of his league. I say these things, but I smile as I say them so they don't pull out a John Roscoe and fill me with more holes than a pin cushion at a porcupine convention. I can see he is sweet on her so what else do you want to know?'

'Why would someone like Crina fall for Smiley?' asked Bobbie, genuinely bewildered. An image of a man who would never be mistaken for a relative of Douglas Fairbanks, swung across her mind. Smiley was, as his moniker suggested, a man who wore a grin as wide as the Mississippi and twice as welcoming. Yet Bobbie knew there was more to Smiley than met the eye. He had a knack for finding trouble, faster than a bloodhound on a scent.

'You know better than to ask a question like that,' said Runyon in a semi-scolding voice.

'I am a journalist, remember?' laughed Bobbie. 'And a woman.'

'I think that this is something me and the office are aware of. So, you're asking me why Crina married someone who is, mistakenly, believed to operate on the wrong side of the law?'

Bobbie decided to let the 'mistakenly' comment pass. She merely raised her eyebrows in acknowledgement, that this was indeed what she was asking.

'This may come as a surprise to you young lady, but Smiley is not the tough guy you think he is. In fact, like me, he does not want to be involved with things that raise your blood pressure. Smiley is strictly legitimate these days. He decides to use the scratch that he has accumulated over the years to buy a theatre. He buys said theatre long before honest people cannot drink. This is a line of business that he is very much against. So, with said theatre, Smiley meets new people, and he likes them very much. One is Miss Colbeck. He likes her very much indeed. And Miss Colbeck, who is needing someone to make her laugh, finds Smiley, very much, a man who can do this.'

Bobbie frowned sceptically at this which made Runyon shrug.

'You are telling me that Smiley is no longer involved in anything that the law, or to be more specific, my father, might deem dishonest?' asked Bobbie, grinning.

Runyon's arms spread out and he said, in a careful voice, 'Do not get Smiley wrong. He is, as everyone will tell you, a straight guy. None straighter. If he wasn't I wouldn't have any truck with him.'

'Unlawful, then?' pressed Bobbie, unwilling to let Runyon off the hook so easily.

'I can tell you, Red, hand on heart, that the cops have nothing on Smiley and that he has a very good relationship with our friends in uniform. If anything, the only bad thing I will say about Smiley is that he is too trusting.'

5

Same morning

New York Police Commissioner's Office, New York: April 1922

Commissioner Richard Enright stood up as his old friend, Inspector Flynn, entered the office. They were both nearer the end of their careers than the beginning. Together, they had been waging a silent war against the forces of corruption, which threatened to engulf the city in darkness.

The prohibition of alcohol hadn't helped their cause one little bit. Intended to curb societal ills, instead it gave rise to a lucrative black market, where bootleggers and speakeasies thrived in the shadows. For some police officers, the temptations of easy money proved too great to resist. Bribery became commonplace, with bootleggers lining the pockets of corrupt officials. They knew that their battle was not one that could be won with brute force alone, but with patience, cunning and dumb luck.

'The Mayor needs results,' opined Enright, grimly. It wasn't the first time he had made such an appeal; they both knew it wouldn't be the last. The Mayor in question was John

Hylan. The two men respected Hylan as intelligent and highly independent, yet they both accepted that there were many points of difference.

'What results exactly, Commissioner?' asked Flynn, grimly. Inside this building, he always referred to Enright as Commissioner. Outside the building they were more informal. 'If he thinks that I can find a link between organised crime and 'the interests' as he refers to them, then we need a thousand more men and all from Harvard, Princeton or Yale. Not with what I have to work with now.'

'The interests,' that Flynn referred to, was the 'invisible' government of big businesses, like banking or oil, that the Mayor believed, operated as a second government at all levels, to further their own interests.

Enright shrugged his shoulders and held his arms out.

'Look, Flynn old man, you know what I mean.'

'But it was him that asked me to get men on the inside of the mob, get them on their payroll, and then go after the head. That doesn't happen overnight and it certainly does not happen if we go after a few cops on the take.'

'He needs some results. Time to go after the low-level stuff,' said Enright wearily.

'Fine, I'm happy to do that. It won't look good on us, but I'll do it. Then we'll have to start over. Meanwhile, us making bootlegging raids and knocking out a few craps games is not going to have Rockefeller or Rothschild quaking in their boots. It's not like they were drinking any of this moonshine, anyway.'

This brought a chortle from Enright and the two men parted soon after a few barbs at some men, who would soon be feeling the heat when the raids began.

Twenty minutes later, Flynn stepped out of the police car and skipped up the steps of Midtown North precinct. The shadows in the entrance hall seemed to linger a little longer, the light struggled to penetrate the gloom and one could not help but feel a sense of melancholy. The sergeant's desk, a relic from a bygone era, stood as the last bastion of order amidst the chaos. Here, the weary custodian of law and order sat, his eyes heavy with the weight of countless battles fought and lost: Sergeant Brendan Aloysius Moran. Bam Moran as all affectionately knew him.

'Morning Bam,' said Flynn.

'Inspector, good to see you,' smiled Moran. 'What brings you here?'

'You're all out of a job,' announced Flynn. 'We've conquered crime. We can all go home.'

'To my old lady?' asked Moran. He didn't sound enthusiastic. "There must be some crime left, surely.'

'I'm sure Erin will be glad to have you around the house. Lots of odd jobs for a capable man like yourself, Bam'

'You're funny Inspector, you know that?' said Bam glumly before breaking out into a grin. 'Couldn't be any worse than these damn reports that Lieutenant Grimm has us filling out all the time.'

'Is he still doing that?' scowled Flynn. 'I thought I'd told him.'

'I wish you would,' replied Moran, wearily.

Flynn headed up the stairs of the precinct and made his way towards the squad room. He walked along the corridor, glancing briefly at the walls which now crumbled and cracked like the resolve of a defeated army. The very air seemed to echo with the sighs of those who had long since given up hope of redemption. How was he meant to fight against an enemy both visible and, if Mayor Hylan was to be believed, invisible, amorphous and powerful, with men that had to work in in the middle of such evident neglect?

In some respects, he wondered if Grimm was not right to enforce structure to the activities of the detectives. Perhaps it would engender discipline, or pride, or dare he hoped, accountability. His resolve to have a word with Grimm once more evaporated. He would leave it. There were other battles to fight and he needed every man he could trust on his side, even martinets like Grimm.

He walked into the squad room and found Captain Frank O'Riordan in his office with Lieutenant Grimm. The other detective there was his old friend, Sergeant Shane 'Harry' Harrigan. Flynn went over to him.

'You still here, Harry?' asked Flynn. It was his standard 'hello' to a man he'd known for decades.

'The Yankees wouldn't have me,' replied Harrigan. He proudly patted a belly that could never have been described as svelte.

'You surprise me,' said Flynn. He glanced down as Harrigan offered him a cigar that Flynn knew to have been pilfered from the Commissioner. He declined with a frown that was less to do with his disapproval at such naked criminology as it was regret that his own sense of morality was denying him what would be a very nice smoke.

'Nolan around?'

'The blue-eyed boy is out crime fighting at the moment, I'm sure he'll be back soon. What did you want him for?'

'More crime fighting,' laughed Flynn. He turned as he heard the door opening to the captain's office and Grimm appeared. An ingratiating smile, immediately, crossed the lieutenant's lips. The air in the office seemed to turn sticky for Flynn, such was the atmosphere of sycophancy, which surrounded the lieutenant. Meanwhile, O'Riordan was certainly not someone who could be described thus. He chewed a cigar and wore an expression that made a bulldog look like a blushing debutante.

'Good afternoon, sir, to what do we owe the pleasure?' asked Grimm. Quite how anyone could ask that, while keeping a straight face, was beyond Flynn.

O'Riordan, to give him his due, looked appalled at his lieutenant's grovelling. This almost made Flynn smile, until he remembered that the reason he was here was to deal with a man who was, certainly, corrupt. The only question that needed to be answered was the extent of his criminality, and who was his paymaster.

Flynn girded himself and pointed to the office.

'Let's go inside. Tell me here about what you have on.'

This was part of his job now that he was a senior policeman. He no longer worked much on individual cases. His job was spent overseeing the men who were in his command. He missed his old job but he knew, too, that his energy was not what it once was. It was a young man's game, and he could by no measure be described as young.

O'Riordan's in-tray was no different than that in most precincts in the city: a murder or two, robbery, shoplifting, drunk and disorderly behaviour, domestic abuse and assault. It was a grim reminder that they lived in an imperfect world.

When O'Riordan and Grimm had finished going through the crime reports, Flynn made good his escape. It was an odd situation in Midtown North. He hated the fact that O'Riordan was on the take because, in other circumstances, he'd have thought him a good cop, albeit rough around the edges. Very rough, in fact. Grimm was too smooth, too political, ever to appeal to a man like Flynn.

There was no sign of Nolan's return, so Flynn exchanged a few more insults with Harrigan, before leaving the squad room. On his way out, he bumped into Detective Timothy Yeats. Flynn was a small man, but hard as nails. Yeats was bigger than a standard issue grizzly.

After rebounding a foot or two, Flynn looked the big detective up and down and inquired, 'You lost a pound or two?'

'No, does it look like I have?' asked Yeats, guilelessly.

'No,' scowled Flynn. 'Where's Nolan?'

'On his way up,' came the reply.

They parted on this moment of mutual respect. The two men liked one another, and Flynn certainly rated the young giant, although not so much for cerebral capabilities as his physical ones. Nolan, however, was someone who unquestionably held up well on both counts. Flynn had hopes for Nolan, although they stopped short of him dating his daughter. This was less to do with the innate qualities that he had identified in the young man and everything to do with his chosen profession. Yet, even now, he sensed a losing battle lay ahead.

He met Nolan on the stairs.

'Let's go outside,' said Flynn. 'I have some work for you. You may not like it.'

6

As Bobbie had been chatting with Damon Runyon, and happily ignoring Ade Barton, she became aware that the editor of the newspaper had come out of the office and walked straight past them. Bobbie and Runyon stopped chatting, and glanced over in the direction he was walking. Kent was a tall, imposing man; good-looking with a temper, which made a wounded bull seem emotionally repressed. He ruled the newspaper offices with an iron glove covering an iron fist. He stopped short of being considered a martinet because, Runyon aside, he was a better journalist than any of them. And they all knew this.

He motioned to Barton to get up from his desk and follow him into the office. Barton was on his feet in a moment. As Kent walked past, he said without either stopping or, indeed, looking at Bobbie, 'You, too, Flynn.'

Bobbie glanced at Runyon and they both raised their eyebrows. Bobbie, like Barton, was not going to risk the editor's wrath by staying seated on Runyon's desk one moment longer than Kent's volcanic temper deemed appropriate. She was up on her feet and followed Kent into his office, with Barton trailing unhappily behind. He ignored Runyon's whispered jibe, 'Looks like he wants Bobbie to hold your hand, Ade.'

'Shut the door,' said Kent taking his seat. Barton did as he was ordered. Neither he nor Bobbie sat down. They were there to take instructions, and then leave.

'I'm hearing that Mayor Hylan is on the warpath. What do we know? Who, what and why?'

How Kent heard these things was a mystery to all, but perhaps not. He had contacts in every major office and business in the city. It was as if he knew where all the bodies were buried and he had markers on all.

Curiously, Bobbie sensed the question was directed more at her than Barton, and this angered her. While Barton was a bit sleazy in Bobbie's view, he was a good enough newsman for the low-level activity that constituted most of the crime committed in the city.

'Why not ask Damon?' said Barton sourly. Another aspect of Barton, that Bobbie did not like, was his evident overestimation of his own abilities, and unconcealed jealousy of Damon Runyon, who was not only a better writer, but also seemed to have very good relationships, with people on both sides of the law. As soon as he asked the question, Bobbie suppressed a grin. This was not how you acted with Kent. Perhaps even Barton sensed this as he seemed to shrink into the seat.

Kent seemed unconcerned by what Barton said, however. In a voice that was more whimsical than angry he asked, 'Oh, how do you mean?'

A question like this was equivalent to an invitation to jump into a crocodile infested river. Barton seemed to wake up to the danger and decided that discretion was the better part of keeping your job.

'Damon could help us too,' he suggested brightly. 'Let's face it, he has better contacts than I do.'

This was a surprisingly deft response from Barton, and surprised Bobbie for being so. It was an admission of the obvious, and not a bad idea at that. She noted that he only mentioned himself in regard to the quality of Runyon's contacts. She wasn't sure if this was because she was someone he abhorred too much to acknowledge or, perhaps, he recognised that she had a trump card of her own in her father.

Her father.

The anger she'd felt a few moments earlier returned. There was no question in her mind that Kent was angling for her to use her father's inside knowledge of Tammany Hall to their advantage. She would not do this. Or, at least, it would be on her terms. She wasn't completely lacking in pragmatism.

Kent's eyes seemed to Bobbie like molten ice. He clearly had not forgiven Barton, notwithstanding his suggestion on Runyon.

'Maybe I should let Runyon run the crime desk, Barton. What do you think?'

'Steady on Mr Kent,' said Barton turning pale.

'Find out what is happening,' hissed Kent. Then he turned to Bobbie and added, meaningfully, 'Both of you.'

Kent's eyes shifted downward to a sheaf of paper on his desk. This signalled the end of the meeting. Barton exited the office first. As she was about to leave, Bobbie hesitated and then she stopped at the door and shut it. This gained Kent's attention. His eyes shot up to her, and they were flashing warning signals.

Just as Bobbie was about to speak, he held his hand up. There was something in the manner that warned Bobbie that it was best she remain silent.

'I know what you are going to say, but don't say it, because we both know it isn't true,' said Kent. He was not angry, which surprised Bobbie. If anything, there was just a hint of resignation in the tone. For a moment, Bobbie felt ashamed. Then she remembered that life was not black and white. Just as she might take advantage of her father's position in the police department to gain insights that would not normally be available to others, so too did her father, with all manner of people on the street, to help solve crimes.

Bobbie nodded and was about to leave the office when Kent added something else.

'Aren't you supposed to be at the sentencing?' asked Kent.

'Yes, but it's not taking place until three,' said Bobbie.

Kent nodded, and then looked back down to the papers on his desk. The subject and her time with the editor had ended. Bobbie closed the door of the office and made her way back through the news room. She saw Ade Barton motioning to her to come over. He didn't look happy but, then again, being humiliated in front of Bobbie was never going to do much for his mood.

'Yes, Ade,' said Bobbie, trying to not seem surly, and failing miserably.

'You know that Kent wants you to find out from your father what's going on with Hylan?'

'Mr Kent was quite clear on that with me just now,' said Bobbie, emphasising the word "mister" and embellishing the truth somewhat.

'What are you going to do, Red? We need to work together on this. It's a big story if we can crack it,' said Barton. He'd called her Red, which he used to do, before she became attached to the crime desk. Then he'd changed that to Flynn. His tone stopped just short of wheedling. He recognised that Bobbie held something of an ace, by virtue of her father's situation, and relationship with the Mayor.

Bobbie saw what Barton was suggesting, which in many ways was worse in her eyes than Kent. He wanted her to use her father to find out more about who Mayor Hylan was levelling accusations against, and then share it with him, so that his name rather than hers would head the byline in the story.

'My father never discusses what goes on in City Hall, Ade. If I ask him anything, he'll know exactly what I'm up to. He's not stupid.' Which, thought Bobbie, you clearly are if you think I'm going to fall for this.

'Kent won't be happy,' retorted Barton.

'I'm sure Mr Kent will be fine,' answered Bobbie and decided that the conversation had reached an end. She moved off before Barton could respond to this. She had a few things to finish, before she left the offices to go over to the orphanage to collect the young girl, who would soon become her ward, Violet Belmont.

On a whim she went to the other side of the offices which coincided in another dip in the productivity of the newsmen. Bobbie was oblivious to this, as she had seen someone she wanted to catch up with, Peregrine Wimslow.

The Honourable Peregrine Wimslow, known to all as Perry, was the theatre and arts critic for the newspaper. He was an Englishman, who had resided in New York since the turn of the century. Perry wasn't a day under sixty, and it was at least four decades since anyone would have described him as slender. Despite the generous expanse of his waistline, he dressed like Beau Brummel's more extravagant brother. He was a confirmed bachelor, yet he loved women and they loved him. Bobbie certainly did.

'You're back, Perry,' she exclaimed.

'Your powers of observation do you credit, Roberta,' said Perry, who took a rather parental view of Bobbie. 'I gather you've been up to all manner of adventures, in my absence. Well, I'm sure dear old Flynn will be delighted to know that I am back in the fold and ready to ensure that proper boundaries are respected.'

Bobbie made a face at Perry and then grinned.

'How was England? Did you meet the King?' asked Bobbie. The theatre critic had been back in his home country for three months, visiting his family seat. His elder brother was an Earl.

'I'm afraid we just missed each other,' said Perry with an exaggerated sigh. 'I'm sure I'll catch up with him on my next visit.'

Perry had claimed to know King George V, but few believed him. Aside from being a bon vivant and newsman, he was also known to be a notorious name-dropper. There was barely a famous person he claimed not to have met or had drinks with. Prohibition had barely made a dent in his prodigious intake of alcohol. In this regard, he differed little from the vast majority of the New York populace.

They chatted for a few minutes as Perry, despite his rampant narcissism, had genuine affection for Bobbie, and was fascinated by the cases in which she had been involved. One of those cases, involving murder and an attempted robbery at the Metropolitan Museum, she had to keep to herself, on the instructions of none other than the NYPD Commissioner, Robert Enright.

When she had finished updating him on the first three months of 1922, Bobbie asked again, 'How was England?'

'Cold and dreary as ever,' replied Perry, sadly. 'However...'

He then proceeded to tell her a few stories that were gloriously indiscreet, and bordered on ribald, which had Bobbie doubled over with laughter.

'You must publish, Perry. I'm sure they'd land you millions.'

'They'd land me in court, paying out millions. No, I shall remain the soul of discretion on these tales.'

The look that accompanied this was enough to set Bobbie off laughing again. Perry knew himself all too well. He was the least circumspect person in any room that he entered.

'Are you going to the opening night of Crina Colbeck's new play, Perry?'

'Of course I am young lady. I wouldn't miss it for the world. I even re-arranged my return to New York in order to be there on the opening night. Crina is a dear, dear friend of mine.'

Bobbie looked at him doubtfully.

'You may look at me in that way if you wish, but I have known that young lady since she was in Vaudeville. I predicted great success for her then and I was proved right, as usual. Of course, back then, no one believed me, least of all dear Crina. She often says to me, "Perry, you were the first to believe in me." And I was.'

'In that case, can you clear up something for me that I've always been curious about? Why did she marry a man that was suspected of being involved in illegal activities?'

'Oh, you mean, Smiley? Well, of course, I warned Crina not to do it. I know of his reputation in games of chance. Oddly, though, having met the man, while not convinced it was a good match for her, I found him not unlikable.'

'Really? And did you take part in any of these games of chance?' teased Bobbie.

'One meets some very interesting characters, when one is with Mr Stanton. Of course, it is a year or two since I last went, but I can remember running into a few state politicians and at least three men that should have been locked away in Sing Sing and the key thrown away.'

'Well, it looks like I shall see you later then, Perry.'

'You shall, my dear, you shall.' And tell me, will there be any young man dangling on the end of your arm this evening?' Bobbie coloured slightly and paused, a second or two longer than was advisable. Perry leaned forward; his eyes shone with mischief. 'There is. Very interesting. Now tell Uncle Perry about it.'

'It's a friend, you understand,' said Bobbie.

'A friend,' repeated Perry doubtfully, 'And what is this friend's name pray tell?'

'Dick,' replied Bobbie. 'Dick Devenish.'

Perry's eyes widened and then his face cracked into a wide grin.

'Dick Devenish, you say. Bless my soul. Who would have thought?'

Bobbie was quite surprised by this and frowned slightly.

'How do you mean?'

Oh nothing. I know Dick and I think he's a splendid boy. You'll have great fun with him.'

7

Nolan's relationship with Inspector Flynn was an ongoing paradox that he had not yet quite fathomed. He liked the old man and he suspected that the inspector trusted him. Why else would he have asked him to work undercover; to be bribed by a fellow policeman, if he suspected he was already on someone's payroll? Yet, there was no question that since the night he'd taken Bobbie dancing, a shadow of mistrust had fallen over them.

That night had been bad for him on a number of levels. The inspector had torn a strip off him for recklessly putting Bobbie potentially in harm's way. Nolan had been blameless of this, as it had been Bobbie's idea, not his. Furthermore, since that night, Bobbie's attitude to him had changed. She seemed to have accepted her father's wish to avoid him at all costs.

The frosty turn in their relationship had confused him, as there was no question in his mind, she was not the type of person to acquiesce easily if she felt strongly about something. And there *had* been something between them. It was undeniable. Even Devenish had seen this at the Metropolitan Museum.

Yet, nearly two months on from that night of dancing, here he was, caught between how he felt about the young woman and acting as her father's agent in an undercover operation, against people in his own department. What could he do? Aside from being Bobbie's father, Flynn was his senior in rank, by around several hundred levels. Nolan said nothing to the inspector, merely nodding acknowledgement and joined him in descending the stairs.

As there were several other policemen coming down or going up it would have looked strange if there was silence between them, so Flynn began to question Nolan.

'Where've you been?' asked Flynn in a voice that was loud enough to be heard by others on the stairs.

'A murder in Central Park,' replied Nolan, understanding what was happening and replying in a similar tone. Flynn flicked his eyes in the direction of Nolan and nodded in approval. Thus encouraged, Nolan spoke a little more about the case until they were outside the building. They made their way around the corner to a small restaurant out of the way of anyone who might be from the Precinct. While they were walking, Flynn said in low voice, 'You'll have to let Harry and Yeats handle the murder, son. I'm afraid we have a more important matter to deal with.'

Flynn noted the frown on the young man's face and felt a mixture of despondency at having to ask him to step away from the case, but also satisfaction that this was the detective's reaction.

'I've been to see the Commissioner. He was with Mayor Hylan,' began Flynn. Nolan closed his eyes and they stayed closed a moment longer than was necessary. 'I agree,' added Flynn, who understood that Nolan saw where this was heading.

'We're getting closer, sir,' pointed out Nolan.

'I know, but Mayor Hylan wants some heads on a plate. He has his own pressures to deal with,' answered Flynn, thinking of the, almost daily, criticism from the press about the levels of crime and corruption in the city. 'One day you'll be dealing with these men, son. You'll have to develop an ability to see things through their eyes. You won't always like what you must do, but there's usually a good reason for doing it. They're not stupid. They know what we're trying to do, but it could take forever to find the men at the top and bring them all down. The longer they think you are on the take the more dangerous it'll be for you. I can't take that risk, detective.'

Flynn found there was a catch in his throat as he said this. He remembered that moment a couple of months earlier when he'd asked Nolan to work undercover and find proof of the collusion between some members of the police department and organised crime. Nolan, he sensed, had the right combination of integrity and capability to manage the delicate balance such a covert role would entail.

He knew that he was putting the young man in a very dangerous situation, yet his own role demanded that he do so. Nolan had accepted without demur. His reaction had only confirmed, in Flynn's mind, the qualities the young man had. Sadly, he recognised that, in her own way, Bobbie saw them too.

The sidewalk was thronged with men and women returning to their offices after their lunch break. They found the restaurant and sat down. Both ordered coffees. For the first minute there was silence. The conversation was not going to be an easy one, for either man.

'Who does the Commissioner want to take down?' asked Nolan, but he already knew the answer. Flynn looked back at

Nolan but said nothing. Then, he stared down at his coffee, and shook his head.

Nolan sighed and felt a crushing weight on his stomach. When Flynn had come to him, in January, to ask him to join some of the other men, who were almost certainly taking bribes, he'd accepted immediately. The thought that any police officer could go against everything they had sworn to uphold appalled him.

Two months later his view had softened. He knew of some men in the precinct who were being paid to look away. Most of them were patrol men who ignored, as most people did, the Volstead Act. A few even went as far as to tip off the bootleggers when a raid was due. Then there were a few who did not work with the mob in circumventing Prohibition. They mainly dealt with the various gambling activities which were illegal in the state. This was low level by comparison to the murderous activities around bootlegging.

A heavy silence fell between the two men. Nolan decided to put Flynn out of his misery.

'So, we're going to take down the captain?'

Flynn nodded. He stared into the eyes of Nolan and asked, 'How do you feel about that?'

'It has to be done,' said Nolan, a little grimly. He had never particularly liked O'Riordan, and he was under no illusion that the feeling was mutual, but a recent bust at the Metropolitan Museum had suggested there was a good cop in there somewhere.

Hidden.

Deeply.

'It does, son. He brought it on himself,' agreed Flynn. There was no hiding the sense of despondency in his voice. 'When do you think?'

'I've heard there's a craps game on tonight. He'll be there, I'd bet my badge on that,' said Nolan.

Flynn nodded at this. He'd heard rumours at City Hall that O'Riordan liked to gamble. Of course, many of the people saying this were probably doing the same.

'And you'll never guess who's running it.'

There were a few men, Flynn knew of who ran games in different parts of the city. Most were low level. The big games, the ones attended by celebrities and politicians and mobsters were buried deep underground. The police only got to hear of them after the event. On the odd occasion that they had advance warning, the Vice Squad were invariably too late. This was almost certainly because some were in the pay of the men running the games. It was another reason why Flynn had selected Nolan. He was not part of the Vice Squad and therefore, in Flynn's eyes, highly unlikely to be tainted.

'Go on,' said Flynn.

'An old friend of yours we thought had moved out of this business,' prompted Nolan.

'Not Smiley Stanton,' said Flynn in surprise.

'The same.'

Flynn shook his head. Everything he'd heard was that Stanton had made his money and decided to pack up his game and put his ill-gotten winnings into the biggest long shot of all: running a Broadway theatre. Flynn had never really been convinced that Stanton had walked away, yet, for two years now, his name had not been mentioned in connection with illicit gambling. This either meant he'd walked away from gambling or he had some very powerful friends protecting him.

'Where is the game?' asked Flynn, with a sickening feeling slowly rising within him.

'I don't know exactly,' admitted Nolan, but Captain O'Riordan has given me two tickets for a show tonight. He said I had to go in case I was needed. 'It must be nearby.'

'The Crina Colbeck play?' asked Flynn wearily.

Nolan nodded, slightly surprised that the inspector was clued up on Broadway opening nights. He could see that Flynn was unhappy about this, and assumed the inspector was feeling the same despondency that he felt about bringing down a fellow officer.

'Yes sir,' said Nolan.

'Well, you should go as planned. I'll get Harry and a few others to cover the place although Lord only knows how we'll distinguish people going to the play and folk going to a room to gamble,' said Flynn.

Raiding a theatre on opening night would require the logistical dexterity of orchestrating a foxhunt in a china shop. Attempting to search the labyrinthine corridors of the Century Theatre would need more men than he could spare. And it would cause the almightiest panic inside. The police would find themselves navigating their way through a blizzard of satin gowns and top hats. This meant the players, ensconced amidst the glittering throng, would vanish quicker than a magician's rabbit, leaving the cops clutching nothing but cigar smoke.

Of course, the police could pretend to be theatre goers, and melt into the crowd themselves. This would, at least, get them inside without raising suspicion. However, this created another problem for the inspector. Flynn suspected that available tickets for Crina Colbeck's return to the stage were rarer than clothes on a stripper.

And for what? They would raid a craps game and catch several powerful men from both sides of the law. All of them would hire the best lawyers and would almost certainly avoid jail. At worst, a few politicians would be embarrassed, but probably gain popularity as they used their presence at a craps game to evidence their man-of-the-people credentials. All Flynn would be left with was, potentially, the heads of a policeman or two. The game would move elsewhere and start over.

And the press would simply go back onto the attack again. This time they would probably complain that the police had ruined the return of a stage legend.

Flynn shook his head. The challenges posed by this location, especially on a night like this, meant it would be a colossal risk, not to say waste of police time.

Nolan studied the inspector, seeming to read his mind. He said, 'You have to admit, it's a helluva cover.'

'Yes, I suppose it is,' came the morose reply.

8

New York County Courthouse, New York: March 1922

It is one of the more idiosyncratic aspects of New York's history that its courthouse on Chambers Street came into being thanks to the tireless efforts of one of the most corrupt politicians the state, in fact any state, has ever produced. In a delightful twist of fortune, the courthouse bears his name.

The Tweed Courthouse was built by Tammany Hall's most Machiavellian leader, William M. "Boss" Tweed. He oversaw the growth of the Tammany organisation, in the middle of the nineteenth century, which resulted in it becoming the dominant political machine in the state. It worked on behalf of the Democrat party, Irish immigrants and big business to ensure, at moderate cost, the regulatory and legislative maze would not act as a block on rapid economic growth.

"Boss" Tweed cheerfully embezzled tens of millions of dollars, over this period, and the courthouse was one of his better wheezes. Carpenters were paid hundreds of thousands of dollars for work on a building which had little wood and the marble came from a quarry, in Sheffield Massachusetts, owned by one Mr W. M. Tweed. But fate is the ultimate court jester. Ten years after work had started in the courthouse, a corruption scandal brought down "Boss" Tweed and he was tried in an unfinished court in the building that would bear his name in future generations.

It was in this monument to justice that Renat Murdrych found himself. On his last trip to the courthouse, the previous week, he had pleaded guilty to the charge of kidnap and false imprisonment. There was little point in denying he had done this, as he had to all intents and purposes handed himself in when he helped rescue the child he'd kidnapped. It was an irony that seemed appropriate in a setting whose establishment was a testimony to the capricious nature of fate.

Today was the hearing where he would be sentenced. He felt a wooden club prod him needlessly in the back as he walked forward into the dock. In front of him was the old trial judge. Beside him was his nemesis in the prison, Sam Sanders, a guard who appeared to have taken an intense dislike to the Russian, for reasons that Renat could not fathom. Renat stumbled forward and stood in the dock to await his fate. As there was nothing better to do, he surveyed the large room. Everyone seemed to be staring back at him. They were all judging him, he realised. And he could hardly blame them. Kidnapping a child. How low could one man sink?

Immediately in front of him was his lawyer, Abel Mankiewicz and the prosecutor, Hermann Fielding. Behind them were a rather large number of pressmen who were a permanent fixture in the court anyway, but this case had enjoyed its fair share of notoriety.

His eyes finally rested on the reason why he was in the dock.

Violet Belmont sat staring stonily ahead. Either side of her was the inspector and his daughter who had been involved in the case. Violet looked up at Renat. She seemed unhappy.

The proceeding got underway, with the judge spending as long summing up as he had at the trial. If Renat had been familiar with the phrase "Get on with it", then he would have shouted it at the old man. But Judge Lance McCleod could have cared less. He had spent a lifetime in this role. He performed it with all the urgency of a tortoise on its morning stroll and the measured calm of a Benedictine monk making wine. After what seemed like an age, Judge McCleod stopped his summing up, and looked meaningfully at the bench.

Abel Mankievicz took this as his cue. He stood up to his full five feet two inches, patted a generous proportioned waist and said, 'If you please, the subject of the abduction, Miss Violet Belmont née Scott, would like to make a short statement to the court.

There was a murmur on the courtroom. This had not been unexpected. Renat glanced once more in the direction of Violet. She stared back at him.

Then she nodded.

Violet Belmont was eleven years old but had piled many decades of living into this short span of time. Brought up in an atmosphere of neglect, she had been adopted by a lawyer and his wife. Life had seemed to be taking a turn in the right direction for the precocious child until fate lobbed a hand grenade into what it deemed an altogether too comfortable arrangement.

Violet was kidnapped by mistake. The intended victim was her best friend, a banker's daughter, Lydia Monk. The perpetrator of the crime, and the mistaken identity, was stood before her in the dock.

By any rights, Violet should have been somewhat miffed by the chain of events that had led her to return, once more, to the Roman Catholic Orphan Asylum. If anyone had a right to complain about the wicked whims of destiny it was this young lady. However, Violet was not just a resilient child, she was a rather idiosyncratic one too. She was about the last person who would ever consider such self-pity, but she did feel sorry for Renat.

She rather liked the orphanage and she adored Sister Assumpta who had taken the young girl under her wing. Additionally, the kidnap had resulted in her meeting Bobbie Flynn and her father: she had hopes there.

Violet, despite her young years, had developed a rather acute mind. This was a lethal blend of street smarts, she was an imp from Hell's Kitchen after all, as well as a deep love of reading. This combination gave her an insight into people that was as shrewd as that of a snake oil salesman. One thing that stood out for her in this whole hot mess: Renat the Russian was as much a victim of fate as she was.

And he was *not* a bad person.

There are various ways one can detect if a person has virtues unseen. Politicians believe it is revealed with every baby kissed on the election trail. Prospective boyfriends do so by showing an interest in listening to the love of their life analyse, in forensic detail, the failings of previous boyfriends.

For a kidnapper, your options are certainly a lot more limited, on the face of it. Yet, Renat had demonstrated possibly more virtue than even those two shining exemplars, the politician and the hopeful boyfriend, through the rather unusual act of saving Violet's life, not once, but twice. A girl from Hell's Kitchen, even one who is only eleven years old, knows when a debt has been incurred.

'Are you sure, Violet?' asked Bobbie.

Violet was sure. Bobbie knew this, but felt she had to ask anyway. She nodded to Abel Mankiewicz. The attorney sighed audibly and nodded, in turn, to the judge and the prosecutor. The latter puffed his cheeks out and blew.

Prosecutor Fielding wasn't happy about the situation, but what could he do? This sense of dissatisfaction stemmed not from any dislike towards Renat. The big Russian had, at least, shown enough decency not to make a trial of something that was clearly a crime. No, it was just that what Violet was proposing to do could set a dangerous precedent.

Where would we be if all kidnappers started to treat their victims well just on the off chance that it might reduce their sentence if they were caught? The whole point of stiff sentences was deterrence. Quite simply, no kidnappings were better than some kidnappings with friendly kidnappers. The logic was simple. Fielding hoped the judge saw it that way too.

'I'm ready,' whispered Violet. She looked once at her notes. She had written out a statement in her best handwriting yet she knew it off by heart.

'Your Honor,' said Mankiewicz rising to his feet, 'With your permission, before the Court passes sentence, the kidnap victim would like to make a statement which we believe should be taken into account.'

Judge McCleod was already aware of the likelihood of this happening and was no more pleased about it than Fielding.

However, it ill behoves any man, least of all a noble representative of American Justice, to stand in the way of an eleven-year-old girl's wishes. He was, after all, a grandfather himself, who had seen four formidable such examples of the species. And then there were their mothers. Life had presented him more difficult choices than this.

'This is very irregular,' intoned Judge McCleod, looking over his half-moon glasses at Mankiewicz. Then he shifted his attention to Violet. He was met with a stare of such ferocious purpose that he decided this was, indeed, one of the easier decisions he would ever make. Still, he decided, all children need boundaries.

'The Court shall permit a statement from Miss..uh...Belmont.' He then shot a warning glance towards Prosecutor Fielding. There would be no objection. In truth, McCleod could have cared less. It had been a busy day and he was going to the opening night of Crina Colbeck's new play. He just wanted to go home. Fielding casually waved away any objection coming from his side.

'Up you go,' murmured Mankiewicz to Violet. 'It's...'

'I know where to go,' said Violet, who leapt from her seat with such violence that Bobbie flinched before grinning widely. She had no doubt that Violet would give a very good account of herself and yet her insides were churning with nerves.

Violet walked up to the steps to the witness stand, which was opposite the dock, where Renat stood. The murmur in the courtroom grew louder, forcing Judge McCleod to bang his gavel, in a casual manner. It would become more aggressive if the noise persisted.

Violet's head just about peeped over the front of the stand. She glanced down at her notes and then she put them down and stared at the old judge.

'Only three people know what happened that day, your Honor: Renat, Bugsy and me. I wasn't happy about being snatched, I can tell you. I was plenty mad at both. But throughout the time I was there, I think I knew that I could trust Renat.'

'How?' asked the Judge, genuinely curious.

'You can tell when someone wants to hurt you,' said Violet, fighting back the tears as memories of her own father and mother, who had mistreated her, flooded through her mind. 'I could tell he was not happy about the situation. And he didn't like Bugsy one bit. Bugsy was a mean man and I've known many of them.'

This brought a ripple of laughter in the court, and a stern look from McCleod at the guilty parties.

'Then I escaped,' said Violet matter-of-factly. 'Renat wasn't very good at kidnapping.'

This brought a roar of laughter, which even the judge joined in, before banging his gavel to bring calm back to the proceedings.

'Well, he wasn't,' confirmed Violet, slightly surprised at the reaction from those attending. She glanced down at Bobbie who gave her a big smile and a thumbs up. Renat did not seem impressed by having his snatching capabilities questioned so publicly, especially by a child. What kidnapper would?

Violet was remorseless, though.

'They were both useless. I mean who leaves a window open for a prisoner? Anyway, I walked a long way and came to a bad area. Some men approached me. I didn't like the look of them one bit.'

You could have heard a flea cough in the silence of the court as they listened to the child speak. Violet's voice tightened as she recalled the moment that they tried to grab her.

'They had me and I thought this was worse than when Renat and Bugsy had me. But then Renat shows up from I don't know where.'

'What happened, Violet? What did Renat do?'

'He beat the hell out of them,' said Violet, which detonated another roar of laughter. Judge McCleod decided against banging the gavel. It was a losing battle against a consummate performer. Even Hermann Fielding found himself swept along by the narrative he was hearing and wondered if he would see as good a performance tonight at Century Playhouse.

Violet described the walk across the bridge and how Renat had now promised to take her home. She described in detail the second attack when they had faced several more men. She described how she had thrown bottles at their attackers, to save Renat's life. And then, with the court held in her thrall, she took them through the moments when Renat had been shot when they finally confronted the people who had organised the kidnap.

The statement took ten minutes. Not once did Violet look at her prepared notes. The telling of the story was as dramatic as anything the courtroom had heard before and the newsmen had lapped up every word.

Violet stepped down from the witness stand. She returned to her seat and received a hug from Bobbie as well as a wry look that turned into a frown from Inspector Flynn. She quite appreciated that from the old detective.

Judge McCleod took a deep breath and began his final speech of the afternoon where he would pass sentence on Renat.

'Renat Murdrych, you stand before this court, not merely as an individual, but as a symbol of a heinous breach of trust and decency,' began McCleod, his words cutting through the silence like a scythe.

'Your disregard for the sanctity of human freedom, for the anguish you have inflicted upon your victim, you should face the full weight of justice which, in this case can be life imprisonment.'

Violet gasped, audibly, at what she was hearing. Tears stung her eyes and she glanced towards the big Russian standing in the dock.

'You shall reflect upon the enormity of your crimes and the life you endangered. We cannot live in a society where the life of a child, in fact anyone, can become a goal that is subject to monetary transaction. But let it not be said that this court lacks compassion. We have listened to the evidence of this extraordinary young girl whose story and whose willingness to forgive is a salutary lesson to us all. The court hereby sentences Renat Murdrych to four years imprisonment and it hopes that you will use the time served as a catalyst for introspection and repentance, for it is never too late to seek redemption, to atone for the sins of the past. Take the prisoner away.'

Renat was led away by Sam Sanders. Out of the sight of the courtroom, Renat felt the wooden stick jab into his kidneys.

The guard snarled into Renat's ear, 'You're mine now boy. All. Mine.'

9

Dick Devenish arrived at the door of the Flynns' brownstone, house in Greenwich Village. He took the steps two at a time, arrived at the door and gave it one almighty rap. It was just before six in the evening. He was dressed in a black dinner suit and black bow tie. His tall, elegant figure filled the suit, in the way it should be filled. He was wide of shoulder, narrow of waist and long of leg. Any woman would have been delighted to be on the end of his arm and he knew it.

All except one, perhaps, he lamented.

And she was his date tonight.

The singularity of women never ceased to delight him.

The door opened and Devenish realised that there were, in fact, two women who were deplorably immune to his charm and good looks. Both lived or worked in the same house.

Mrs Garcia cast a wary eye over Devenish, before saying cryptically, 'Oh, it's you.'

This wasn't quite the red carpet that Devenish might have hoped for but, in his heart, he wasn't expecting one, anyway. He'd met the formidable housekeeper before and had, happily, thrown barbs in her direction and received them back threefold.

'May I come in dear lady?' asked Devenish, before adding wryly, 'Or would you prefer I stand here and wait while Cinderella escapes your clutches?'

Mrs Garcia shook her head slowly and turned away before adding, 'I suppose you should come in. Wipe your feet.'

'On your head?' murmured Devenish.

'I heard that,' retorted Mrs Garcia.

Devenish entered the living room which he'd been in once before. It was a room that he had liked on first acquaintance. From the rich, dark parquet floor to the floor to ceiling bookshelves filled with books, this was his kind of room. In fact, he had one just like it in his 5th Avenue apartment. Sadly, Bobbie had deftly turned down every invitation of his to peruse his leather-bound tomes.

Devenish did not have to wait long. Bobbie soon appeared, fragrant and beautiful in a long emerald-green dress. She was, quite simply, breathtaking. Of course, Devenish was not about to show anything but amused disdain. There could be only one centre of attention in any room he was in.

'Nice dress. Have I seen it before?' he said casually.

'Nice suit,' replied Bobbie, 'Have I seen it before?'

'If you don't mind me saying, the colour suits you to a tee, Red. And may I compliment you on your modesty. So many young women are in a mad rush to reveal more skin than a poor man can handle.'

Bobbie's eyes narrowed and a half smile appeared, 'Thankfully, you are not poor and I'm sure you would cope manfully with the skimpiest of costumes.' She glanced in the mirror and saw that while it was hardly skimpy it might still have raised eyebrows in an Amish village.

'I try,' agreed Devenish, pretending to take an interest in a book on a nearby shelf.' It was John James Audubon's *Birds of America.*

'Are you interested in birds, Dick?' asked Bobbie, noting the direction of his gaze.

'This is a very rare and rather beautiful item. I imagine many would like to get their hands on it,' he said, turning his gaze back to Bobbie and smiling.

'It's not for sale,' re-joined Bobbie, an amused frown gently creasing her forehead.

'Who says anything about buying? I'd certainly spend a happy afternoon leafing through its pages enjoying the art,' said Devenish.

'I'll bet you would too,' grinned Bobbie, lifting her clutch bag from a table. 'Anyway, let's go. Where are we dining?'

'I booked *Une Belle Gosse*. I thought it appropriate,' replied Devenish.

This prompted a giggle from Bobbie. Whatever Dick Devenish might be, she thought, he was never anything less than entertaining.

'Where is that dreadful ogre of a father of yours?' asked Devenish, as he helped Bobbie on with her coat. Devenish thought the world of Flynn, and the feeling was probably mutual, but it was not something the old detective would ever admit to either in private, never mind in public. It was much easier to be grumpy in the presence of the rampant ego that was Dick Devenish.

'He didn't say, funnily enough,' said Bobbie, almost musing out loud. 'Not that he ever does or has too. After the sentencing, he gave Violet a hug, and said that he had to go.

Then he just left, without a word on where or why. I hope he'll be okay. When he does that it's usually something big.'

'How did Violet take the sentencing?' asked Devenish. His tone changed and it was not the usual jocular, semi-mocking, one that Bobbie was used to. He liked the young girl and had cause to admire her, following their encounter at the Metropolitan Museum. Bobbie glanced at Devenish and wondered if she was being too hasty in dismissing his semi-amusing, semi-mocking advances. If only he took himself, and others, a little more seriously...

They started to walk down the stairs to the entrance hallway. Bobbie said, 'She was upset. It was too much to hope that Renat would be let off and I think she knew this herself but, well, she's young. Really smart. But young. There was no way that Renat could possibly hope to escape some punishment. Given that the judge could have given him life imprisonment for kidnapping a child, I think he was remarkably lenient.'

'Which judge did you have?' asked Devenish, he remained more serious.

'Judge McCleod.'

'McCleod? You were fortunate. I like him. Decent old boy. Who was the prosecutor?'

'Mr Fielding.'

'Fielding? And he raised no objection to this?'

Bobbie shook her head. There were tears in her eyes now as she said, 'He would have been lynched, I think. You had to hear Violet in the witness box. She was so brave.'

Devenish nodded at this. They were outside the door now and they walked over to the waiting cab.

'You won't get an argument from me on that score,' replied Devenish. 'How much longer before I will have to run the gauntlet of that little lady in Flynn Towers?'

Bobbie burst out laughing at this. The cab had set off now and they were on their way towards Broadway.

'I haven't quite asked Violet if this is what she wants. But I understand it will go quite quickly once she agrees. The fact that daddy is a policeman means that we can cut through the red tape a lot more quickly than most.'

The journey to the restaurant went quickly and soon they were stepping out of the cab. At the doors of the restaurant a man wearing a tuxedo exited before them. He and Devenish recognised one another.

'Hello there Dick,' said the man. He was around fifty years of age, his accent was very much upstate New York, clearly from a wealthy background. He was not tall but he had a genial manner that made him more handsome than he might otherwise have appeared. 'If you're having dinner, I can recommend the salmon. It was excellent.'

'I shall look at that old boy,' replied Devenish. 'May I introduce this young lady.'

'I was hoping you would,' laughed the man, removing his hat.

'This is Miss Roberta Flynn, also known as Bobbie, also known as Red. Take your pick.'

'Well, I shall be guided by you Miss, and ignore this rogue. He is a rogue by the way,' laughed the man.

"I had noticed,' agreed Bobbie. 'But a charming one, I'll give him that. And Bobbie is fine, by the way.

'Bobbie it shall be, then.'

'And this, Bobbie, is Felix Stanton, otherwise known as "Smiley".' Bobbie's eyes widened in surprise. Of course! She should have recognised him. 'Anyway, Smiley, we might see you later.'

They did.

Only he had a knife sticking out of his chest.

10

Felix "Smiley" Stanton was a man to whom words such as "scrupulous", "integrity" and "honour" were exactly that, just words. Despite all the advantages of a wealthy background, an expensive education and a solid God-fearing family, the affable "Smiley" had chosen another path, from the one that had been earmarked for him in the family business, of manufacturing bathroom commodes.

The market for indoor conveniences was a lucrative one. It had been spotted by his father, Ernest, a few decades earlier. This astute individual had foreseen a huge demand for indoor latrines, as Americans began to enjoy the fruits of the country's prosperity. The growing economy was matched by an enormous decline, in the great and the good's desire to perform their natural functions in a cold, insect-ravaged outhouse.

Much to the disappointment of his father, and three elder brothers, Felix found the world of the indoor privy too confining. He was flushed with a desire to see the world. This was partially forced on him as he was sent down from Yale, where he had been studying law. His crime had foreshadowed what was to become a lucrative career as the twentieth century began.

Illegal gambling.

Felix by now, was known as "Smiley" by friend and foe alike. While there were many of the latter, even his bitterest enemy did not have it in his heart to dislike the man. His genial manner was all too clearly written on his face. Win or lose, Smiley never stopped smiling.

He rarely lost.

Choosing to read law at Yale had been a mistake; a failure to recognise where his true talents lay. And they lay in mathematics. Specifically, the mathematics of probability. This discovery was as enjoyable as it ultimately proved to be profitable. At least, this was so, until his final year, when the University uncovered a craps game, he was running, where bets of several thousand dollars were routinely being made.

The game was stopped. And young Smiley's smile, for once, left his face. Rather than deal with the wrath of his parents, he took his gains, which were close to fifty thousand dollars, and headed to New York, where he felt opportunity lay, for an enterprising young man such as himself.

It did.

There were a few bumps and bruises along the way, but soon Smiley was running the biggest craps game in town on behalf of businessmen who were keen to diversify and make, as Mark Twain once said, their vocation a vacation.

For fifteen years he enjoyed himself at the pinnacle of New York's gambling scene. During this time, his affairs had been many and as brief as decently possible. Love had not so much eluded him as been deftly avoided, by a man keen to sidestep any long-term entanglement.

Until he met Crina Colbeck.

At a craps game.

He hadn't been expecting to meet the great actress at one of his games. This is not to say the world of entertainment was not averse to playing games of chance. Far from it. Many Vaudeville performers, even more show girls, often found their way into Smiley's floating craps game. But never anyone with the star power of the great Crina Colbeck.

And she clearly did not want to be there.

The man she was with had insisted that she give it a try. However, love's light was extinguished for the star when the man in question, someone who she had met while still mourning for her late husband, proved to be a gambler and a drunkard.

As she watched this man get progressively more ossified during the game, losing thousands as he went, as well as his temper, another man took her home that night. That man, that saviour, was Felix "Smiley" Stanton.

He'd done this as he saw the tell-tale signs that the game was threatening to spill over into violence. This was an occupational hazard for floating craps games. How often had he seen someone losing more than they believe the laws of probability dictate? Their reaction was all too predictable, and Smiley was an expert in probability. Things began to turn hostile. Given that some of the players were armed to the teeth, the situation was, in Smiley's view, febrile and certainly no place for a beautiful leading lady.

Sir Galahads come in all shapes, sizes and types. Crina Colbeck was still beautiful and retained all the grace of someone who was theatre royalty. She should never have been there, and that was not just her view. Smiley took it upon himself to protect the actress. And he did so rather forcefully.

He knew his way around a punch up. And a few men were taught this, as he escorted his damsel from the scene.

Crina was very grateful to her rescuer. Smiley, meanwhile, was bedazzled. Unbeknownst to her, the man she thought of as Galahad was, in fact, not just the game organiser, he was the premier game organiser in Manhattan. This discovery did not happen until a year later. By then they were married.

Smiley promised to give up running craps games. And then he'd told her he was buying a theatre. Crina was delighted by this news. Her absence from performing had not dimmed her love for the stage. Perhaps, just perhaps, she would return.

Not once, in all this time, did Crina ever stop and think to ask the one question which should have been uppermost in her mind.

Smiley, how can you afford to buy a Broadway theatre?

There was a reason why Smiley could afford to buy a Broadway theatre and it certainly was not because he had come from a wealthy family or had made tens of thousands of dollars running craps games. As he crossed the road to the theatre, he "owned", Smiley felt his guts churn. He was going to meet the real reason he was now a theatre impresario.

And it would not have impressed his ever-loving wife.

'Felix, there you are,' said the man. He was sitting in Smiley's office, in Smiley's seat, behind Smiley's large antique oak desk. Around the room were publicity posters for many of the shows that Smiley had put on, in his two years running the theatre. This was the first time that he'd been visited by the man before him. Smiley did what he always did. It was what came most naturally to him.

He smiled.

'I didn't realise you had a ticket,' said Smiley, opening his cigarette case and offering the visitor one. It was declined.

'I had trouble getting tickets. Looks like it's a full house, Felix,' said the man. There was a smile on his face, but it could not have been chillier. 'Tell me Felix,' said the man, in a voice that was pleasant, educated even, yet utterly chilling, 'You have a beautiful wife, she is going to perform in this beautiful theatre which you own and, I gather from speaking to your books man, Clement, that the show is sold out for all of its five-week run: where did it all go wrong?'

And there was the nub. *Where had it all gone wrong?*

Smiley walked forward, his heart pounding, like a middle-distance track runner in the home straight. He sat down opposite the man and tried to, at least, give the appearance of being in control.

'Is it such a bad thing if we have a hit show?' he asked, trying not to sound plaintive.

'This isn't what we planned, Felix, is it?' murmured the man.

'I know, but look here, it's getting mighty suspicious if we produce one losing show after another. I'm getting asked questions. Pretty soon no one will believe the accounts. And no one will believe that our backers will happily sit by and...'

'Watch their ill-gotten gains getting washed clean and having substantial tax write off's because of the losses incurred,' finished the man.

When you put it that way, thought Smiley, it probably wasn't the best idea to have put on the hottest show in town. He still had one ace to play.

'The one mistake you are making,' he said and immediately wished he'd found other words to express the point, 'the issue you are not considering is that we are not going to make much money on this. Yes, it will be profitable, but not so much that it will transform our year. Crina is entitled to a percentage of the house because she's a star, but that will go through our joint company and I can make sure that we make losses elsewhere so as not to draw suspicion upon us. Honestly, you have nothing to worry about.'

The man nodded at this and, perhaps it was Smiley's imagination, he was almost reassured.

'Perhaps Felix,' he intoned, 'But why did you take so long to inform your backers that ticket sales were going so well? It's almost as if you were hiding things from us and that would not be a good idea.'

'It's been a busy time. We lost the young female support and two understudies last week so I was running around trying to audition and hire replacements.'

The man nodded again and seemed dissatisfied by the answer. Then he stood up. He was tall and dressed very elegantly. Quite how he ever ended up in this world was beyond Smiley's guess. Quite how *he* ever ended up running a loss-making theatre on behalf of the mob was beyond him also.

'I'll take my seat now, Felix. Is it a good show?' he asked coldly.

'Best thing in town,' replied Smiley, and realised this was not what the man wanted to hear. So Smiley smiled, and the man departed.

It was a half an hour to curtain up. Smiley went down the stairs to the backstage area. On his way, he bumped into a pretty young woman with a dark bob haircut. This was Polly Buckley, the young actress suggested to him by Crina after he had lost his previous choice.

'Hi Polly, how's things back there?'

'Oh, great Mr Stanton. We're all a bit nervous, well, except Miss Colbeck. She seems so calm.'

'How's her mood?' pressed Smiley.

'Seemed fine with me,' replied Polly.

They parted and Smiley wandered into the corridor where the dressing rooms were located. His nostrils were immediately assailed by the unmistakable aroma of recent emulsion. The scent, a potent concoction of industrial zeal and aesthetic ambition, hung in the air like a Wagnerian opera — impossible to ignore and difficult to escape.

Lane Vidal was outside the dressing room he shared with Wickham McNeill, smoking a cigarette, with the composed air that would have done justice to a cow in a meadow. If he was nervous, then he hid it well. He was an experienced actor and had done this many times, thought Smiley. An opening night was like water off a duck's back to him. Even if his co-star was Crina Colbeck.

'Hey Lane,' said Smiley. 'You look like you've just been told your stocks are up.'

Vidal smiled at this. He replied, 'Well, I've certainly picked a winner here old boy. So have you.'

This was a reminder that Smiley did not need at that moment after his earlier encounter. He laughed this off and made his way to the dressing room of his wife, the star of the show, Crina Colbeck. He knocked on the door and said, 'Hey, honey, can I come in.'

'Enter,' said a voice from behind the door.

Smiley stepped in. The dressing room was large and beautifully furnished as befitted a star of such magnitude. A leather Chesterfield sofa for guests, an oak coffee table, a drinks cabinet and a *chaise longue,* upon which Crina had stretched out languorously, smoking from a long cigarette holder.

'Everyone is so relaxed,' said Smiley. 'I'm a bag of nerves.' This was certainly the truth and Crina would never have guessed why, he concluded. He bent down and kissed her proffered cheek. He would like to have done more. She radiated an aura of unassailable glamour even though she was clad only in a silk Japanese kimono. Smiley perched on the coffee table and stared into those wondrous green eyes. He never worried about how many other men had done as he had done. He was the one looking at her now and that was all that mattered. He was the luckiest man alive.

'I'm happy to be back, Felix. Thank you for giving me this opportunity,' said Crina. While the sentiment suggested humility, it was difficult to avoid the suspicion that it was Crina who was doing Smiley the favour. However, Smiley was too star struck; love's light shone brighter, in his eyes, than a well-polished chandelier.

'I won't stay,' said Smiley, rising, 'I just want you to know that I love you, and I know you're going to be a sensation.'

Smiley left the room a minute later. He had one more stop to make. He walked down the corridor to a door that led to the area beneath the stage. He opened the door and entered a realm that could only be described as a blend of Aladdin's cave and an attic after a children's party. The air was thick with the musty scent of dust and antiquity, mingled with the faint whiff of greasepaint and stale popcorn.

The space was a labyrinthine tangle of ropes, pulleys and mysterious contraptions whose purpose was as inscrutable as a vegetarian's dietary preferences. Old set pieces, relics of past productions, loomed in the shadows like the forgotten dreams of a once-great thespian. Here a battered chaise longue reclined with the weary grace of an aging diva, there a faux-Grecian column tilted precariously, threatening to topple over at the slightest provocation.

Cobwebs festooned the rafters like the decorations of a, particularly indolent, party planner, and the occasional scurry of a rat, moving with the stealth of a cat burglar, added an element of furtive activity to the scene.

He walked through to the other side and reached another door. Taking some keys from his pocket, he opened the door and walked into a short, dark corridor. At the end was another door which was also locked. Keys still in hand, he opened this door and found himself in a room that had once been used for rehearsals but now had another purpose. There were no windows to this room. It was dark inside. He switched on the light.

The room was about the size of half a basketball court. There were a few chairs and small tables scattered about. One large piece of furniture dominated the middle of the room. The top of the table was cut in with a green baize with enigmatic markings.

Smiley ran his fingers along the green baize and felt his heart leap. This was what made him happiest. It was how he had made his fortune.

He stared at the craps table and thought about the game that would take place later that night while his wife performed above them.

11

Evening – end of the performance

The screaming in the theatre grew louder as the realisation dawned that someone had been murdered.

Except the man hadn't been murdered. Dick Devenish, a few seats down from where the man sat slumped, immediately went to him. He bent over to check for signs of life.

'Good Lord,' he called back to Bobbie. 'It's Smiley. He's alive.' He stood to his full height and tried to shout above the din of the screaming. 'Is there a doctor in the house?' It took a few attempts but soon noise in the theatre began to dim as several of the people began to make shushing sounds, which gradually rippled through the audience. Then Devenish's call for a doctor could be heard more clearly.

On stage, Crina was being comforted by Polly Buckley while the male actors stood around somewhat dumbfounded as their triumphant performance had suddenly been forgotten by the extraordinary turn of events.

A shout from the back of the stall indicated there was one doctor in the house. A second came from the circle. The audience was now caught in the paradoxical desire to remove themselves from the scene of the crime, as well as morbid curiosity as to what had happened. The area around Smiley began to clear and several people moved past Bobbie, who had been sitting near the end of the row.

Another voice, an all too familiar one to Bobbie, was now audible. It was Detective Nolan, who was calling for people to let him through as he was a detective. The seas parted to let him through. Bobbie glanced in the direction of the young woman that had accompanied Nolan to the play, she was still sitting in her seat, staring ahead as if unmoved by what was happening.

Bobbie saw Nolan arrive to Smiley. He exchanged a few words with Devenish and then nodded. Nolan quickly looked around him at the sea of faces and towards Crina Colbeck on the stage. Her head was buried in the shoulder of Polly Buckley. Nolan motioned for the actress to lead Crina off the stage. He spoke quickly to Devenish who then turned to Bobbie. He gestured towards the stage.

Bobbie understood immediately. She made her way slowly past the many people crammed in the corridor to the side of the theatre and towards the steps that led up to the stage. As she did this, she heard Nolan shouting above the noise.

'Ladies and gentlemen, I am Detective Nolan from the New York Police Department. Please can I have your attention.'

This brought more shushing from many in the theatre and soon the noise levels reduced enough for Nolan to make himself heard by everyone in the audience. His voice was calm and measured as he addressed the theatre. Bobbie realised he might have made a fine actor as she listened to his voice carry throughout the auditorium.

'Ladies and Gentlemen, please try and remain calm. You are aware that there has been a violent assault on a member of the audience. Can I ask patrons up in the circle to exit the building quickly and calmly. Can I also ask everyone in the stalls from rows E to the back row also to leave unless you believe you have seen or heard something that may help with the inquiry. I would also ask that anyone in rows A to D from seat 40 to the aisle on the far left to leave also unless you believe that you are a witness to what has happened. Ushers, can you please help get the audience to leave the theatre calmly.'

Bobbie was on the stage now and glanced towards Nolan. He was standing on one of the seats near where Smiley lay injured. Beside Smiley was Dick Devenish and another man, dressed in a tuxedo, who appeared to be examining Smiley. Another man was making his way along the seat row. Bobbie guessed he was a second doctor.

Bobbie realised many of the audience were now staring at her and wondering what was happening. She quickly turned to the cast and walked towards them.

'My name is Bobbie Flynn. I am a friend of the two gentlemen near Mr Stanton. One of them is Detective Nolan who is a personal friend. The other is Private Investigator Dick Devenish who has supported the police in several murder cases. Mr Stanton is in good hands. I, too, do have some experience in these matters and they have asked me to come up here and handle matters until more police arrive.'

Bobbie spoke with such authority that the only person more surprised by her tone than the cast was herself. Everyone on stage was staring at her but the looks on their faces which had initially been somewhat hostile soon changed towards something approaching reassured. Bobbie turned to Crina and Polly.

'There are doctors with Mr Stanton. There's nothing else to be done. Miss Buckley, please can you take Miss Colbeck to her dressing room and stay with her. If she has a dresser, can you ask her to obtain something medicinal.'

Polly frowned slightly at this and then it dawned on her that Bobbie was asking to find some alcohol. She nodded to Bobbie and whispered into the ear of Crina. A few moments later, the two actresses slowly made their way from the stage. The three male actors stood like they were dressed in fancy dress at a funeral. Uncertain about what to do next they turned to Bobbie who, at least, gave the impression that she knew what she was about. Bobbie twirled her finger around to a young man standing in the wings. Moments later, the curtain came down on the most extraordinary opening night that anyone had ever seen.

Bobbie then turned to face the three actors.

'Can I ask you to return to your dressing rooms? The police will be along shortly to take statements.'

One of the men clearly looked a little displeased at Bobbie ordering them around.

'Who are you may I ask? Why should we take orders from you?' This was Jason Crane, the oldest member of the cast. He was around sixty, tall, slender and still handsome. A pencil thin moustache clung to his upper lip like a leech. His tone had an inbuilt sneer that had been apparent during the play. Bobbie had thought this a trait of the character he was playing, it was, in fact, a character trait of the actor. She took an immediate dislike to the man and she was in no mood to give him an inch, publicly.

'Go if you wish, Mr Crane. But you are a key witness to what appears to be attempted murder. The police will be happy to interview you down at Midtown North precinct where Detective Nolan is stationed. It would be unfortunate if the press were to hear that you were there, wouldn't it? As it happens, I am a member of the press.'

Bobbie watched in satisfaction as Crane's face turned pale. She also noted how a few of the other cast members smiled as Bobbie said her piece. Clearly, Crane was not loved.

'Perhaps the rest of you, unlike Mr Crane, would prefer not to be photographed going into Midtown North. If you could make your way down to the dressing rooms, I'm sure the police will be along shortly to listen to your statements.'

'Listen young lady,' snapped Crane at Bobbie. 'I shall have words with the police about your attitude.' He strode towards Bobbie in a manner that put in mind a particularly repressed English butler. This image somewhat reduced the sense of threat in Bobbie's eyes while, at the same time, increasing her sense of amusement, at his affected manner. He was now very close to Bobbie. 'And I have a number of very good friends in the police force, I can tell you.'

'Do you Mr Crane?' said Bobbie sweetly. 'Well, do you know Inspector Flynn? He has made the news on a few occasions; you may have seen him. He's my father. He is close friends with the Commissioner, Mr Enright, whom I have had occasion to help more than a few times myself. I'll introduce you if you like, or perhaps you know him already?'

It sounded like Wickham McNeill who laughed first. He walked past them both and murmured to Crane, 'I think it's time to pick yourself off the canvas Crane and get your cornermen to throw in the towel old chum.' McNeill's fruity

81

English accent made this all the funnier to Bobbie, but she managed to stop herself smiling.

Crane merely scowled at Bobbie, before following McNeill and Vidal into the wings, where there were stairs that would take them backstage to the dressing rooms.

This left Bobbie alone on the stage. She had a choice now between going to the front to re-join Devenish, but this would mean having to come face to face with Nolan once more. She wanted this desperately. Yet, how could she? It would mean confronting the reality that he had, insofar as he was ever close to Bobbie, moved on. And boy had he moved on. The girl he was with seemed like a goddess, but one who had no idea just how beautiful she was. Bobbie felt like a cheap imitation by comparison in her shiny dress.

Then another thought struck her. The young man who was operating the curtains. He was potentially a witness. She glanced across the stage but could see no sign of him. He had been standing at the same side as the one the actors had exited from.

Decision made; she headed across the stage, without glancing out into the auditorium. She was sure that Nolan would have matters in hand. And anyway, one other thought was spinning around her head which meant that meeting Detective Nolan was unavoidable.

She, too, was a witness.

12

Reaching the side of the stage, Bobbie quickly confirmed that the young man she'd seen operating the curtains was no longer there. As she had not seen him attempt to leave via the stage, she assumed that he had gone backstage. The wings were quite large and had all manner of props and sets that she'd seen used earlier in the play. Mrs Garcia would have had palpitations at how untidy it was.

Bobbie passed a control panel which operated both the curtain and, she suspected, the lighting. She wondered if the young man had been the one to turn the theatre into darkness, as the play reached its final moments. There were several questions that Bobbie needed answers to.

She saw a light above a narrow set of stairs and headed towards it. Soon Bobbie was descending the stairs, which took her out into a corridor, where she saw two of the actors she'd seen on stage earlier, but not Crane.

Wickham McNeil saw Bobbie appear and grinned towards her.

'If you're looking for Crane, I think he's gone to lick his wounds, young lady. Bravo by the way. Best entertainment I've had in a long time. My name's McNeill,' said the actor, holding out his hand to Bobbie. His face had the flushed look of a Vaudeville drunk, which probably was not too far away from the truth, in Bobbie's judgement. However, he seemed to be pleasantly inebriated. Bobbie had seen a few mean drunks in her time, and it gave, a small part of her, some sympathy towards the lobby that had advocated Prohibition. Only a small part of her, though.

They shook hands with Bobbie who said, 'Very pleased to meet you Mr McNeill. I enjoyed the play immensely up until, well, you know... I saw you in Henry IV. You were wonderful as Falstaff.'

'Thank you my dear,' beamed the actor. 'But let's be honest, it wasn't much of a stretch for me and this is not to disparage the wonderful character created by Shakespeare or blow my own trumpet. I doubt I was sober at any point during the run.'

Bobbie laughed at this. She replied with a chuckle, 'It didn't look like you were under the influence, that's to say you were just right, if you know what I mean.'

'I do and you are very kind. Now, my dear, is there any way I can be of assistance to you before the US Cavalry arrive?'

'I was wondering if you had seen a young man come here. I saw him operating the curtains earlier.'

The old actor nodded. He said, 'Ahh you mean young Mr Hart. Yes, I saw him a moment ago. I think he may have gone to the stage door. There'll be a riot outside soon, with those jackals from the press. He'll have his shotgun loaded I hope.' McNeill said the word "jackals" with a great deal of feeling. And that feeling was hatred.

Bobbie decided that now was probably not the time to mention that the press had already made an incursion backstage, in her own slender form. She decided to forgive the elderly actor, as it was not beyond the realms of possibility that his view of the Fourth Estate may have been borne from a bad review or several.

'Where would I find the stage door – is it at the end of the corridor?'

'Oh yes,' waved the actor airily.

Bobbie thanked him and moved down the corridor, past the room marked with Crina Colbeck's name, through a set of double doors into an area that was a little more run down looking. Instead of stuccoed walls, there was brick. The floor was concrete and there were several storage cupboards. It was dark and Bobbie could just imagine the size of the cobwebs above her. Not just the cobwebs, the spiders too.

Up ahead was the stage door, if the sign was to be believed, and above it was another sign saying exit. Beside the door, there was a small office with large windows to view who came and went. There was a light on. Bobbie marched forward and knocked on the door.

'Yes,' came a male voice.

'Hi, my name is Bobbie Flynn, I was on the stage earlier after the attack on Mr Stanton. Can I speak with you a minute?'

'Sure, come in,' came the reply.

Bobbie entered an office that looked bigger inside. There were two tables, one with a typewriter. There were also more cupboards, and a bank of drawers. The office was very tidy however, unlike much of what Bobbie had seen backstage.

There was a young man seated at one of the desks. Bobbie would have put his age at twenty, or perhaps a little older. He had freckles and friendly eyes which crinkled as he smiled when he saw Bobbie enter. He rose from his chair. Bobbie appreciated the good manners from the young man and, immediately, felt reassured that he would not prove difficult.

'Yeah, I remember you on the stage, Miss. How can I help you?'

Bobbie smiled at the young man and sat down at the other free seat. 'Are you Mr Hart?'

The smile on the boy's face widened, 'Mr Hart? Well, probably, but maybe you could call me Tommy. Everyone else does, except Mr McNeill, that is. I like him.'

'Yes, he's very nice,' agreed Bobbie. Then she leaned forward and studied Tommy for a few moments. Her initial impression that he was a teenager was borne out by his voice and guileless smile. He was quite tall, certainly six feet or more, but very slender. There were just a few freckles on his face and his straw-coloured hair, and clear green-blue eyes might have suggested a country boy, had it not been for a mild New York accent, which was not so very different from her own.

'Are you the stage manager?' asked Bobbie, trying not to look or sound sceptical.

The boy laughed, 'Oh no, that would be Mr Crispin. I'm his assistant. I've been working for him for six months now since I left college. He's showing me the ropes, Miss..uhhh.'

'Call me Bobbie. Mr Crispin, is he not around tonight? I mean, a big night like this...' asked Bobbie, unable to hide her surprise.

'Oh, he's around, at least, he was earlier. He saw all the actors arrive and then he went through with me again about the curtains; I already know all that.'

'So, you operated the curtains tonight?'

'Yes, that was me,' said Tommy, proudly. 'I've been doing this for a few months now so it's no big deal.'

'Who does the lights? Do you have someone for that, like a lighting manager?'

'No, that's me too. We don't have a lot of people working at the theatre. Only me, Mr Crispin and Miss Haynes, who is the dresser and helps with makeup. And there's Mr Jeffries who is our Property Manager.'

'Props?' asked Bobbie.

'Yes, that's it. He's somewhere backstage now, I imagine,' answered Tommy.

Bobbie nodded at this. She thought for a moment, while Tommy happily smiled back at her. He obviously was keen to help her. She did not have long, before the police would be here, so now was her chance to glean as much as she could, before the police shooed her away and she had to face Detective Nolan, as a witness rather than a partner in crime, so to speak.

'Tommy, you switched out the lights just as Miss Colbeck was doing her final soliloquy?' She saw the boy nod. 'And who managed the prop with the gun firing?'

'That was Mr Vidal. But you never know that in the play.'

'Strange,' replied Bobbie and smiled when she saw Tommy's eyes widen and head nod. He clearly agreed. 'What do you remember about what happened, just before, and after you switched out the lights. Tell me, who was on stage that you could see. Who was off stage? What do you remember hearing, not just what you were seeing.'

'Gosh. Well, I was the only one in the wings.'

'So, Mr Crispin and Mr Jeffries were not there.'

'I didn't see Mr Jeffries but I think I caught sight of Mr Crispin across in the right wing.'

'Is this normal?'

'I suppose it is although maybe on the opening night, both are around more. Anyway, I didn't see anyone else except the actors and Miss Buckley on the stage. And there was no one at the other side, aside from Mr Crispin, that I could see. But, then again, I wasn't really paying attention. All I could think about was making sure that I hit the lights at exactly the right moment.'

'What moment was that?' asked Bobbie.

'Well Miss Colbeck's character, Petronella, says something like, "*You see, this is how it must end.*" And then I hit the lights, on the word "*end*", then there is a gunshot a few seconds later. I wait for Miss Buckley to scream, and then I hit the lights again, so that we can see Miss Colbeck lying on the floor. Then I lower the curtain, after a few moments – just long enough for the audience to see that Petronella, Miss Colbeck, is dead and that the others are in shock.'

'We all were, trust me,' laughed Bobbie. 'So let me recap, Tommy. You were managing the curtain and the lights at the time of the attack. There was no one else around you, aside from the people on stage. Tell me, what did you hear, or sense when the lights went out. Could someone have thrown a knife from the stage?'

Tommy laughed at this, albeit a little nervously. Then he replied, 'I think I would have heard someone move on the stage or around me. There's no way anyone went past me to reach the stage and then disappear before the lights came back on.'

'Could anyone have been hiding in the set at upstage? Theoretically?' pressed Bobbie.

'I suppose, but they still would not have had time to get to the front of the stage, and throw a knife, into the darkness, by the way and then get back without anyone seeing, or hearing, them on the stage. Maybe they could have done it from the other side of the stage, but they would have to have been waiting there throughout the play, and they would have had to have gone to that side before the play began, as I was in the wings throughout.'

'I see,' said Bobbie. She stood up at this point, much to the evident disappointment of Tommy, who was rather enjoying being interrogated by a young woman who was easy on the eye. 'I should get back to see what is happening with Mr Stanton. Just out of curiosity, who told you to come back here?'

'Mr Crane suggested I should, and Mr McNeill agreed. He said it was going to get busy. I had to stop the press getting in.'

Too late, thought Bobbie who merely smiled sympathetically.

'Where do you think I might find Mr Crispin? And what do I look for?'

'Mr Crispin will either be in the corridor, you came along or, perhaps, he'll be in the green room, where the performers go, before the performance begins. I imagine the police will want to question people and they'll do it there. Mr Crispin is probably in his sixties, quite small, with a grey moustache and bald.'

'Should be easy enough to find. Thanks, Tommy, for everything,' said Bobbie and meant it.

Tommy looked please to have helped. He seemed like a very sweet boy, thought Bobbie. She wondered how he would cope with the so-called jackals.

Just after Bobbie had left the stage manager's office, she heard a voice from behind her. She turned around and saw Tommy at the door, 'You could also try underneath the stage. He might be there also if he's not around backstage.'

'Thanks,' said Bobbie and headed back into the backstage corridor.

13

Clement C. Crispin spent twenty years of his life working as a clerk in a bookkeeping firm. As the third decade in the firm beckoned, a talent for discretion, finally, reaped the appreciation his work so richly deserved. It occurred when he discovered that a firm, for whom his company were doing contract bookkeeping work, was involved in a number of activities that might be deemed somewhat illegal, that he showed his mettle.

Rather than immediately hounding off to the local law enforcement precinct, he decided that the police, admirable fellows though they may be, possessed too much rigidity of outlook when it came to understanding the numbers he was looking at. Instead of bringing it to the attention of his boss, a horrible lay preacher called Smith, he decided to take the bull by the horns, which is to say, his life in his hands and bring his discoveries to the attention of the firm in question.

Delighted by the level of prudence shown by Crispin, they hired him on the spot, for double his salary, to continue showing this dedication to well-maintained books, accompanied by silence.

The next fifteen years flew by, until that moment when a gold watch beckoned. His employers recognised that newer and younger blood, using more up to date bookkeeping systems, would require Crispin to step aside. This was disappointing, but inevitable, he judged. There were no hard feelings, on either side.

Then Fate, whose humour undoubtedly tends towards the sardonic, intervened. The purchase of a theatre, by several different elements of the Mob, presented a new career path for the retiring bookkeeper. His well-known passion for the performing arts, he was a regular theatre goer, prompted one of his bosses to ask if he fancied taking over as stage manager. For double his salary. The job required that he work rarely more than twenty hours a week.

Crispin accepted the post delightedly. The cost of putting two children through college had badly dented his finances. So, too, had a bad run at the craps table. The boss, who had suggested he join him, was none other than Felix "Smiley" Stanton.

It was like a small boy being handed the keys to a candy shop, with a two-word instruction and those words were, 'Help yourself.'

One moment, the birds were chirping, the bees were buzzing, and the world seemed as radiant as, a freshly polished, silver teapot. The next, a metaphorical dark cloud began to loom on the horizon, casting a shadow over his otherwise sunny disposition. It was the sort of cloud that arrives unbidden, bringing with it the, unmistakable, whiff of impending doom.

Smiley wanted to escape from the treadmill of running a floating craps game. Crispin wanted to spend the rest of his working days in the theatre. Specifically, to be in the same universe as, the wondrous, Crina Colbeck.

When the lights went out, Crispin had been in the right wing, unseen by the cast, gazing at Crina, rapt, just like the audience, at her extraordinary performance. It would certainly rank among her great roles, and he had seen them all, often many times.

Now, as part stage manager, a job that he could never have predicted would come his way, he'd had the privilege to attend the rehearsals, and see her work almost on a daily basis. The differences between those days and what he had witnessed on this night astonished him.

Most good actors can lose themselves in a character; from this, truth emerges. And it is a magical process, certainly.

A star shone, however, so brightly that it did something else to the performance, that actors could only dream about. They created memories. This was achieved by playing characters that somehow, took from the real world its desires and its anxieties and portrayed this through their character. Petronella Rothschild's death was the death of an old-world giving way to the Jazz Age. Crina had somehow made Petronella become something so much more than an aging woman.

This was the difference between Crina and the others. He'd seen her many times on stage, often several times over one run. He adored her, and always had. Of course, he was but an audience member then, but now he was working with her.

She even knew his name.

While Crispin was standing in the wings, he knew his job, that night, was not to manage the curtain or the lights. Young Hart was now, thankfully, trained on such mundane matters. His job, that night, was to keep an eye on the audience, to ensure that the unthinkable would not happen.

A police raid.

That night the unthinkable had happened. Someone had attempted to kill Smiley. It was Crispin's job now to inform the craps game patrons. Because as sure as there was murder, police would follow soon after.

When the lights went up, and the commotion started, Crispin stood back from sight, crouched down and made his way beneath the stage to the door that Smiley had used, a couple of hours earlier, that led to the secret room that housed the craps game. He, too, had a set of keys that allowed him entry to the corridor, where the room was located.

At this point, it is worth noting that entering a room where a craps game is in progress is not a simple matter of walking in. This is not a good idea when so many of the patrons are packing Roscoes and are feeling mightily twitchy, as it is without some, emptyheaded, man with a death wish interrupting proceedings. Crispin's heart was already beating at a rate of knots that was decidedly unhealthy for a man nearer seventy than sixty.

Crispin gave three loud knocks, loud enough to cut through the noise on the other side of the door. He received one knock in return. Crispin stepped inside the room and was confronted by the sight of around twenty gentlemen, all dressed in tuxedos. There were a few young ladies there too, but the smoke and the smell of the room shouted male.

Standing at one end of the table was a man with a cigar pressed between his teeth, his arm in the air, dice in hand and a look on his face that would have melted stone, because he did not like to be interrupted, mid-throw.

Crispin addressed this man directly.

'Captain O'Riordan, we have a very serious situation.'

Nothing, on O'Riordan's face, suggested that there was anything more serious than his next throw. He gave a Crispin a look that said "this-better-good".

It was.

'Captain, someone's just tried to kill Mr Stanton.'

Silence.

O'Riordan's arm fell, he slowly removed the cigar from his mouth and looked Crispin square in the eye.

'Say that again.'

'Someone just tried to kill Mr Stanton.'

'How do you know?' asked O'Riordan, still not quite comprehending the turn of events. And who was to blame him? Here he was mid throw, on a run that was recouping his not inconsiderable losses for the evening when, suddenly, fortune had thrown a curve ball at him.

'How do you know?' asked O'Riordan. The captain had many qualities, but quick thinking and flexibility of mind were not in among them. He was not unaware of his limitations and sensed that the room was already losing patience, with this ponderous line of questioning.

'He had a knife sticking out of him.'

Well, that seemed fairly irrefutable, by any standards. Silence followed this statement, as its implication became all too clear to everyone.

'We need to pack up,' said O'Riordan. 'Quickly.'

This had already been anticipated by a couple of local state politicians, who were clearing money off the table. Some of it was even theirs.

And then disaster struck.

Now, one may say that having the host of a craps game sitting with a theatre audience, a knife sticking in his chest while a craps game is taking place in a secret room nearby, probably constitutes a disaster. Not so.

The disaster occurred moments later when the door leading out into an alleyway burst open. Into the room rushed a lot of patrolmen all wielding batons and shouting while, paradoxically, everyone was to be quiet.

The situation was somewhat febrile. The cocktail of baton-wielding policemen, nervous politicians and hard guys whose disposition is permanently mean, was incendiary. At any moment gunfire was possible.

This possibility simmered for seconds until the final couple of policemen walked in. One of them was Sergeant Shane "Harry" Harrigan. The other was Inspector Flynn.

Very quickly, hands that had gently descended towards pockets containing something deadlier than a white handkerchief, swiftly moved away. Flynn was not a man to be messed with.

Flynn walked forward into the room where silence had fallen like, well, a theatre curtain. He surveyed the men in the room. Nodded to the two politicians and then he turned to O'Riordan. Sweat beaded the captain's head and trickled, like a tear, down the side of his face. The two men stared at one another, before O'Riordan looked away. Flynn shook his head sadly.

'The game's over Frank,' said Flynn. There was a sigh in his voice.

Just as he said this, he looked up and stared dumbfounded at something on the other side of the room. Someone he had not expected to see had just walked in.

'What the...' began Flynn.

14

Bobbie retraced her footsteps along the corridor. Wickham McNeill was still there, finishing the last drop from a hip flask. He put it in his pocket and took out another. He spied Bobbie returning and held up the second flask.

'Break in case of emergency,' he said with a wink.

'Bottoms up,' smiled Bobbie before adding, 'Have you seen Mr Crispin anywhere?'

'No, I can't say that I have,' replied McNeill, but his eyes were not on Bobbie and this was not just to do with the fact that his ability to focus was diminishing with every swig. Bobbie decided not to pursue the matter at that moment, but she did wonder why he was being so obviously evasive.

Lane Vidal appeared and smiled at Bobbie.

'Did you hunt down young Mr Hart?'

'I did, thanks for the suggestion. I was wondering if you had seen Mr Crispin anywhere.'

There was a short pause which, once more, made Bobbie think that something was afoot.

'Was he not with Tommy?' asked Vidal. This deftly removed the need to lie outright. Once more, Bobbie decided not to lose a potential ally by pressuring too hard for an answer.

She shook her head, unsure if entering the dressing rooms was an option to consider. A better option occurred to her, whereby she could put the onus on Vidal to tell the truth. She pointed to the dressing room of Crina, and then the one shared by Vidal and McNeill.

Both were met by a shake of the head. Vidal had little choice, as Bobbie would simply have had to look in to see if it was true or not. She pointed to Jason Crane's dressing room. As the other major star, he also had a dressing room to himself.

Once more, Vidal shook his head. This left three options. Either Crispin had left the building, or he was out front with the police, or under the stage somewhere. Bobbie was still keen to avoid Detective Nolan, which is to say she was desperate to see him, but this would not do. She smiled her thanks to Vidal and headed down the corridor, past the green room and towards the area beneath the stage, which led to the orchestra pit.

She tested a door at the end of the corridor and found that it was open. She went to the other side and found herself in a dark, cavernous room below stage. She wondered how many spiders inhabited this area too. The area was a mess and looked to be a dumping ground for all manner of props. Whatever Mr Jefferies duties as a props man were, keeping things tidy was, obviously, not high on the list.

The area was dark and the ceiling was low enough so that even Bobbie, who was barely five foot three herself, had to duck a little. She took a deep breath to calm her anxiety about the dark and the vicinity of large, killer spiders who could trap intrepid reporters in a giant steel mesh of cobwebs, and then devour them over a period of months. Such things existed in Bobbie's fevered imagination just then.

As it happened it was another killer who she met first.

She stepped forward nervously and immediately trod on something large, dark and furry. There was a howl of outrage from a gigantic rat, it seemed. Bobbie stopped from screaming only because she was in a state of shock.

Or not.

'You've just stepped on Thomas Jefferson,' said a voice nearby.

'We didn't need a Declaration of Independence, anyway,' replied Bobbie, nervously.

The Thomas Jefferson in question was not the architect of America's stated desire for self-government, but a black and white cat who was decidedly unhappy that Bobbie had trodden on his tail, while he was taking a break from his rat catching duties.

'Thomas Jefferson?' replied Bobbie, trying to sound like she was chatting to a friend she'd just bumped into in Central Park.

'Yes,' said the man, coming closer to Bobbie. In the dim light she saw that he was in his thirties, rather short and a little plump. Normally Bobbie would not have felt threatened in such a situation. This was different though.

He was holding a knife.

The man saw the look of alarm on Bobbie's face, which made him smile. A decidedly odd reaction thought Bobbie. Then the man used his index finger to press the blade downwards.

'It's not real.'

'It looks real,' responded Bobbie, a little more irritably than she had intended.

'That's the point,' replied the man and Bobbie saw that he did, indeed, have a point.

'Are you Mr Jeffries?'

'I am. If you don't mind me asking, who are you?' He had a funny drawl of a voice yet his accent remained distinctly New York.

'My name is Bobbie Flynn. There's been an attempted murder in the theatre. I've been sent by the police,' which was a lie, but Bobbie had never been one to quibble over such minor considerations. 'I must find Mr Crispin. I think you should also make your way backstage so that the police can interview you.'

'Why should I believe you? How do I know you are not the murderer?' said Jeffries. There was an odd smile on his face. The shock of hearing about the attempt on Smiley's life had, clearly, worn off.

Bobbie was taken by surprise with the question. She replied by deflecting it, 'There wasn't a murder, for a start. But Mr Stanton looked in a bad way,'

This appeared to shock Jeffries.

'It was Mr Stanton?'

'Didn't you hear?'

'No, I was in the room back there,' said Jeffries.

'You'd no interest in the play?'

'I do, but I have four weeks to see it and I've already seen the rehearsals,' pointed out Jeffries.

At this point, Thomas Jefferson reappeared and walked over to Bobbie. He took her in for a few moments and then walked towards her, brushing past her legs.

'He doesn't think I'm a killer anyway,' smiled Bobbie.

Jeffries laughed and replied, 'He's a good judge of character. I'll take his advice. And, no, I haven't seen Clement anywhere'.

'Thank you, Mr Jeffries. Tell me, where does that door lead. The one over there.'

She pointed to a door at the other side of the tarp room.

'It's always locked,' replied Jeffries. His voice was a little cagey, in Bobbie's view. An awkward silence fell between them. Bobbie wanted to try the door. She knew that the man before her knew this too. What would he do if she started for it?

'I must find Mr Crispin. Please excuse me Mr Jeffries and do make your way over to the back stage area as soon as possible. As I said, the police did ask me to help them on this.'

'Why would they ask you?' asked Jeffries. His tone was different from before. There was a hint of a sneer in his voice. Bobbie's heart was beating faster now. It had occurred to her that the man she was speaking to might have been the one to throw the knife. Initially she had felt this unlikely, but she remembered that her father was always steadfast in not judging people by how they looked, only by evidence.

'As you ask,' replied Bobbie, stepping forward to show she was not afraid and had nothing to hide. This was a trick she had learned from her father. He did this when he wanted to wrongfoot people who were trying to be threatening. It usually worked. 'My date tonight is with the police. And my father is Inspector Flynn. You may have heard of him.'

The man was silent for a moment. Then something in his face changed that, even in the dim light, Bobbie could see was recognition.

'You were involved in that kidnap case,' he said pointing towards her. 'I remember you now.'

This was not the time to reminisce. Bobbie was keen to find Crispin and find out what was happening. There was still a loud murmur from the auditorium, but it was clear that Detective Nolan, and Dick Devenish, had managed to calm the horses.

Bobbie pointed to the door and asked, 'Do you have a key?'

'No, Miss Flynn,' said Jeffries. 'Only Mr Stanton and Clement have keys.'

'I see. I think I'll try anyway,' said Bobbie.

It was clear that Jeffries was a little uncomfortable with this. He replied, 'Shouldn't you wait for the police to do this. I don't think Clement is likely to be going anywhere too far.'

It's possible that a fundamental law of physics came to Isaac Newton as a child when he was told not to do something and it prompted an equal and opposite desire to do what he had been told not to. Wild horses stampeding away from a pack of grizzlies would not have stopped Bobbie from seeing what was behind the door. This, she recognised, was a character flaw of hers, that might one day land her in trouble. In fact, it already had, many times.

'You better head backstage Mr Jeffries,' said Bobbie, with a smile that she hoped looked more genuine than she was feeling.

She turned and walked towards the door, half suspecting that Mr Jeffries would try and dissuade or block her. He did neither. She reached the door and twisted the handle.

It opened.

She entered a short corridor with a door at the end. There was a lot of noise coming from behind the door. Men. Then a sudden silence. She felt like Alice in Wonderland. There was no turning back now. She marched forward towards the door. There were muffled voices now.

When she reached the door, she paused and considered whether it would be wise to wait and see what was being said. Then something she heard made her change her mind. A voice that she knew all too well. She was astonished.

How could he be here, of all places?

She opened the door and stepped inside. At first no one noticed her. Everyone in the room was facing in the other direction. They were all staring at the inspector. Bobbie could hear him saying something about the game being up.

Then Flynn saw his daughter, standing across the room. His mouth almost dropped open. Everyone seemed to turn at the same time towards Bobbie as her father said, 'What the...'

'Hi Daddy,' said Bobbie brightly. 'Someone's just tried to kill Smiley Stanton up in the theatre.'

A few heads turned from Bobbie to Flynn and then back to Bobbie. It was as if they could not quite believe that Inspector Flynn, a man whose perpetually furrowed brow and thunderous countenance could curdle milk at a hundred paces, had produced a daughter of such radiant beauty.

Flynn's face went through a series of transformations that Bobbie had seen many times before but are worth dwelling on, for the historical record.

Inspector Flynn prided himself on his ability to command any situation although he would have acknowledged a tendency to volatility on occasion. But dealing with his daughter was an entirely different campaign.

At first, there was a flicker of bewilderment, as if he were trying to translate a, particularly tricky, piece of Sanskrit. His eyebrows knitted together and his eyes took on the vacant look of a man who has been asked to explain the finer points of Einstein's General Relativity, to children at a birthday party. This phase of befuddlement was short-lived, giving way to a more alarming transformation.

As the full import of her words sank in, the inspector's face began a remarkable conversion. His complexion shifted from its usual ruddy hue to a dangerous shade of puce. His eyes, previously clouded with confusion, now sparked with a fury that could ignite dry timber. The furrows on his forehead deepened, resembling freshly gouged trenches on a battlefield.

'Have you taken leave of your senses, Bobbie?' he thundered, his voice echoing around the room, like an irate Swiss yodeller.

Bobbie remained unperturbed and unflinching. She smiled serenely, the very picture of rebellious serenity. It was a smile that did nothing to soothe Flynn's escalating temper. His transformation was now complete, his visage a tapestry of paternal ire. One could almost see the steam rising from his ears and it was clear to any observer that Flynn was a man at war; alas, this time, with his own flesh and blood.

Then Bobbie noticed Captain O'Riordan for the first time. He was standing by the craps table. O'Riordan looked mortified, as if he'd just been caught with his hand in the cookie jar. His hand opened listlessly and a pair of dice fell onto the table. For the record it was a four and a three.

'This probably isn't a good time,' said Bobbie, with a slight grimace.

15

'Do you know much first aid?' asked Devenish, as he and Nolan stooped over the wounded man.

'Only what I learned in the war,' replied Nolan grimly.

'Me too,' sighed Devenish. 'He looked down at Smiley who had turned very pale. He was semi-conscious. 'Sorry old boy, we'll have to leave the knife in there. Smiley must have heard them for he nodded weakly at this. The arrival of the two doctors had been an enormous relief to the two young men.

'I'll go and make sure there's an ambulance on the way,' said Devenish. 'I'll be back soon.'

The two men got to their feet. While Devenish headed off towards the front of house, Nolan turned to address the crowd who remained following the murder attempt. In the background, he could hear Devenish telling people to let him through. His language was a little less elegant than his usual dandyish foppery. Nolan smiled bleakly. He liked Devenish. It was a bitter pill to swallow that the man was dating Bobbie. Yet, he had to accept that if it was going to be anyone, best that it was someone he could respect.

Nolan went to the front of the orchestra pit and addressed the people who had returned to their seats.

'I'm sorry that you are being forced to stay on. Mr Stanton has been attacked, as many of you will have seen. He is receiving medical attention and an ambulance will be on its way soon. Just to repeat. My name is Detective Nolan, second grade. I am stationed at Midtown North Precinct. I must ask you to remain a little longer and give statements. You are all potential witnesses to this attack.'

Potential murderers, too, thought Nolan.

For the first time, he surveyed the men and women who were before him. In particular, his eyes fell on the men who were sitting directly in front of Smiley. With a sudden intake of breath, he realised that he recognised them. They were men that most police officers in the city would recognise for the very good reason that they were part of the Mob.

The first man was heavily built without being overweight, but it made him seem older than his forty years. The eyes that stared back at Nolan had already worked out what was happening. This was Arnold Rothstein, a fellow with the intellect of a chess grandmaster and the moral compass of an unscrupulous ferret. Rothstein headed up the Jewish Mafia and Nolan instantly discounted him as a killer. He was simply too smart, too careful, to consider such a foolhardy act, in full public view. Of all the men from the Mob, he feared Rothstein most because he was the opposite of the violently volatile caricature of a Sicilian.

The man to his right was a different story altogether. He was a protégé of Rothstein: younger, dark-haired with eyes like twin shards of ice, glinting in the winter sun. Nolan had no doubt that the man born Salvatore Lucania in Sicily but known to the Mob, and NYPD alike, as "Lucky" Luciano was capable of murder. Yet even Nolan had to admit, something like this was not his style. Rothstein had chosen to mentor Luciano for a reason. He was smart. The two men, from very different backgrounds had come together and were a very powerful, highly connected pair, dressed like movie stars, sitting in the front row of the most major of Broadway shows.

To the other side of Rothstein was his wife, Carolyn. Beside her was another man, that Nolan was all too familiar with. Rothstein's bodyguard, a man that you would dread to sit behind at the theatre owing to his size. This was Lenny Choynski, another man with a conscience as soft as a diamond-studded anvil. Nolan had, in the past, been helped by Choynski on the Violet kidnapping case. Their relationship, like the one with Rothstein, could best be described as "complicated".

'Detective Nolan,' began Rothstein, his voice cutting through the hubbub. 'These are truly unfortunate circumstances in which we meet. Is this not always the case? May you be so good as to permit me to turn around and see how my old friend, Felix, is? I think you can trust that neither I, nor my friends, nor Mrs Rothstein will attempt anything stupid.'

Nolan nodded. He had to. Technically speaking, he was in the pay of the man in front of him via Captain O'Riordan and probably another few levels besides. He knew this, Rothstein knew this, but proving it was probably a task so difficult that it would have had Hercules reaching for a restorative brandy.

Still, he was a detective. And he had a job to do. He strode forward to the three men and tried to look them squarely in the eye. This is much easier if there's only one, of course, but he made a decent fist of showing that, firstly, their reputation did not faze him and, secondly, the arrangement by which they were connected would in no way prevent him doing his job, even if he did not think they were directly responsible.

The man to Luciano's right, was not someone Nolan recognised, and he did not appear to have much respect for law enforcement officers. As soon as Nolan stepped forward, he was out of his seat as if someone was about to attack Luciano. Three things struck Nolan about the man. Firstly, he was as large as Lenny and, if anything, even meaner looking. He was fairly bursting out of a tuxedo. His biceps alone would have made a blacksmith weep. Secondly, the murderous look in his eyes would have cleared a room within seconds of his entry. Finally, and most alarmingly of all, he had a gun in his hand.

This, rather unusual, gentleman's progress was interrupted by the left leg of Luciano, who stuck it out causing the heavy to trip over and tumble at Nolan's feet. The gun flew from his hand. Nolan calmly bent down and picked it up. He nodded to Luciano who nodded back. Neither were given to idle chatter; indeed, they approached verbosity with the same enthusiasm one might reserve for a visit to a poetry reading.

Rothstein looked at the fallen man with an undisguised weary dismay.

'You'll have to excuse Sideways. He has more enthusiasm than a Labrador, only less brains. Up you get Sideways and leave Detective Nolan alone to do his job.' Then Rothstein fixed a steely eye on Nolan, who calmly handed the gun back to the man called Sideways.

'I trust you have a licence,' was Nolan's only comment.

'Doubtless you wish to know what we saw and heard. I doubt you think me so stupid as to try and murder my friend Felix in such an obvious manner.'

'No sir,' agreed Nolan. 'Not in such an obvious manner.' This drew a smile from Rothstein, Luciano and Lenny, but Sideways merely scowled in what he hoped would be a threatening manner. Nolan almost laughed.

A noise at the back of the auditorium caught the attention of all the men. More medical help was arriving in the form of three ambulance men and a stretcher.

'At last. Some help for Felix,' said Rothstein, turning around to the wounded man.

The men shuffled down the aisle while Nolan noted the return of Devenish. He made his way directly to the group of witnesses to speak to them. Nolan felt his regard for the private detective increasing. The only person remaining in the auditorium was the young woman he'd brought to the performance.

'Perhaps Mr Rothstein, if you could oversee the removal, I must have a word with someone,' said Nolan.

Everyone's eyes turned to look in the direction that Nolan's eyes were staring. The sight of the young woman drew a low whistle from Luciano and a smile. Rothstein glanced at Nolan and looked him up and down.

'My compliments, young man,' for this comment he received a dig in the ribcage from Mrs Rothstein, but she accompanied it by the stern smile so well recognised by husbands, the world over.

Nolan departed, but, as he did so, he heard Rothstein tell the two ambulance men to take Smiley to the Mount Sinai Hospital, and that he would pay. The detective stopped by the waiting audience members.

'My apologies, the police are on their way.'

'Tell them to hurry up,' shouted one annoyed man. Nolan ignored him. He continued on his way and arrived at the seats where the young woman was waiting.

'Sorry Aisling, I guess you've been listening in to all that.'

'Fascinating,' came the reply. 'What do we do now?'

'Do you mind waiting a little longer? I'll have to arrange for someone to take you back. I'm sorry.'

'No rush,' laughed Aisling. 'I've often wondered what you get up to. Now I know.' She smiled in the direction of Nolan. He sat down beside her and took her hand.

'Trust me, it's not usually like this, Aisling. You read too many detective books.'

'I wonder why,' said Aisling, which made the detective laugh. Out of the corner of his eye, he saw that Smiley was on the stretcher ready to be moved.

'They're taking Stanton away,' murmured Nolan. As he said this, he saw something happening up on the stage.

Police.

Or to be more precise, it was Inspector Flynn along with a few patrolmen. He was not surprised to see Flynn. He'd known about the raid. Now they had another problem much bigger than just raiding a floating crap game. An attempted murder.

And Nolan had a problem of his own to deal with.

Bobbie had just walked onto the stage alongside her father. She was staring directly at him, or to be more precise, at Aisling.

He realised he was still holding her hand.

16

While Sergeant 'Harry' Harrigan and Detective Yeats dealt with the floating crap game downstairs, Flynn, reluctantly it must be reported, took Bobbie and two patrolmen, Mulcahy and Reiner, along the corridor that Bobbie had just come along to the Trap room. On their way they met Jeffries. The props man had decided not to go to the dressing rooms, as Bobbie instructed, but to listen to what was happening. The arrival of the police raid had caught him on the hop, just as much as it had the gamblers.

'Who are you?' snarled Flynn, as he passed Jeffries underneath the stage. Flynn, whose mood could sometimes be described as annoyed, was definitely in a bad mood. He, already, felt a degree of conflict, over the use of such manpower on a raid that was more about politics than impact. Few of the players would be charged with anything more than a misdemeanour, the people running the game had plausible deniability and the only obvious casualty would be a man that he did not particularly like, but who was not the worst cop in the world either, Captain Frank O'Riordan.

'Jeffries,' answered the props man, nervously.

'How do I get to the auditorium from here?'

Jeffries pointed to a door, which seemed to be hidden, behind a lot of wooden crates.

'Don't you ever tidy this place?' grouched Flynn. 'What about the back stage area? The dressing rooms.'

Jeffries pointed in the direction of another door on the other side of the Trap Room. It was the same door that Bobbie had used a few minutes earlier.

Flynn turned to Mulcahy and pointed towards the door, 'You deal with the actors. Mr Jeffries, you will come with me.'

They filed through the door and up the stairs. Soon they were in the wings. The stage was empty, but they could hear the hubbub in the auditorium. As soon as they walked through onto the stage, they saw all eyes turn towards them. I could never be an actress, thought Bobbie. This was not a million miles from what her father was thinking, also. Then his attention was drawn to the front of the stage, where he was confronted by a couple of quite astonishing sights.

Smiley Stanton was lying in a stretcher with a knife sticking out of him. Three men were attending him. Yet that was less shocking to Flynn than the sight of the men directly in front of the theatre owner. He knew these men all too well.

Bobbie, meanwhile, had caught sight of Nolan by the young woman he had come to the play with. He was holding her hand. Nolan and she had exchanged looks before Bobbie had to look away. She glanced over towards Devenish who was with the remaining people in the theatre. He smiled at Bobbie and then he did an odd military salute. Bobbie's eyes shifted towards her father and she saw his salute had been directed towards Flynn. Her father sighed audibly at this which made Bobbie smile a little.

'At least you'll have some help Daddy,' she said. This was greeted with a sour look from her father, but she detected, just a hint of, humour in his eyes. As much as the old detective professed to find Devenish a great source of irritation, something that the private detective played on with unrestrained glee, he did recognise his abilities and had benefitted from his help in a few cases, over the years. In fact, he could almost hear Devenish saying, six cases, Flynn: six.

Devenish began to make his way over towards the front of the stage. Bobbie noticed that Nolan, likewise, had risen from his seat with the beautiful young woman and was heading in their direction also. Bobbie steeled herself for the inevitable meeting with Nolan. She forced her hands apart as she realised that they were perilously close to wringing. Nolan would notice this. The situation was close to intolerable for her.

Her emotions raged between anger at Nolan for his disloyalty to her father, by taking bribes, and now jealousy. She was not going to deny that this was what she was feeling. Had Nolan's date been of the show girl variety, it might have made things easier for her. In fact, Bobbie felt more like a show girl than the young woman accompanying Nolan. Her anger at this was directed inwardly. She was blaming only herself.

Her father was on the move now, climbing down the steps at the side of the stage that led down to the front row where Rothstein and Lucky Luciano had been sitting. Bobbie followed him and Patrolman Reiner.

The greeting to Flynn from the mobsters varied in their levels of warmth. Rothstein clearly respected the inspector and greeted him as warmly as was possible, given the circumstances.

'Inspector Flynn, I am pleased that you will be the man who will handle this unwarranted attack on my dear friend Felix,' said Rothstein.

The unfortunate Smiley was already heading out up the aisle and Flynn decided there was no value in stopping to see more of what had happened. Time was probably of the essence anyway. He'd get a report from Nolan and Devenish, not to mention the Medical Examiner.

'Thank you, Rothstein,' replied Flynn. 'Although you may not feel so warm towards me when you hear that I have just broken up one of your floating crap games. And you've lost one of the cops that is on your pay.'

Rothstein's smile remained fixed and he showed barely a flicker of emotion upon hearing the news.

'You must have me mistaken for a man who runs gambling in this city,' replied the mobster.

'I wonder why,' replied Flynn, grimly happy that he had put one over a man who was very much his nemesis.

'May I ask who the traitorous law enforcement officer was?'

'I think you know it was O'Riordan,' replied Flynn before putting his hand up to interrupt any denial from Rothstein. 'Not your game, you say. Well perhaps Luciano, it's you who will miss the captain most. Or perhaps it will be Smiley. How was he, last you saw?'

'Not well,' replied Luciano. 'Someone just tried to put a hit on our dear friend, Smiley. A knife in the chest is a serious matter.'

'Very serious,' agreed Flynn. 'I don't suppose you gentlemen can shed any light on what happened?'

'I hope Inspector Flynn,' began Rothstein, amiably, 'that you do not imply we are in any way responsible for this tragedy. As you may appreciate, Inspector Flynn, there is no percentage in us putting a hit on an old and dear friend like

Felix in full view of the theatre. I may not be the smartest man...

'Enough of the phonus balonus, Rothstein, you are the smartest man here and, no, I don't believe that you are so stupid as to do this.'

'They could have,' piped up Bobbie, at this point, causing all the men to turn in her direction. Bobbie took a deep breath and enjoyed the shock on the face of her father. Then forged on, before the pin came out of the grenade. 'If you remember, Mr Rothstein, the lights in the theatre went out and there was a gunshot on the stage. They were out for a few seconds if you think about it. Plenty of time for someone to stab Mr Stanton.'

'Is this true?' asked Flynn, turning back to Rothstein and Luciano.

Both men shrugged, in a manner that might have been a choreographed movement, confirming in Flynn's mind that there was more to this attempted murder than he knew.

'No one is accusing you Mr Rothstein, of course,' continued Bobbie, uninvited, it must be said. 'The question is what you might have seen, or heard, or felt when the murder attempt took place. For instance, could the knife have been thrown from the stage, or the orchestra pit?' Bobbie was thinking of Jeffries at this point. Then she added the final clinching point that no one had considered yet. 'And was Mr Stanton the intended target?'

Rothstein glanced towards Luciano and then fixed his eyes on Flynn.

'Your daughter makes an interesting point that had not occurred to me. You know, Inspector Flynn, if they ever decide to let women into the police force, I will join you in opposing this as I think they could be very damaging to a lot of business in this town.'

'I'm not opposed to women joining the department,' snapped Flynn before adding. 'Well, maybe one in particular.'

'Bravo, Bobbie,' said Devenish. 'I was wondering who would spot this.'

Bobbie looked wryly at Devenish, but she suspected he had probably thought of this too.

'Mr Devenish,' said Rothstein, turning to the private detective. 'It is a great reassurance to me to know that you will be involved in this case.'

'He won't be,' interjected Flynn. 'This is a police matter.'

Rothstein ignored Flynn and kept his attention on Devenish.

'If I hire you to find out who put the hit on our dear friend Felix will you accept? Perhaps ten might persuade you?' suggested Rothstein.

'Ten would persuade me,' confirmed Devenish, without much hesitation.

Ten thousand dollars? Bobbie decided she was in the wrong line of business. She frowned at Devenish, who smiled shamelessly back at her. She could not help but smile and shake her head in response. She noted that Nolan did not look happy at any of this. He was obviously earning a lot less from the mobster, she thought bitterly.

Inspector Flynn was listening to this, with a growing sense of frustration. Part of this was borne of the fact that Bobbie had arrived at an insight he should have considered himself. First things first though, he had to organise the questioning of the witnesses.

'Detective Nolan,' said Flynn. 'I'm afraid I'm going to need you for questioning. You'll have to let that young lady you brought to the play know.'

Nolan glanced from Aisling to Flynn and nodded.

Devenish also noticed Nolan's date for the first time.

'I say, Nolan, you're rather punching above your weight there,' commented Devenish, wryly.

'Come and meet her,' said Nolan, turning to go.

'Are you sure you can handle the competition?' laughed Devenish.

'I'll manage,' murmured Nolan. The detective seemed remarkably untroubled by the prospect of Devenish meeting her, which pricked the private investigator's ego, more than a little.

The two men went off, leaving Bobbie with her father and the show-going mobsters. An unusual set of theatre goers at the best of times.

'Excuse me,' said Flynn to Rothstein.

'Do not worry, Inspector Flynn. I think I can vouch for all of us when I say we will not make a run for it.'

Bobbie suspected what was coming. It was the usual speech from her father not to become involved. She'd heard it a few times already this year and each time she had, somewhat, rebelled and helped solve a crime in the process.

'I want you out of here now, young lady. It looks like Devenish is here to stay, so your date for the evening is busy and I don't want you involved.'

Bobbie said nothing although the glare she gave her father was probably as eloquent a response as any. Just then she saw Devenish motioning for her to come over. He seemed to be sharing a joke with Nolan. Anger raged within her. As swiftly as she felt the rage, it died within her, as she realised something that her father had said earlier.

Bobbie turned and checked to see who was within earshot. She lowered her voice.

'Daddy, there's something I have to tell you about Detective Nolan,' said Bobbie. Her heart was not racing. It felt like it had stopped all together. Flynn stopped and eyed his daughter closely, dreading what she might say to him. I saw him with Captain O'Riordan one day outside the police station. He took money from him, Daddy. You can't trust him.'

Flynn's mouth, almost, fell open with the shock of what Bobbie had just related. Before he could reply, he heard Devenish shouting over to her.

'Hurry Bobbie, you're needed here.'

Flynn's eye flicked in the direction of the two men and the young woman, then he looked back at Bobbie.

'Go Bobbie. I'll talk to you about this later.'

Bobbie stared at her father for a moment and then, angrily, spun around before stalking off, in the direction of Devenish, Nolan and Aisling. Flynn watched her go and then joined Rothstein, Luciano and the others. Rothstein's wife, Carolyn, spoke first.

'I think you are in a great deal of trouble, Inspector Flynn,' said Mrs Rothstein, a half-smile creasing her face.

This brought a few chuckles from Rothstein with even Lenny and Luciano smiling.

'It looks like it,' said Flynn, tipping his Trilby to the back of his head.

Bobbie was acutely aware that, as she walked up the aisle, most everyone in the auditorium was looking at her. She could sense their amusement at her evident anger and this made her angrier still. And now, to cap it off, she was to meet the beautiful young woman that had stolen Nolan's heart. Life's vicissitudes never felt more complicated, nor more malevolent to Bobbie, than at that very moment. She was travelling rapidly along a road with no exit.

Devenish's beaming smile did little to appease Bobbie as she approached the group. Nolan, at least, had the decency to look serious while his girlfriend stared stonily ahead.

'Nolan, perhaps you should do the honours for this beautiful young lady. Listen up Bobbie,' said the private detective gleefully.

Bobbie, just about, managed to avoid scowling at Devenish. How long could she maintain her composure, she wondered. It felt like an explosion was imminent. On one side, she had Devenish, evidently enjoying the sight of Bobbie's jealousy. On the other, she had a man who was going to partner with her father when he had an enormous conflict of interest. She couldn't trust Nolan. What if he betrayed her father? He already had, she supposed. But if he was cornered, what would he do? At least, she had voiced her suspicions now. Her father would know what to do.

She hoped.

But she could not leave her father alone with Nolan. She had to find a way to get back into the theatre. These thoughts ran through her head as Devenish spoke to her. Then she turned her attention to the young woman.

On closer inspection, she was even more ethereally beautiful than Bobbie had first thought. There was an air about her, that radiated tranquillity and intelligence. Bobbie felt her self-control waver, in the direction of tears rather than anger.

'Miss Flynn, meet my sister,' said Nolan. Bobbie nearly collapsed at this news.

'Hello,' she stammered.

'Aisling, this is the young lady I mentioned, Miss Bobbie Flynn. She helped us clear up a few cases this year.'

Bobbie's legs felt like they had just walked the length of Central Park. Twice.

The face of Aisling lit up into a smile that made her seem even more radiantly beautiful. Aisling held her hand out to shake Bobbie's hand. And that's when Bobbie experienced her next shock.

Aisling was blind.

17

'Rather typical of men that they assumed you would be the one who would take me home, don't you think?' said Aisling, as she and Bobbie walked through the entrance foyer of the theatre.

There were still people milling around, one of whom was her friend, Damon Runyon. He waved over to Bobbie as she was heading towards the exit. Beside him was a patrolman who he was sharing a joke with.

'Bobbie,' said Damon, 'It disappoints me greatly that New York's finest will not, once more, call upon your talents.'

'Me too,' replied Bobbie, laughing ruefully. Then, realising that this may seem a rather mean-spirited comment towards her companion she added quickly, 'But at least I get to help Miss Nolan.'

'Miss Nolan,' said Runyon. 'I did not know that the ever-handsome Detective Nolan was married.'

'He's not,' laughed Aisling. 'I'm his sister.'

'This is Damon Runyon, he writes on the same newspaper as me,' explained Bobbie. Aisling smiled and held out her hand, whereupon it became immediately clear to Runyon about the young woman's condition.

'I noticed that some friends of mine were kept behind,' said Runyon. 'I hope that they are not considered suspects for this diabolical act.'

'Witnesses, more like,' replied Bobbie. 'Mr Stanton was one row back from them. It's possible he may not have been the target either if you think about it.'

Aisling frowned at this and asked who Bobbie and Runyon were referring to.

'Let me, Damon. I suspect if you say who they were you'll make them sound like choirboys. They're anything but. Arnold Rothstein is...'

'A businessman,' interjected Runyon.

'A businessman,' continued Bobbie without pausing, 'With business interests that interest the police, shall we say. His associate, Mr Luciano, is similarly employed. I've met Lenny before, but not the other gentleman.'

'Gentleman is not a word I would use, in connection with Sideways. He is someone I do not have much truck with,' said Runyon.

'Why is that?' asked Bobbie.

'He thinks he is a tough guy and maybe he is, especially around dolls. Personally, I think Sideways is not so tough as he thinks and Luciano can do a lot better when it comes to personal protection. Anyway Red, you have a big story tomorrow. Show me, before you show Mr Kent.'

'I shall,' laughed Bobbie, and led Aisling away from one newsman, only to bump into another.

'Perry,' exclaimed Bobbie with a smile.

Perry kissed Bobbie on both cheeks and said, 'Roberta, how good to see you. I don't suppose you can shed much light on what has happened. And who is this enchanting young woman?'

Bobbie rolled her eyes and introduced Aisling to the theatre critic. Then she quickly explained what had happened.

'How horrible,' said Perry. 'A great pity too. Crina was extraordinary tonight. Which is more than I can say for the play. The writing had all the subtlety of a falling anvil.'

This made the two ladies chuckle. They parted soon after and they walked along the street, Aisling holding Bobbie's arm. The cold air bathed their skin, giving both goosebumps following their time in the hot, stuffy theatre.

Much of the theatre crowd had melted into the night, taking with them all the cabs. Bobbie was not disappointed about this as it would give her a little more time to get to know Aisling, whom, on first acquaintance, she had taken a liking to. There did not appear to be any bitterness about being blind, and she clearly had a wry sense of humour when it came to the male of the species.

'Sean has told me about you, you know,' said Aisling. There was hint of mischief in her voice, that Bobbie picked up on, probably as she was meant to.

'Really? I almost dread to think what he said,' replied Bobbie, which was about as big an invitation for Aisling to tell her as she could decently get away with.

If Aisling suspected this, then she did not mind. She was more than happy to relate what she'd heard about Bobbie, and the cases that had brought them together, in a manner of speaking, since they had first met on New Year's Eve. Her knowledge of the cases was surprisingly detailed, too.

'Sean tells me everything,' she explained when Bobbie laughingly asked her how she knew so much. 'He knows how much I love detective stories. I think I've read all of Sherlock Holmes half a dozen times. Sean even read out to me your articles that you wrote on them.'

Bobbie's heart sank as she listened to Aisling say this. The two women were walking along Broadway now and attracting a lot of attention from young men who were not slow in inviting them for drinks at one speakeasy or another.

'We can get a cab if you like.'

'I don't mind walking,' said Aisling, 'Unless all the male attention you are getting is too much.'

'I think you are probably getting more than me, Aisling. I doubt there was a more beautiful girl in the theatre tonight.'

'Thanks,' replied Aisling, but she accompanied the comment by a shrug. Bobbie felt tears sting her eye as she realised that her companion would have no idea what it meant to be beautiful.

'How long have you been blind?' asked Bobbie.

'My eyesight started to deteriorate when I seven and then, by the time I was eleven, I was barely able to see anything. Just shapes, not much more.'

'Is there nothing that can be done?' asked Bobbie, wondering if this was why Nolan was taking money.

'Nothing,' confirmed Aisling. There was no rancour in her voice, or self-pity. Just acceptance.

So much for that idea, thought Bobbie, trying not to feel disappointed, because it meant Nolan was on the take for financial gain rather than altruism.

'I'm sorry,' said Bobbie and she hated herself, just at that moment. For meaning more than just her sympathy towards Aisling for her condition.

'I'm sorry that I'm taking you away from the crime scene,' laughed Aisling, changing the subject deftly. 'I'm sure you would have been a help to them.'

'My father hates it when I get involved,' admitted Bobbie.

'Yes, Sean told me. I suppose I can see his point of view, but then you have helped solve the other cases.'

'I wouldn't go that far,' said Bobbie.

'Sean said you did,' replied Aisling. 'He really likes your father. I suppose it's why he agreed to work for him.'

This sounded strange to Bobbie. To say that Nolan worked for him was stretching things a little. Her father was many levels of seniority above Nolan. It was almost pure chance that they had worked together so often, although Bobbie suspected that her father had a high regard for Nolan's capabilities.

'Sean wasn't sure about becoming involved in the corruption case.'

Bobbie stopped suddenly when she heard this.

'Is something wrong?' asked Aisling. Her heightened senses picked up in a change in the breathing of Bobbie, the strange silence.

'You know about the corruption case?' asked Bobbie, trying to control her voice.

'Yes, I'm never likely to meet any of the individuals concerned. And Sean was desperately sad about having to pretend to be one of them when it meant he would be responsible when they went to prison. I think at first, he was not too sympathetic to the Captain.'

'O'Riordan?' asked Bobbie.

'Yes, but I think he's changed his mind a little about him. He prefers the captain to Grimm, anyway.'

'Is Lieutenant Grimm one also on the take?'

'Not according to Sean. It's only O'Riordan and half a dozen patrol men. I can't remember their names; they don't work out of Midtown North as far as I know.'

Bobbie's mind was whirling with what she had heard. She could not stop herself saying, 'I hadn't realised my father had asked Detective Nolan to work undercover.'

'He did. It's connected with gambling. Your dad couldn't trust anyone in the Vice Department so he chose Sean because he was in Homicide,' said Aisling. Then she added, almost brightly, 'Also because my big brother is wonderful.'

Bobbie did not know how to respond to this so remained quiet. They walked along in silence for a few minutes and then Bobbie suddenly burst out laughing.

'I don't know where we're going,' she exclaimed.

Aisling laughed also. She replied, 'Well if you don't know then I certainly won't know. Perhaps we should get a cab after all. To be honest I just wanted to go for a walk in the fresh air. It was nice to meet you. Sean has spoken of you often.'

Bobbie glanced towards Aisling and wondered if this was meant to be an invitation to say something about her brother. She decided to take it.

'I've been perfectly awful to him of late,' she said and felt a sense of exultation at saying this.

Aisling was silent for a few moments and then she asked why.

Outright honesty is, of course, the first resort of the unimaginative. Bobbie decided full disclosure, given what she had just heard, was inadvisable.

'My father hates the thought of me involved with his world,' replied Bobbie, opting to stick to the truth without really answering the question.

'Mr Devenish works as a private investigator. Is he not in your father's world?'

'He is,' admitted Bobbie. 'As much as I like Dick, he's not anything to me other than a good friend.'

'Oh,' said Aisling. 'I thought he was...'

'No,' interjected Bobbie. 'Definitely not. Dick's not someone I envisage settling down easily. I like him, but he's not what I have in mind for me, nor my daddy, I suspect.'

The two ladies laughed at this. As they walked, Bobbie hailed a cab. As ever, there was almost a pile up as cabs made a beeline for her.

'That was quick,' noted Aisling as Bobbie helped her in. Then Aisling addressed the cab driver, 'Do you know where the Catholic Institute for the Blind is.'

'Would I be doing this job if I don't?' came the reply, which prompted the two ladies to smile.

'Do you teach there?' asked Bobbie.

'Yes, I've been teaching children to read Braille for the last three years. It's wonderful.'

'You live there too?'

Aisling nodded brightly, yet Bobbie wondered if this was a little forced. She wanted to ask her about things most young women would want to know, but how could she? They had only just met, although Bobbie felt that she wanted to be with her again.

'Is it true you are to adopt that little girl Violet?' asked Aisling as the cab set off. It felt like she wanted to change the subject. Bobbie was relieved and she chuckled, as she thought of Violet.

'You make her sound like an innocent little angel. She's smarter than a Mississippi card sharper I can tell you. And yes, I hope to. I hadn't realised Detective Nolan was aware of this.'

'He and Violet may have had a chat about this,' said Aisling enigmatically. Bobbie glanced towards Aisling. There was a half-smile on her face.

'I think my little angel has a king-sized crush on your brother,' laughed Bobbie.

'I remember my brother was very good-looking,' said Aisling wistfully.

Bobbie paused and tried to think of something to say. The air seemed to leave the cab just at that moment. Then she filled the enormous vacuum that seemed to have arisen with a whisper.

'Yes, he is.'

18

The next morning, Bobbie arrived to work just after eight. After returning home the previous evening, she had written some notes on the evening in preparation for writing the story the next day. Her father had not come home when she went to bed just after midnight. The next morning, there was no sign of him either. According to Mrs Garcia he'd left early without taking her prepared breakfast. The old housekeeper was still angry at him.

This was typical of her father. When he was directly involved in a case, he became obsessed. Thankfully, this was increasingly rare, as he had moved up into a leadership role. She hoped that he would be handing over the reins of the case. But to whom? She knew he didn't rate Lieutenant Grimm. And then there was the captain. What had become of him? Bobbie was not yet aware that Captain O'Riordan was languishing in a cell, just at that moment, waiting to be questioned by her father.

Bobbie went straight to the main newsroom, in the hope of finding Thornton Kent. The editor's moods swung as wildly as a metronome in a hurricane, but she had made it a point to confront him whenever possible. At those moments, it felt as if she was taking her life in her hands but the feeling afterwards, when she survived to fight another day, was bordering on euphoric.

As ever, the air was thick with the scent of newsprint and the clatter of typewriters. Again, the noise dimmed appreciatively a little, as she walked through the room.

Bobbie marched up to the door and gave it an urgent knock. Before the editor had time to send her on her way with two carefully chosen words, that he normally used for such unscheduled interruptions, Bobbie entered, heart-a-thumping.

'I was at the Crina Colbeck show sitting in the same row as Smiley Stanton when someone tried to kill him last night.'

To be fair, if you are going to try and get the attention of an editor with a story pitch, this one was not the worst by any means. Her voice carried through to the newsroom.

The room fell silent, as the final clack of the typewriter keys died away. Heads turned, pencils paused mid-scribble, and even the perennial grumblers in the corner ceased their mutterings.

For a moment, Kent said nothing, simply drumming his fingers on the desk in a rhythm that matched the pounding in Bobbie's chest. Then, with a dramatic sweep of his arm, he cleared a space amid the clutter of papers and ink pots.

'All right, Flynn,' he said, a hint of reluctant admiration in his voice, 'I want the story on my desk in twenty minutes.'

'Front page?' asked Bobbie in a low voice, accepting that this might be the spark that lit the tinder.

'Out,' snarled Kent.

It wasn't an outright refusal. This was a consolation. Nor had he shouted at her. On the whole, she viewed the meeting as an unqualified triumph.

Bobbie made her way to a desk near Damon Runyon's, who was not in yet. She grabbed some paper and put it in the typewriter. Then she extracted her notes from her handbag and began to type up the story that she had been writing in her head all the way over to the Tribune Building.

It took fifteen minutes to write a few hundred words covering the main points of the story. Yet, a part of her remained unsatisfied. It felt incomplete. And she knew what it was. What had happened to Smiley? She reached for the telephone and rang Midtown North. She knew it was a risk that she might end up speaking with Nolan. Yet, she wanted to speak to him also.

A familiar voice came on the line. It was Moran the desk sergeant.

'Bam, it's Bobbie Flynn. Is my dad there or Detective Nolan?'

'Hey Red, where've you been? It feels like ages since we saw you,' said Moran.

There wasn't much that Bobbie could say to that, so she didn't try. Instead, she said, 'You know I miss you, Bam. Anyway, who's around?'

'I can't interrupt them. They're down in the cells with Captain O'Riordan.'

'Have they got a suspect?'

'You are misunderstanding me, Red,' replied Moran. 'It's the captain who's in the cell. They caught him at the game last night. He's been hand in glove with the gambling rackets all this time. Who knew?'

Nolan and my father, for a start, thought Bobbie. So, they had caught O'Riordan. This was a new story entirely. She listened, as Moran explained, a little more, about what had happened last night, in parallel to the Smiley case. Bobbie was astonished. Not so much that O'Riordan was on the take. This much she had guessed. It was that the operation had occurred last night while she was watching Crina Colbeck on stage. And her father had said nothing. It also explained Nolan's presence at the theatre last night. It was all so much to take in that she almost forgot the purpose of her call.

'What about Smiley, Bam?' Any news on how he's doing?' asked Bobbie when Moran had finished.

'No news yet, but that's good, I suppose. Tell you what, Red. Call me in half an hour and I'll try and find out what's goin' on.'

'Bam, your ever-loving wife is the luckiest lady alive,' laughed Bobbie.

'Don't I know it,' said Moran. 'But would you mind telling her, Red?'

Bobbie had enough to complete her report on Smiley now. She quickly polished it off and went into Kent's office feeling a lot less nervous than usual. Big stories did that to her. Excitement trumps anxiety every time.

'Here's the story Mr Kent and I have a second one building,' said Bobbie handing him the typed sheets.

Kent started to read, pen poised dangerously over the copy, like an eagle, poised to swoop, at a moment's notice, on an unsuspecting grammatical error or hyperbole. It stayed there, as he read.

'The other story?'

'Captain Frank O'Riordan, of Midtown North, is in a police cell at the moment. He's been questioned, on his connection with gambling rackets. Apparently, my father found him at a floating craps game at the theatre last night. It looks like the theatre is being used as a location for gambling.'

It's not often Bobbie had seen the editor lost for words. Usually, these situations occurred when he was confronted with something or, more likely, someone of such stupidity that he was stunned into silence. This was not such an occasion.

For a moment, Kent did not react. It was a moment that seemed to stretch into an eternity, filled with the silent hum of the newsroom and the distant clatter of typewriters. Then, slowly, like a great engine awakening from slumber, Kent's head lifted. His eyes, sharp as daggers, fixed on Bobbie with a look that could only be described as Olympian incredulity.

'Drop everything you have on this afternoon. Wait for the call from Midtown and then get down there to find out more. Go to the hospital too. See if you can get in to visit Smiley. Speak to the doctors there – who saved him? What will happen now? We also need to know what happened last night with the police. Who did they speak to? Who do they suspect?'

There was a knock at the door.

Bobbie and Kent both turned to look at Damon Runyon standing framed in the doorway. There was a smile on his face.

'I will help Red on that,' said Runyon. Kent fixed his eyes on Runyon and then nodded. Runyon said to Bobbie, 'Meet me in Lindy's at one pm.'

The meeting ended with Bobbie rising and returning to the desk she had just left. She sat there for ten minutes, her fingers drumming on the table as she waited for a call from Moran. When the phone rang, Bobbie nearly jumped from her seat.

'Hey Red,' said Moran

'Bam, what news?'

'I couldn't get through to anyone but I found a message that was left earlier this morning. Smiley's out of danger. I hear he's pretty weak but he'll live.'

'Has Crina Colbeck been to see him.'

'No, but I guess she was told not to go.'

'Thanks, Bam. I owe you one,' laughed Bobbie before hanging up. She added another paragraph to her story before showing it once more to Kent. While he read it, she updated him on what Moran had said about Smiley.

Kent sat back and thought about what they should do next. They had the story they needed for the front page. The real story was just starting. The floating craps game that had seen a police captain caught red-handed. They would need to follow this one as it was not just possible, but likely it was connected to the attempted murder of the man who was once the king of this racket in the town.

'Get down to the hospital for the latest then go to the theatre. I doubt you'll get near anyone connected to the O'Riordan arrest. They'll want to keep that quiet anyway. When you're at the theatre see what you can find out about the craps game. Who else was there? How long has it been going on under everyone's noses?'

As Bobbie was leaving the newsroom, Ade Barton was just arriving. He barely gave her a look as he walked in which amused Bobbie. He would be in for quite a shock when he heard the news about the extraordinary events at the theatre.

Outside, Bobbie descended the steps, two at a time. A cab was waiting and she jumped in.

'Can you take me to the Mount Sinai hospital?' asked Bobbie, settling down into the seat.

'Hope it's not serious,' said the driver.
He was joking.

19

While Bobbie was writing up her latest front page, her father was meeting Detective Nolan for a coffee, before they went to interview Captain O'Riordan. Both men were tired, from the late night they'd had at the theatre, and the subsequent early start, that had seen Nolan visit the hospital to check on the condition of Smiley Stanton, while Flynn had tried, and failed, to see Crina Colbeck. The actress had been taken away from the theatre in shock and been given a sleeping draught by her doctor. She was still out for the count.

Nolan quickly reported the latest on Smiley.

'They removed the knife last night. It missed the vital organs, but he lost a of blood. He'll make it but they're keeping him in for a few days. He'll be too weak to see anyone today. The earliest is tomorrow afternoon.'

'It's as well for him. He's got questions to answer on that damn game,' said Flynn. 'There's something else. I've been thinking about O'Riordan. You know, you don't have to interview him with me. You've done what you had to do. O'Riordan only has himself to blame for this.'

Nolan shook his head. Flynn was offering him a chance to avoid being blamed by O'Riordan, targeted even.

'No sir. He'll know it was me. Why hide the fact? If not now, then later he'll know, if he doesn't already. I'll have to testify. My days undercover are finished, let's face it.'

'I'm sure you'll miss it,' said Flynn.

'Like I'd miss a toothache,' laughed Nolan, bitterly.

They finished their coffees and got up to return to the precinct. As they left the restaurant, Flynn stopped, forcing Nolan to stop also.

'One thing I meant to ask you. Where did O'Riordan normally pay you?'

'Always in his car, three blocks away. He wasn't taking any chances.'

Flynn nodded and said, 'Every time?'

Nolan was confused by the line of questioning, but then a thought seemed to strike him.

'The first time, at the start of February, I think, he paid me near here. We were in a doorway. He handed me the money, but I think he was in a rush that night. He never did it that way again.'

'Beginning of February, just after we finished on the Bonaty case,' said Nolan. He was looking at the inspector with a few questions in his eyes. He said nothing because he could see that Flynn had a faraway look in his eyes. Then something changed and the hard glint returned.

'Bobbie saw you that day,' said Flynn. Nolan's eyes widened momentarily as he took this in.

'Miss Flynn told you this?'

Flynn nodded slowly. His voice was low, almost inaudible, 'Yes. Last night.'

Nolan could not disguise the look, of incredulity, on his face. He was aware that Flynn was studying him closely.

'Miss Flynn never said anything to me, sir,' responded Nolan, after he had fully absorbed what Flynn had said.

They walked back to the precinct in silence. Nothing else was said on the subject. The two men now had much to think about on why it was that Bobbie should have waited almost two months to reveal to her father what she knew.

Captain Francis Patrick O'Riordan also had a lot to think about, as he sat in a cell at the Midtown North precinct. He'd been in this cell countless times, with men and some women, who had erred from the path of true righteousness, as his local parish priest, Father McCarthy, might have said. The captain wondered what the priest would make of this when it became public, as it surely would. He had a lot to think about, all right. A glance around his present accommodation did not provide much inspiration.

The cell itself was a cheerless affair, possessing all the charm of a dentist's waiting room and none of the promise of eventual relief. O'Riordan sat on the narrow, wooden bench, which seemed to have been designed by a malevolent carpenter with a deep aversion to comfort. The walls, a drab shade of institutional grey, closed in on him with an oppressive air, as if they had been, specifically, tasked with sapping any remaining vestiges of hope from their occupants.

O'Riordan viewed his surroundings with a mixture of disdain and resignation. The cell's sole window, a small, barred affair set high in the wall, allowed a meagre shaft of sunlight to filter through, casting a dim, prison-stripe pattern on the floor. He considered, not for the first time, how it was that he had come to be in such a situation. He knew the answer of course.

He was in debt. In debt to gamblers, to be precise. The only way he could pay this off was to work for them and recruit others to do the same. All in all, he'd been able to reconcile his conscience to this dirty work, because he did not believe that what he was doing was, essentially, wrong. Why could a free-born American not choose how he would spend his money? It was not as if the many politicians he had met at the craps tables were in any disagreement with him.

A faint rustling, from the other side of the bars, heralded the approach of Nemesis in the diminutive shape of Inspector Flynn and, no surprise, the ever-handsome Detective Nolan. The sight of the young detective provoked a mixture of emotions in O'Riordan. Initially, it was anger. The young man had put the finger on him. Who else could have done it? What had he been thinking when he recruited Nolan? The boy with the picture-house looks, and the halo over his head. How could a wise guy have ever fallen for a sob story, like Nolan needing extra scratch?

As quickly as the anger rose in him, another emotion enveloped him: guilt. This took him by surprise as he watched the two men enter the cell. They went over and sat on the bed, opposite the bench.

'This is a mess,' began Flynn. O'Riordan nodded but said nothing to this. 'You'll go down for this,' continued Flynn remorselessly. 'How much do you owe them?'

'Two,' replied O'Riordan.

Flynn shook his head angrily. He said, 'And your solution to that was to keep gambling and making it worse, so that you would never be off their hooks?'

When you put it like that, thought O'Riordan, I don't sound like such a wise guy, after all.

'Yeah, something like that,' muttered O'Riordan, staring at the floor. He knew what was coming next. In fact, it's all he had been thinking about since the moment the game had been raided.

'You'll have to give us names, Frank,' said Flynn. The last time he had used O'Riordan's name was never. His tone was softer, it was as sympathetic as he'd ever heard the inspector.

O'Riordan sighed and shook his head. He would tell them all he knew. There was no other way. It had already occurred to him that they would piece together things, anyway.

The cell fell silent for a minute or more. Nolan noted how Flynn had stopped talking. He sat still, immutable, his expression sombre. The usual grumpiness and the mischief were absent now. His eyes met O'Riordan's. Flynn could see the weariness there, the defeat. The pouches underneath O'Riordan's eyes were saddlebags, his face stripped of its arrogance and vain deceit. The time had come.

'It is Smiley's show,' said O'Riordan. 'It always has been. I think he would leave it if he could, but the mob have their hooks into him, as much as they do with me.'

'Who?'

'I don't know, Inspector. Look, if I had evidence I'd say. I know the score. Is it Rothstein? Probably, but he never goes anywhere near the games. Not once have I seen him there. Luciano, yes. A few times. He plays but he does not look at me. I only deal with Sideways and Smiley. This game has been running from the theatre these last two years. In the back room where you found us. They have a floating game too for the suckers, but this is for the smart guys, the rollers.'

'We'll need more than that,' said Flynn. His tone was harder now. It was a grim and pleasureless task, as much for Flynn as it clearly was for O'Riordan. Nolan could see the strain on each man's face. O'Riordan was sweating profusely while Flynn appeared to have aged ten years. The lines on his face seemed deeper. The hair that bit greyer.

O'Riordan put his hands up to his face and breathed audibly. He said, 'I ain't got more than that, sir.'

'Aside from Nolan, who else is on the take?' snapped Flynn, trying to fight back any feeling of pity he had for the man before him.

O'Riordan's head shot up and his eyes blazed at Flynn. The old inspector did not take his eyes from O'Riordan. The captain was suffering and there was no one else he could blame but himself. And he knew it. He was alone now. The defiant tilt of the chin was gone. In the creases of his forehead lay the understanding, that his career was over. Possibly his marriage. All that lay ahead of him were the questions - who, when, how? And why. This was the biggest question of all.

The conversation lasted another ten minutes that felt like hours. O'Riordan provided seven names along with details of payments received and given. By the end, O'Riordan's voice was barely a whisper, and there were tears in his eyes.

This was how they left him.

Broken.

They trudged along the corridor in silence, then upstairs to the entrance hall of the station. Both waved to Moran, the desk sergeant who was on the phone to someone. He smiled and waved back at them. Just as they were leaving the building, they heard Moran shout to them.

'Inspector, come back.'

Flynn turned around and saw Moran gesticulating wildly to him. This was unusual. Something was wrong. He could see it in the sergeant's eyes.

'What's wrong?' asked Flynn.

'That was the hospital. Smiley's dead.'

'Dead?' exclaimed Flynn. 'How? I thought he was stable.'

'He was,' came the answer. 'Then someone stabbed him this morning.'

20

Mount Sinai Hospital, Jefferson St, New York

Bobbie had expected there to be at least a couple of policemen at the hospital. After all, someone had attempted to murder one of their patients, the previous evening. However, the police presence at the hospital was way beyond her wildest speculations. There were half a dozen police cars parked outside and two policemen were barring anyone from entering, including what looked like genuinely ill people.

The cab parked as near as it could to the hospital. Seeing the crowd outside, the cabbie asked the question that was uppermost on Bobbie's mind.

'What's going on here?' he asked.

'Can you wait here; I'll go and check.'

'Sure – it's your money.'

Bobbie leapt out of the car and made her way towards the entrance. She had no expectation of gaining entry, but there was at least a chance she could quiz the policemen on duty. She knew one of them.

'Paddy!' shouted Bobbie waving at a burly, middle-aged officer with dark hair and bushy eyebrows that made him look ferocious, which is probably why they had chosen him for the task of guarding the hospital entrance. This was Officer Jakub "Paddy" Paderewski. The large paws and his thick fingers suggested that he would never be able to play the piano like his famous namesake.

'Red,' exclaimed Paddy. 'Two Flynns in one morning. You after your father?'

'He's here?'

'Sure is.

'Is he interviewing Mr Stanton?' asked Bobbie.

'He'll only be able to do that through a medium,' said Paddy with a grim smile. 'Someone hit Smiley this morning. Finished off what they started last night.'

'Good lord,' aid Bobbie. 'How?'

'Scalpel maybe or something like that. Some nurse found him when she went in to give him breakfast.'

'Any ideas on who might have done it?'

'None,' admitted the big patrol man, before shouting at some people who were trying to gain entry. He was having none of their claims to being ill. He turned to Bobbie and said, 'The cheek of that guy. I've seen him before. Press.'

Bobbie laughed at this and said, 'So am I.'

'Your family, Red,' said Paddy. 'Hey, do you want to go in?'

'My dad and will only chase me out of the building. Is Detective Nolan with him?'

'Yes,' said Paddy. 'He's in a bad mood, Red.'

He would be. If it was true and Smiley had been hit, then this was a disaster and not just for Smiley. Bobbie tried to smile at the patrolman her thanks. He nodded grimly.

'It's not good, Red. Not good at all. Look, get in there before anyone sees you.'

This was too good an opportunity to pass up. She quickly went down the steps to the cabbie to pay him and then returned to the entrance. To the highly vocal dismay of a dozen people being refused admittance, Paddy let her through.

She went over to the reception area to introduce herself. Bobbie was a firm believer in the concept of equivocation. While she did not lie to the lady on the reception, she did not quite tell the, full, truth either. When Bobbie did her moral accounting, she always felt vindicated as she believed firmly in her proven ability to help investigations, whether or not her assistance had been asked for, by her father.

'Hello,' she said, smiling brightly to the receptionist. 'My father Inspector Flynn and Detective Nolan are here. He asked me to pop over and bring him this notebook.' Bobbie duly fished her notebook out of her handbag. She opened it and the receptionist saw that it was, indeed, full of notes. It also had the name Flynn, embossed on the front. This had been a present from her mother two years ago, a half a dozen reporter's notebooks with her name on them. 'Where can I find him?'

'I can put a call out to him,' said the receptionist helpfully.

This would not do.

'Oh, no problem. I think he's with the person who found poor Mr Stanton.'

'Oh, you mean Nurse Williams,' said the receptionist.

'Yes,' smiled Bobbie. 'Where can I find her?'

'She was in the canteen, I think. They were speaking with her there but I think they left her to speak to other staff.'

'I'm sure they'll be back. Where can I find the canteen?' asked Bobbie.

The receptionist directed Bobbie, adding offers to send for Inspector Flynn but Bobbie was already moving away towards the canteen. The canteen was a largish rectangular room, with around forty tables, where the smell of bacon fought a valiant battle against disinfectant and tobacco for olfactory supremacy. Bobbie was less worried about the odd aroma in the dining area than she was relieved by the absence of her father and Detective Nolan.

She wandered over to a young nurse, smiled and said, 'Do you know a Nurse Williams?'

'That's her over there,' said the nurse, indicating three nurses, one of whom was around Bobbie's age. Tears were streaming down the young nurse's cheeks. Bobbie thanked her and walked over to the table. She was still hiding the notebook. Needs must, thought Bobbie as she approached the table.

'Excuse me, Nurse Williams?' asked Bobbie

The young nurse looked up.

'I have to type up some notes on this morning's statement,' began Bobbie. This was technically true. The young nurse looked at the name on the notepad and put two and two together, as she was meant to. Bobbie then picked out a page where her writing was particularly poor and she showed it to the nurse.

'Can you help me with some of the details?'

The nurse smiled, wiped her cheeks and nodded hesitatingly.

'His writing is worse than a doctor's,' she said, which seemed to relax her. The other nurses departed leaving Bobbie alone with Nurse Williams.

Bobbie pretended to consult the notebook. Then she asked, 'What time did you find Mr Stanton. Who else was with you? How long had he been dead do you think?'

'I was on duty most of the night. I found him this morning around eight thirty. We'd been told by a doctor around six to let him rest. When I found him, it felt like he'd been dead for an hour, maybe more.'

'Which doctor was this?' asked Bobbie, 'I don't see a name down here.'

'I don't know. He must be new. Inspector Flynn wanted to know too, I guess that's why you don't see the name.'

Bobbie pretended to squint at the notebook. She said, 'I can't read the description of the doctor.'

The prompt worked and the nurse replied, 'He was tall, well-spoken like most doctors. He was still wearing surgical garb, so I didn't see his face. He had blue eyes.'

Bobbie frowned. Then she said, 'Is it normal to have surgery during the night?'

'It depends if it's an emergency. It can happen at any time of the day or night. There's always a surgeon on duty and sometimes we have visiting surgeons. That should be down there because I told that to Inspector Flynn and that cute detective with him.'

'Detective Nolan,' said Bobbie, rather more grimly than she'd intended.

'That's the one. He can handcuff me any time. I'll come quietly,' said the nurse, a trace of a conspiratorial smile on her face. She began chuckling to herself, so Bobbie felt duty bound to do likewise. When the moment passed, Bobbie pretended to consult the notebook once more.

'There weren't many more questions then.'

'No, they just went to see the head of the hospital, I guess to find out who the surgeon was. I mean, you don't think that he...?'

There was a sudden catch in the young woman's voice as the thought, that she'd met the murderer, finally occurred to her. Bobbie patted the nurse's hand and said, 'Don't worry. I'm sure there's a simple explanation for all of this. Perhaps the wound was deeper than anyone suspected or it had hit a part of his heart. Who knows?'

Nurse Williams smiled gratefully back at Bobbie. The tears had returned and she sobbed quietly. Bobbie stayed with her for a few minutes until she regained her composure then she departed. There was little point in risking being caught by her father or Detective Nolan. Once news of the story broke, and they would have to admit this soon, then Pandora's Box would open.

Questions would be asked of the hospital. Was it negligence on their part? Or was Smiley likely to die anyway from the original attack. The autopsy would confirm this. If his death were caused by a second attack then the police would have questions to answer and her father would be in the front line for all of that. Her mind was a fugue of worry for her father.

She marched out of the hospital into the sunlight. A nod of thanks to Officer Paderewski and a whispered, 'Don't tell my father.'

'I won't Red, but he'll find out anyway. You can't hide anything from fathers generally and you certainly can't hide anything from him.'

'Lucky me,' smiled Bobbie, but inside a creeping feeling of desolation was rising within her.

Bobbie gazed up at the cloudless April sky hoping for inspiration from the heavens. A storm was about to break over her father's life and, at that moment, there was nothing she could do to stop it.

21

It was after eleven when Bobbie walked back into the Tribune Building. She already felt weary. More than that, she was worried about what she was about to do next. The story, regarding Smiley's death, would break soon anyway. There was little point in avoiding this. She would have to file the story, as she knew it from Nurse Williams. It would not alter the position of her father with regard to the outcry that would follow. She knew it was murder. This was not a mistake from the hospital. Someone had gained entry and committed murder. At the very least, she could present the story in a better light.

Her first stop was the editor's office. Kent was in a meeting with a few other men, who did not look like newsmen. Their shirts were too well starched. Bobbie waved to Kent and indicated she needed to speak with him. Much to her surprise, he put a hand up and paused the meeting. There was still the frown of course, but he was too much of a newsman not to want to know what had happened.

Bobbie knew she had to make this quick. She took a deep breath as the door to Kent's office opened. He stood in the doorway, expectantly. Bobbie risked further wrath by motioning him to come outside. Perhaps there was just a hint of amusement in his eyes, but he shut the door behind him.

His eyes had the ever-present look that read this-better-be-good.

'Smiley Stanton died earlier. It may have been from his wounds, but my dad is there and I think someone killed him.'

'How do you know?' demanded Kent. This was nothing without some evidence.

'I spoke to the nurse that found him. His wound was bleeding again like he'd been stabbed. There's no murder weapon. Anyway, my dad and Detective Nolan are looking for a man who was dressed as a surgeon. He spoke with the nurse that found Smiley but she did not recognise him. This isn't unusual, apparently.'

'Wasn't there someone guarding him?' said Kent frowning.

This was the question that Bobbie had been dreading. It potentially could lead to criticism of her father.

'There was, but either this man, if he was a killer, convinced the policeman guarding him that he was a doctor, or he needed a break to go to the rest room. I don't know and I guess my father will be looking into that now.'

Kent nodded at this. His eyes were fixed on Bobbie's, in that unerring way that suggested he was indulging in mind reading.

'You know what this could mean.'

She did. Only her view altered from Kent's in one crucial aspect. She would not sit idly by and watch open season declared on the police or, specifically, her father. She was going to help him find the killer whether he liked it or not.

The report was finished by just after midday and left with a sub-editor. As Damon Runyon was out of the office, there was little Bobbie could do, until she met him at one in Lindy's. To fill in the time she went to the office she shared with Buckner Fanley.

Fanley barely looked up when she entered the office. He said, 'I thought you were with Barton today.' There was no rancour in his voice, but there was, just, a hint of his usual sardonic tone.

'I need to check on a few things, if it's ok.'

Bobbie interpreted the silence, which followed this, to mean that it was no problem. She went over to the large storage drawers which contained, alphabetically, all the obituaries of both living and dead. She picked out a few of the people associated with the case.

Unsurprisingly, there was no obituary for Smiley Stanton. He was a known crook, and it was a policy of the Hearst newspapers not to give any eulogy to criminals. Their death would be reported and not much else.

Of the remaining people in the case, only Crina Colbeck, Wickham McNeill and Jason Crane had any written tribute. Bobbie re-read the article on Crina, before moving on to the English actor, McNeill.

The obituary was rather short and very incomplete in Bobbie's view. It followed a similar style to the one on Crina. It was clearly written by her predecessor, Marjorie Theakston, who retired just after Bobbie had joined.

```
Wickham McNeill (1859-
Wickham McNeill was a popular English
actor, best known for his many
performances on American stages.
He was born Colin Bates, on January
18th, 1859, in London, England. After he
```

took to the stage, he adopted the stage
name Wickham McNeill.

McNeill emigrated to the United States
at the age of forty-two following a
national tour with his repertory company,
The Priestley Players, in 1901.

The actor captured the imagination of
New York theatregoers with his memorable
performance as Falstaff in the 1904
production of "Henry IV" parts one and
two. It was a role he would return to
many times, in New York and nationally,
over the next two decades.

McNeill married three times and was
divorced three times. He leaves no
dependants.

Bobbie glanced, once more, at Crina Colbeck's obituary. While they may have played New York at much the same time, it was difficult to see where they would have been together. Bobbie wasn't sure why she was looking at this, but her intuition was telling her to check.

The obituary of Jason Crane was a little bit more complete, albeit very much like the previous article.

Jason Crane (1869-
Jason was a popular actor, best known
for his many performances on American
stages.

He was born Hector Nilsson on March
29th, 1869, in Chicago, IL. His father,
Sven Nilsson, was a noted businessman who

married local actress, Miss Florence Crane. The family's fortune was lost, following the great fire of Chicago in 1871. Crane's father took his own life, a year later, and the family were left in financially straitened circumstances.

Crane's mother, Miss Crane, returned to the stage, in this period, and had a modestly successful career in New York. She remarried in 1882, to Mr Ronald Harrison.

Crane left school at the age of sixteen, to join a circus. Later, he joined various travelling repertory companies that toured around the United States, between 1890 and 1899. He adopted the stage name Jason Crane, around 1901.

His big break came in New York, when theatregoers and critics acclaimed his memorable performance of Iago, in a 1903 production of "Othello". Major parts followed, including Hamlet (1904), Anthony in Anthony and Cleopatra (1907) and Macbeth (1911), as well as many other, non-Shakesperean, roles.

Mr Crane had a, short-lived, stint in California, where he played a number of supporting roles, in the burgeoning moving picture industry. This included a small part in the Babylon section of DW Griffith's "Intolerance" in 1916.

The actor went to the war in France in 1918 to entertain the servicemen over

there. He returned to New York in 1919
and had, numerous, supporting roles in
major productions on Broadway and on
tour.

Crane was married to Lily Keats, in
1912, but the marriage ended in divorce,
three years later. Crane never remarried
and leaves no dependants. Miss Keats
passed away in 1919 a victim of the
Spanish flu epidemic.

Bobbie finished the article on Crane and pondered her next move. The obituaries were more revealing than she had imagined. And her imagination was running a little wild, she realised. She quickly re-read the articles and then, when Fanley's attention was diverted, she put them in her handbag.

It was time to head over to Lindy's, on 49th Street. She left the offices of the newspaper, and hailed a cab to take her uptown, to meet Damon Runyon. She arrived just before 1 pm. When she walked into the restaurant, she spied Runyon in his usual seat. That he was with Arnold Rothstein and Lenny was less of surprise than the fact that the other person at the table, smiling over at her, was Dick Devenish.

22

Mount Sinai Hospital, New York

It was murder now.

While he had no love for Smiley Stanton, Flynn felt a sense of despair, that the mobster had been killed under his watch. He'd spent a lifetime trying to put murderers behind bars. Successfully. His reasoning was simple, the more people he caught the fewer there would be to commit these appalling crimes. And yet, like the tides of the sea, they kept coming. For every man he caught there would be half a dozen others to take his place. Most of them were people who never dreamed they would be killers. But there were some for whom this was their trade.

Everything about the murder of Smiley pointed to this being a 'hit'. A planned murder by the mob. How else to explain this? The gambler turned theatre impresario had retained his connections to the mob, had continued to run illegal craps games. A major one had been busted and now Smiley was dead.

The manner of the murder was as daring as he could remember in his long career. The attempted murder, in a public theatre. The successful completion of the task was in a hospital while the victim was, supposedly, under the protection of New York's finest.

They were not looking so fine now. And nor was he. The fact that the press would have a field day over the murder hurt him less than the idea that he had, somehow, let Smiley down. Whatever Smiley was, he, at least, had deserved some form of protection.

Flynn and Nolan were sitting with the young policeman who had allowed a doctor to enter the victim's room unaccompanied. He'd believed what he'd been told by the man, because he was dressed in the garb of a surgeon, and he'd seemed plausible.

The boy, for he seemed no more than that to Flynn, was inconsolable. And what could either he or Nolan say that would comfort him? The autopsy would, almost certainly, confirm what Flynn suspected. Someone had stabbed Smiley, in the same place of the original knife wound and then replaced the bandages, to make it look like the wound had merely reopened. The murder weapon would have been something long and sharp. A suture needle would probably have been enough to finish the job, started at the Century Playhouse.

Everything pointed to it being a 'hit'. The mob wanted Smiley silenced. The pieces seemed to fit, even more, by the fact that Rothstein and Luciano were in the audience when the first attempt was made.

Although, Flynn had to concede, it was unlikely, based on the evidence of other people in the audience, that none of Rothstein's party had been heard to make any movement that would suggest they were responsible for the original stabbing. In fact, no one had heard, or sensed, anything. Finding Smiley with a knife in his chest was a complete surprise to everyone around in the audience. Of course, they would check out each statement, but Flynn did not believe the killer had been sitting in the audience.

This created another problem, in Flynn's. mind. The raid on the craps game had taken place at almost the same time as the first murder attempt. This felt strange to Flynn. He glanced up at Nolan, who was pacing the corridor outside the hospital mortuary.

'What's on your mind?' asked Flynn, tired of listening to himself think.

'The timing of the first attack.'

'Yeah,' agreed Flynn. 'That's got me too.'

'Why hit Smiley when they didn't know there was going to be a raid?' Nolan was asking the very question that Flynn had been pondering.

'Indeed,' said Flynn. 'What do you think?'

Nolan let out a sigh and sat down. He rubbed his eyes, with his inner palm.

'There are a few possibilities,' said Nolan, finally. 'A mob hit to silence Smiley. Yet that only makes sense if there wasn't the first attempt on his life. Someone else in the audience with a beef with Smiley. Maybe the background checks on the witnesses will turn up something. Perhaps it's one of the cast. They were facing Smiley and only a few feet away. Don't ask me about motive on that one. Perhaps it was the Stage Manager, Crispin. He was in the wings watching the play according to his statement. He's with the mob.'

'He's an accountant,' said Flynn glumly. 'I know you shouldn't assess guilt based on how people look but I might just make an exception for Crispin. There was no one in the orchestra pit?'

'Crispin says he didn't see, or hear, anyone else. He was too wrapped up in Miss Colbeck's performance.'

'Might be a motive,' said Flynn, before adding, 'Jealousy.' He didn't sound convinced, and nor was Nolan.

The door, to the hospital mortuary, opened. It was a man in surgical garb. He pulled his mask down from his face and then removed the surgical hat to reveal thick dark hair matted by sweat.

'Come in and see,' said the surgeon, whose name was Evans.

'Thanks Dr Evans,' said Flynn. He rose, wearily, from his seat.

'Has the next of kin been informed?' asked Evans, walking towards the table where the body of Smiley lay, partially covered with a sheet which was, only marginally, whiter than he was now.

'Yes,' said Nolan. 'They're on their way.'

'Put those on, would you? Caps also. I hardly think an identification is necessary.' He put the mask back on his face and pointed to a box containing other masks.

'No, I suppose not,' said Flynn, reaching over to the masks, and grabbing a surgical hat. 'Can you tell us what happened.'

'I'm not a pathologist, you understand,' said Evans. 'This is pretty clear cut, if you'll excuse the pun.'

'Go on,' said Flynn. He wasn't smiling.

'It looks as if Mr Stanton received a second stab wound in the place where the knife was originally inserted.'

'How was the knife originally inserted?' asked Nolan.

'I was the surgeon who dealt with Mr Stanton last night. I should have been off duty an hour ago but no matter. In my opinion the original wound was caused by a knife that had either been thrown or it was inserted by a woman. The depth of the wound was not so great that the knife could severely damage any of the internal organs although there was, obviously, a lot of bleeding.

Evans pointed to the cleaned-up wound and began to explain, in more detail, what had happened.

'Looking at the wound again, I can tell you that the width and depth have changed significantly and that a blade had penetrated the heart. The blade penetrated the pericardium and then entered the left ventricle of the heart. It was inserted, and then withdrawn, in such a way as to try and disguise its entry, but you can't hide something like that, especially, as I say, as I saw him last night when I operated on him, and then again later, when I inspected the stitches.'

'What type of blade?' asked Nolan.

This brought almost a chuckle from the surgeon, but he stopped himself.

'It wasn't a scalpel if that's what you're asking. It was one of those,' he said, pointing to a, bloodied, thin metal suture needle. 'That would be my bet. It would certainly do the job. Given his earlier injury, his loss of blood and the internal bleeding, I estimate death would have been measured in seconds, rather than minutes. The level of rigor was not advanced. I would put it at between after five and seven in the morning.'

Flynn nodded and thanked the surgeon. Just then, there was a knock at the door.

'Come in,' said Evans.

The door opened, and in walked the young patrolman, who had been guarding Smiley. He appeared nervous.

'Inspector Flynn,' he began. 'Miss Colbeck, Mr Stanton's wife, is here with her agent. What shall I say?'

What was there to say, thought Flynn? The patrolman had a strange look on his face. Nolan noticed this, and assumed it was because he was tired and upset.

'Sir,' said the patrolman. He was pointing to Dr Evans. 'That's the man I saw last night. The surgeon.'

Flynn and Nolan both turned to Evans in surprise.

'Is this true?' asked Flynn.

23

Lindy's, New York: April 1922

Lenny and Rothstein edged down the booth seats, to allow Bobbie some space to sit. Both were large men but, thankfully, Bobbie's frame was slender enough not to require much seating real estate. Bobbie eyed Dick with a frown.

'Hello Mr Devenish. This is a surprise. Have you not solved the case yet?' said Bobbie wryly.

'I acknowledge the compliment on my abilities, Red, and you are quite correct. Normally these matters would be wrapped up by now. This one has complications.'

'You mean the death of Mr Stanton, in the hospital?' asked Bobbie.

'That would certainly qualify,' agreed Devenish. He looked sternly at Rothstein as he said this. An unspoken rebuke hung in the air, like a storm cloud about to burst.

Bobbie sensed that both Rothstein, and Lenny, were shifting a little uncomfortably in their seats. There could have been a few reasons for this, but the most alarming one was what Bobbie was thinking at that moment. Perhaps something in her face changed, but Devenish, immediately, noticed something in Bobbie and quickly guessed the reason why.

'Before you go jumping to assumptions, Red, I think you should listen to Mr Rothstein. This is not what I think you are thinking,' said Devenish

Bobbie turned to Rothstein, and it would be fair to say that his tough exterior had melted away, replaced by an expression more suited to a schoolboy, who'd accidentally thrown a baseball through the principal's window.

'The stage appears to be yours Mr Rothstein,' said Bobbie, grimly.

Now, a twenty-two-year-old young woman is probably taking her life in her hands in addressing a mob leader in such a dismissive manner. However, Rothstein was a happily married man, which is to say that he was used to being on the receiving end of criticism from the infallible sex, whether explicit, implied or even unjustified. There was more chance of beating the weather in an argument than women, so he wisely avoided any direct entanglements.

'Miss Flynn,' he intoned as he did not want the whole of Lindy's to hear either what he had to say, or the sorrowful manner in which he said it. 'Felix was a valued partner. I have no more interest in putting a hit on dear Felix than I have in leaving my, ever-loving, wife.'

This was pretty vulnerable stuff for a mobster and even Damon Runyon inhaled audibly.

'I know Felix twenty years and not one argument do we have in this time. When he tells me that he wants to run a theatre, I say, good luck Felix, you go run a theatre.'

'And can we put a craps game in one of the rooms?' interjected Bobbie. Runyon's eyes widened at this, but she could see Devenish smiling.

'Felix is a businessman too. He sees the benefit of this suggestion and together we run a very successful operation which gives pleasure to many men and women both front and back of house. Where is the harm in that?'

Bobbie was not keen on gambling, but she had no moral objection to people who chose to spend their money in this way, although she did worry that, for some, it was more than just a game. She stayed silent, but retained her look of scepticism, which Rothstein recognised all too well, after a decade, or more, of wedded bliss.

'Your father and I, we cross swords many times and I like him. He's straight. I respect that. It seems young Nolan is straight too. Well done. They win this one. All I can say is I am glad your father does not gamble. But I do not blame Felix for this. And you must understand that the raid is a big surprise to us. So, answer me this, Miss Flynn - how can we put a hit on Felix when we do not know a raid is taking place? We are not fortune tellers, Miss Flynn. There is no crystal ball here. If there was, I make a lot of money at the track and stop running craps games. I can see that you see my point, Miss Flynn.'

Bobbie's facial expression had turned from scepticism to a frown. This was the one thing that she had been wondering herself. Why would the mob try to silence Smiley if they were not aware of the raid. And if they had been aware that a raid was taking place, just cancel the game and move it elsewhere. It was a floating craps game after all, although it had found a semi-permanent space.

However, Bobbie was still feeling a sense of despair, for her father. He was likely to receive a lot of criticism for the level of protection that was given to Smiley, whatever the level of human error involved.

'Why didn't you do more to protect Mr Stanton?' asked Bobbie. Under normal circumstances, such a question may have been deemed unwise to ask of someone whose business interests included illegal gambling and bootlegging. However, just at that moment, Bobbie's eyes were blazing, like fiery beacons atop a castle turret. She was defending her father's honour as if it were a priceless family heirloom under siege. More importantly, Rothstein, with the benefit of hindsight, agreed with her. He should have done more.

The question was met with a sad shrug of the shoulders. This acted to spike Bobbie's guns, as she realised that the crime boss did feel genuine sorrow over the death of Smiley. Or perhaps it was a pragmatic reaction to the mess that they were in, that went far beyond the raiding of a craps game, and the death of its host.

'Look Red,' said Damon Runyon, acting as a peacemaker, 'I think we are all on the same side. Mr Rothstein is unhappy that someone has hit Smiley. You are unhappy that your father will be asked how this can happen. It is in all our interests to know how such a terrible deed was done, and who is the guilty party.'

Bobbie nodded at this, and she began to feel, a little, remorse at having attacked Rothstein. It is a curious quirk of their character that women, particularly Bobbie, possess an unshakeable conviction in the infallibility of their opinions. They are custodians of truth and rightness, rendering the act of contrition as alien to their nature as snow in July. The apology, when it came from Bobbie, took the form of a frown and a nod, in the direction of Rothstein. He nodded his acceptance back.

Now that the armistice was in place, discussions began on who, as writers in the noblest, most sophisticated form of literature might term "dunnit".

'It wasn't us,' said Rothstein once more. 'Your father and young Nolan they speak to everyone in the seats around us. No one sees anything.'

'It was rather dark, Mr Rothstein,' pointed out Devenish.

'True, but no one hears anything. You see statements Mr Devenish. If me or Lenny, or Lucky, or Sideways turn around, stand up and stab Felix then, trust me, you will hear it. Lenny, here, cannot reach for the salt without it sounding like a cavalry charge.'

Lenny half-smiled at this. He was a serious man. Even when his boss cracked a joke.

Dick Devenish had been unusually silent during all of this, but you can't keep a good man down for long, especially one as thoroughly enchanted by his own verbal prowess as he was. Conversations with Devenish were less about dialogue and more about providing him with an appreciative audience.

'Just before you arrived, Red, I had been outlining my own theories on this topic. Would you like to hear them?'

Not that there was a choice here but Bobbie barely had a second to reflect or answer before Devenish plunged ahead, smiling at the flash of anger in her eyes. Even Bobbie had to smile at his shamelessness.

'Your father and that young Adonis, Nolan, did a fairly thorough job in exonerating their sworn enemies Mr Rothstein, Lucky, Lenny and Sideways. It must have a bitter pill for them. No one, it seems, heard anything that would point the finger at them as potential killers. Where does that leave us Red?'

'With the people who were either on the stage or backstage.'

'Correct,' acknowledged Devenish. 'I believe that the underwhelming Lieutenant Grimm and the underrated Detective Yeats are down at the theatre now, with said performers, running through what happened. I'm sure it's all very Sherlock Holmes yet, no disrespect to them, I rather doubt they will be able to beat a confession out of any killer among that lot.'

'What about Mr Crispin the stage manager? Where was he?' asked Bobbie 'And there's also Mr Jeffries, the props man. Tommy Hart also. I've spoken with him and Mr Jeffries. I didn't get a chance to speak to Mr Crispin,' said Bobbie.

'That's because he arrived to tell the people, in the craps game, that Smiley had been attacked,' said Devenish.

Bobbie pointed at Devenish, for reasons that she probably wouldn't have been able to explain herself, but the gesture suggested that she had an idea.

'Which means he was in the vicinity of the stage. How else would he have known that Mr Smiley had been knifed?' said Bobbie, trying to keep the excitement from her voice.

Devenish looked more doubtful, as did Rothstein.

'I know you shouldn't judge a book by the cover, but Clement Crispin is the sort of person who would apologise if you stepped on *his* foot. Mild-mannered barely covers how docile this man is, Red. He makes a cow look like a four-year-old after bingeing on espresso.'

'My father says you can never tell,' replied Bobbie. She felt like a mother, scolding a child. This was something she found that Devenish brought out in her. Sometimes it was amusing.

'Oh, I don't know about that. One look at your father and I can tell he doesn't think much of me,' replied Devenish with a rueful grin.

The table erupted into laughter which helped the mood. Bobbie felt it was time to share her thoughts. She took out the files that she had borrowed from the obituaries office and showed them to Devenish.

'Don't tell Mr Fanley,' warned Bobbie to Runyon.

'My word is my bond,' replied Runyon.

Devenish poured over the three obituaries of people who had not yet left this mortal coil. Then he motioned to Rothstein who declined the offer with a murmured, 'I'm paying you, remember.'

'What do you think?' asked Bobbie.

'Aside from how morbid it is to read or write an obituary of someone who is still living, I did notice one thing. Probably you did too. The circus.'

Bobbie nodded and said, 'What if one of them was involved in a knife throwing act? That would explain how they were able to put a knife into poor Mr Stanton without being beside him.'

'In darkness?' said Runyon, doubtfully. 'Some act.'

'No different from being blindfolded, old boy,' responded Devenish.

'Exactly,' said Bobbie. 'It's the only way this could have been done.'

'Are you really accusing either Crina Colbeck or Jason Crane of being the killer?'

Bobbie paused for a moment, 'No. We need to check a few things first. I mean, we don't know if either were part of a knife-throwing act and we don't know where they were this morning when Mr Stanton was murdered. The knife-throwing I can believe, but the idea that they are cool assassins who were able to avoid security and calmly walk into Mr Stanton's room and kill him seems a little far-fetched. That bit has me, I'm afraid.' Bobbie turned to Rothstein and smiled sheepishly, 'That part seems more like a "hit" if you don't mind me saying.'

Rothstein did not appear to take offence at this, but his face remained sombre.

'What will you do now?' asked Rothstein.

'Can you tell us what you remember of the moments that led up to the attack last night?' asked Bobbie.

'Lenny, you've been quiet,' said Rothstein. 'What do you say?'

Lenny was not given to the art of small talk or, for that matter, any talk. He had perfected the fine art of non-verbal communication, a skill set rooted in the vigorous application of knuckles to jaws or a glower of violent intent.

He was, to put it mildly, the sort of chap who made silence not only golden but an absolute necessity. Conversationalists who attempted to engage Lenny in anything beyond a terse nod or a monosyllabic grunt, found themselves swiftly introduced to the persuasive eloquence of his right hook. It was with marked reluctance that he began to speak.

'I am watching the broad talking one minute. Then the lights go out. Just as I reach for the old equaliser, they comes back on. The broad is lying on the stage like someone had put a hit on her. I am thinking that, maybe, I need to move Mr and Mrs Rothstein out of the theatre as there is someone who is acting in an ungentlemanly way. Then the curtain comes down. I get to my feet and so does everyone else, but they are clapping. I never see a hit clapped before. Then the curtain goes up and the broad is alive. I put the Roscoe back when the screams start. I think they are screaming at me, but then I see Mr Stanton with a knife in his chest.'

'Any idea how it got there?' asked Devenish. There was no hint of accusation in his voice and, given that Lenny was a good deal over six feet and built like a well-fed lumberjack, it was probably for the best that there wasn't.

Lenny's burst of eloquence had clearly fatigued him for he shrugged by way of answer.

'This is what I told Inspector Flynn, too,' said Rothstein. 'I have no idea how my friend Felix found himself with a knife sticking out of him. Lucky and Sideways said the same, and I believe them. You ask me, the knife was thrown. From the stage. I like this idea of the circus. You should look at that. You should speak to these actors and see what they have to say for themselves. Maybe we can help you.'

Bobbie and Devenish could just imagine what form that help would take and both put their hands up immediately.

'We'll bear your kind offer in mind, Mr Rothstein,' said Devenish, 'but for the moment I think we'll try speaking to them first.' Then Devenish turned to Bobbie and added, 'What do you say to a trip down to the Playhouse?'

24

It was around two in the afternoon that Bobbie and Devenish arrived at the Century Playhouse. There were a lot of people milling around outside the box office looking for refunds or simply curious to find out what was going on. Across each of the posters was a small notice that read:

PLAY CANCELLED UNTIL FURTHER NOTICE

The entrance to the theatre was guarded by two patrolmen, that Bobbie did not recognise. There were a couple of reporters trying to gain access, without much success. The two patrolmen were of the tight-lipped variety who preferred to let their batons do the talking.

Bobbie and Devenish went around to the side of the stage to see if they could gain access via the stage door. It was locked and despite banging on the door for a few minutes there was little joy.

'Why don't we go see if we can gain entry via the door, they used for the craps game,' suggested Bobbie.

'Lead on Macduff,' replied Devenish. 'I hope you know where you're going?'

This necessitated walking around the block to the other side of the theatre. Finding the door used by her father in the raid proved to be easier than they'd imagined. The clue was in the big policeman standing by it. Luckily, Bobbie knew this patrolman. His name was Sarbiewski, and he had once had to babysit Bobbie when she was seven. His solution, when she had misbehaved, was to put her in a police cell.

Her behaviour improved quickly.

'Hey, Red,' greeted the big patrolman. 'What brings you here?'

'As if you don't know,' replied Bobbie. 'Can you let us in?'

'Your pop won't be happy.'

'As if that ever stopped me, or you for that matter,' laughed Bobbie. 'Do you know Dick?' Bobbie turned to her companion who held out his hand.

'The legendary Dick Devenish, this is indeed an honour,' said Sarbiewski, with a wry grin.

'Yes, it must be an honour for an honest yeoman like yourself,' replied Devenish.

Sarbiewski grinned while shaking his head and looked at Bobbie ruefully, 'I don't know what your pop would like less, me letting you in or you keeping company with this meathead.'

'He has his uses,' said Bobbie with a grin.

'It is I who am honoured now,' replied Devenish as they entered through the door. They both murmured their thanks as the door shut behind them. They walked along a short corridor to another door. It was unlocked.

The room that they entered was windowless and dark. It took a moment for their eyes to grow accustomed to the light. Devenish found a light switch and finally they could gaze upon the room.

Both were surprised at how small the room was. It was dominated by the craps table in the middle. There were a few seats scattered by the wall but it was clear that those attending were there to gamble and, if the small bar was any guide, to drink.

'Lovely,' said Bobbie, taking in the fragrant aroma of stale cigarettes and spilt alcohol. Her second visit to this games room revealed it to be no more prepossessing than her memory of the previous evening when it was throbbing with noise and people.

'Charming,' agreed Devenish. 'I must bring a few friends down here sometime for cocktails.'

There was nothing for them in the room, so they passed through into the corridor that led to the Trap Room underneath the stage.

A minute later they were back stage, having climbed the short set of stairs that led from the Trap Room. They weren't alone. On stage were half a dozen people. And one cat. Thomas Jefferson was sitting at the front of the stage watching proceedings like a juror watching a trial.

If only cats could talk, thought Bobbie, as she and Devenish made an entrance, of sorts, from the wings. Their arrival was enough to stop Lieutenant Grimm mid-flow. His eyes flared and there was definitely a hint of steam spitting from his ears as they interrupted his flow. Just as he was about to suggest that they find another place to go, or something not very like that, he realised that it was Inspector Flynn's daughter he was addressing. He quickly reverted to his usual deferential manner.

Grimm was a man whose every action seemed carefully calibrated to curry favour with those above him. This had earned him a reputation as a sycophant of the first order. His shirt was always pressed to a degree that suggested it might crack open if he made one false move.

If Grimm was surprised at how Bobbie and Devenish had managed to make it past the men, he'd installed at the doors then he certainly did not show it. However, he did make a mental note to haul the men responsible over some, particularly hot, coals.

'Miss Flynn, it is a pleasure to see you once more,' began Grimm. He ended it there too. Devenish smiled ruefully at Bobbie as he realised that this warm welcome was not going to extend to him.

Bobbie now had a chance to see who was on stage. Aside from the two policemen, there was Polly Buckley, Lane Vidal and Wickham McNeill. Across in the wings, she saw Tommy Hart by the curtain. There was another older gentleman, whom she took to be Clement Crispin. What remained of his hair was perpetually tousled and his face conveyed a sense of quiet bewilderment. If Bobbie had ever harboured any suspicion that he was a killer then this disappeared in an instant. He looked about as violent as an old cardigan.

'Are you reconstructing the attack on Mr Stanton?' asked Devenish to Grimm.

'In a manner of speaking, yes,' replied Grimm. In fact, the cast had only just arrived and Grimm had been wondering how he would go about questioning them. Devenish had just supplied him with a jolly good idea.

'Perhaps, Miss Flynn and I could assist. We should take our seats in the auditorium,' suggested Devenish.

'Yes, agreed Grimm. 'That would work.'

Bobbie and Devenish descended the steps leading to their seats. Sitting in the front row was Frida Haynes, the dresser and make up lady. Through a haze of her own cigarette smoke, she cast a sideways glance at Bobbie and Devenish and rolled her eyes. The cigarette she was holding only enjoyed a brief tenure between her lacquered fingers, it was not destined for a long life. She drained the remaining quarter inch in a summary manner and cast the remains onto the ground with a restrained violence. Bobbie concluded that if she had ever worked in a circus then they had their man.

'Where is Mr Crane?' asked Devenish. 'Shouldn't he be here?'

'He should,' agreed Grimm who seemed unhappy. Whether this was because Devenish had interrupted proceedings or frustration at the absence of the other major star was a matter of debate.

'So, we are missing the leading man and leading lady,' surmised Devenish who, much to Bobbie's amusement, now appeared to be wresting control from the lieutenant. 'Perhaps if Detective Yeats could take the place of Mr Crane and could I ask you young lady,' he was speaking to the formidable Mrs Haynes, 'to take Miss Colbeck's place on the stage, so that we can establish where everyone was at the crucial moment.'

Frida Haynes raised one sceptical eyebrow and received smiles from Bobbie and Devenish, in return. Well, she thought, the pup had called her young. She rose slowly to her feet and climbed the steps up onto the stage. Wickham McNeil courteously went over to lead her to the spot where Crina had been standing.

Grimm, to his credit, did not demur. It was almost a relief to him for someone to organise matters. Wickham McNeil was happily getting into the spirit of things. This may have been because a lot of spirit had got into him that morning. Whilst his feet may not have been so steady, his memory could not be faulted as he placed everyone in their positions.

Finally, McNeill had performed his duty organising everyone and he nodded, first to Grimm, and then to Devenish. This meant that Frida as Crina was at the front and centre of the stage with her back to the audience. Crane was immediately to her right but several feet in from where she stood. Centre right and further back was Polly and to her left stood Vidal and then McNeill. Crispin stood at the side of the stage and indicated that he had been further back in the wings left while Tommy Hart was wings right as the audience looked.

Bobbie made a quick drawing of where everyone was in relation to Smiley. It was immediately clear that, barring some miracle of speed and stealth, neither Vidal nor McNeill could possibly have thrown the knife. And unless McNeill was an even better actor than he appeared to be and his semi-ossified manner was just for show, then he certainly could not have thrown a knife from where he was standing.

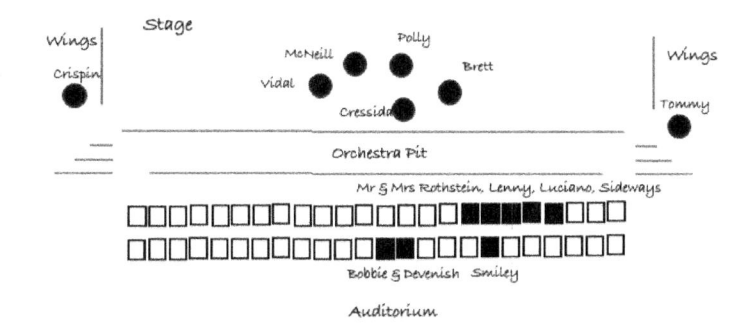

That left Crina, a former circus performer, Crane who also may have been a circus performer and Polly Buckley. Tommy Hart was in the wings and would need to have moved rather quickly and without making any noise, in order to throw the knife. This seemed unlikely.

And then there was Jeffries – where was he?

And where was Crane?

The answer to the latter question came moments later when everyone heard a commotion at the side of the stage and a theatrically angry voice. Jason Crane was in the building and he wasn't happy.

He stormed onto the stage and looked around him. He stared at the side of the stage and then down to Bobbie and the seat that had been occupied by Smiley when the attack took place. And then, astonishingly, his manner changed, like a storm subsiding at the flap of a seagull's wing. He became pale and where once his back was ramrod straight, he became hunched and defeated.

'Are you unwell?' asked Grimm, for it looked for all the world like Crane might be about to decorate the stage in a manner that would not find favour with anyone present or, indeed, the cleaner.

'I did it,' said Crane in a whisper that seemed to carry to the back of the theatre. 'It was me.'

'What do you mean?' snapped Grimm, not sure if he was hearing correctly.

Crane looked up and there were tears in his eyes. And from what Bobbie could see, they were genuine. Crane was almost shaking now.

'It was me. I tried to kill Stanton,' said Crane.

25

Mount Sinai Hospital, New York

Reed Crotch III had spent a lifetime angry. And who wouldn't having been angry, saddled with that surname? There had been a target on his back since his schooldays. If there was any benefit from being so lumbered, it was that he had developed a skin thicker than a rhinoceros in armour. The slings and arrows of outrageous fortune, not to mention the barbs of disgruntled actors, bounced off him like bullets against a dreadnought.

The name, strangely, had been a source of immense pride to his father and grandfather, both of whom possessed similarly armour-plated skin and who had assured him that it would be his making.

In some senses they were right. No one messed with this Crotch.

Financially, it made sense to retain, however reluctantly, the hateful name. It was written into his father's will that if the son ever changed his name, a not ungenerous allowance would immediately be cancelled and donated to the Teamsters Union, a body that both father and son viewed as a communist front.

So, Reed Crotch III was stuck with his name. And it made him resentful. To say his character was prickly was like saying Alaska gets a bit chilly in winter. This ongoing sense of umbrage was allied to an even less pleasing temperamental streak that made a firecracker look like a paragon of stability.

His one act of rebellion against the father and grandfather, who had cast such a shadow over his life, was to abandon any intention of working for the family business. The Crotch family were big in men's underwear. It was the principal reason why Grandfather Crotch, Reed Crotch I, had gone into this business. It was nominative determinism in its impurest form.

When Crotch exited underwear, he went into the one business that could make best use of his vituperative tongue and a hide like a seasoned warship. He became a theatrical agent.

His first client was Crina Colbeck.

If the story of Crina Colbeck were truly to be told, then enormous credit was due to Crotch. He had handled her career from the moment he'd seen her perform, in a burlesque show in upstate New York. What he'd seen that evening as she sang, danced and recited lines from poetry had convinced him he was watching a star in the making.

From that day forward he'd bullied, begged and beguiled theatre managers and producers into using Crina Colbeck. It didn't take long for his original view of Crina to be shared by the people who most mattered.

As Crina's stardom grew, Crotch took on a select few other clients and guided them on a similarly stellar path. But his number one priority was always Crina. He guided her career while, at the same time, trying to protect her like a knight guarding a damsel against a recalcitrant dragon. While she had, against his advice, married other men, he was the one she had always turned to in her life, when the fates had turned against her.

It was with mixed feelings that he walked alongside Crina into the hospital morgue. He and Smiley had disliked one another from the off. A little bit of Crotch went a long way as far as Smiley was concerned and the feeling was definitely mutual. However, he genuinely cared about Crina. This was not just an economic imperative.

He had met Crina when she was a young woman who had an enormous talent but had made mistakes of the male variety. Their relationship was never romantic. He loved her too much for that. And he was, when he met her, twenty years her senior. This would not have helped either her career, or his.

Although his heart was broken for Crina, he could not avoid feeling a certain amount of relief that Smiley was out of the picture. He'd never trusted the man.

And then there was the theatre. The Century Playhouse now belonged to Crina as far as he was concerned. That created a paradox that needed to be resolved. On the one hand, this was wonderful news. His client owned a theatre albeit one that seemed, inexplicably, to be making a loss. At this juncture, Crotch had no idea that the ownership was a tad more complicated than he suspected. All of which was for the future. Right now, he had another potential problem.

Would Crina fall under police scrutiny? The taint of suspicion would be a disaster for her career. And she still had decades of it to run. Because Crotch knew something that the old police inspector, he was facing did not know but would likely soon find out.

Crina had worked in a circus.
In a knife-throwing act.

Patrolman Adam Parks may have had worse days than this, but for the life of him he couldn't remember one. A night spent guarding a man who had nearly been killed had ended catastrophically, for both the man, and him. Smiley Stanton was dead and the finger of blame was hovering like the sword of Damocles over his head.

All he wanted to do was to go to bed and stay there for a month, hidden underneath a pillow. How would he ever be able to show his face at the precinct again? The boys would be whispering behind his back, pointing at him, even.

That's the boy who let Smiley die.

As if this wasn't enough, he was just about to go home when a nurse approached him and asked that he accompany a woman and a man to the morgue to see the body of Smiley. She was introduced as his wife. Not that he needed the introduction. He recognised Crina Colbeck immediately. Patrolman Parks was shocked at how small she was. Still beautiful though. Even with eyes red with tears. The tears for a husband who'd been murdered while he was supposed to be guarding him.

He couldn't say anything to her except sorry. Nothing else. Then, while he wanted to be anywhere but there just at that moment, he led them both to the morgue. They walked in a silence broken only by the sound of her crying. He felt like crying too.

They reached the morgue and the patrolman asked that they stay in the corridor while he informed Inspector Flynn of their arrival.

The second thing Patrolman Parks saw when he walked through the door to announce Crina Colbeck's arrival was the surgeon he'd met earlier that morning. His mouth dropped open in shock. He saw the inspector look askance at him. He even said something, but Parks could barely hear him for the sound of blood rushing around his head. He could barely breathe. And then finally he was able to speak.

'Sir,' said Parks, pointing to Dr Evans. 'That's the man I saw last night. The surgeon.'

He saw Flynn and Nolan both turn to Dr Evans in surprise.

'Is this true?' asked Flynn asked the surgeon. 'You were the man that saw Stanton?'

'The surgeon frowned for a moment and replied, 'Yes. What of it?' There was a sharpness to his tone. It was a reaction to the odd look on Flynn's face. He stared at the surgeon for a second or two longer than decorum probably deemed acceptable. 'I called in on him around five this morning. I met the policeman. What of it?'

'And Stanton was alive?' asked Flynn, conscious that this was probably one of the stupidest questions he'd asked in a long and successful career.

'Of course he was. I hope you're not implying I did something to him, Inspector.'

Flynn was about to explode at the tone of the surgeon, but then he realised that the case had changed in a moment.

Patrolman Parks was not sure whether to laugh or cry at this news. On balance it was perhaps worse for him. It meant that someone else had got past him, not just the surgeon.

Flynn nodded to Evans but said nothing about accusing him one way or another. Then he addressed Parks.

'Ask Miss Colbeck to come in.'

Parks disappeared for a moment. The next person to enter was Crina Colbeck. Flynn stepped forward and said with great solemnity, 'My name is Inspector Flynn of the New York Police Department. Please accept our condolences for your loss. I promise you; we will bring the killer to justice.'

Crina barely heard what was being said. She nodded and then looked towards the door that led to the room where her husband lay on a table, dead.

'May I?' she asked. Her voice was barely a whisper.

Flynn nodded and Evans opened the door for Crina to enter. She left the men and walked inside. This left Flynn with Nolan, Parks, Dr Evans and Reed Crotch III.

Flynn glanced towards Crotch and introduced himself once more. Crotch hesitated before introducing himself. He hated these moments when he said his own name. It was always the same. The hesitation in their voices. The moments of silence while they processed what they had just heard.

The mute mockery in their eyes. Crotch? Are you serious?

'I'm Crina's agent and friend. Reed Crotch,' said Crotch. Before the policemen could reply he continued. 'I want to meet the surgeon who is responsible for this botched operation.'

'Excuse me?' snapped Evans, whose dander was already up following the testy exchange with Flynn. 'What do you mean botched? I did not botch anything.'

Crotch turned to Evans, his eyes blazing. He wasn't really that angry, but he could be a performer himself when the occasion demanded and he smelled money now. What's my motivation? Money, here, now and always.

'I mean botched, mister,' snarled Crotch. 'That man came into your hospital alive and now he's dead because you screwed up the operation. He's dead, ain't he?'

Evans took a step back almost as if he expected that the madman before him was about to lash out. Regaining his composure he said in a hard voice, 'That man, as you put it, was most certainly alive when I last saw him. If you want to know why he is dead then I suggest you ask these policemen who were charged with guarding him last night. It seems as if someone came in this morning and did what you are accusing me of doing.'

Crotch's eyes widened and his head jerked towards Flynn.

'Is this true?' he asked, in wonder.

Flynn took a deep breath and then nodded.

'You mean to tell me that Stanton was alive and you allowed some guy to waltz in here and kill him. Tell me you are kidding me?'

Flynn shook his head and confirmed what had happened.

'Sometime between five and eight, someone came into the hospital and killed Mr Stanton.'

Crotch was standing eerily still. He held Flynn's gaze for a moment or two. One thought swirled around his mind like a leaf in a tornado, he was staring at the mother of all lawsuits.

'I promise you Fynn, we will sue you for so much money that your great-grandchildren will be working off the debt,' snarled Crotch.

Flynn could see that this was inevitable. His country was becoming increasingly litigious. There was no way he or the department were going to stop the inevitable outcry, the condemnation and, if Crotch was to be believed, the law suit.

And then all that changed in an instant.

The door opened and Crina Colbeck stepped out. If she sensed tension in the air, she did not show it. The tear-streaked face indicated her mind was elsewhere. The silence that greeted her sudden arrival was like an earthquake, thought Flynn. It felt like a primal force that was shaking the room, shattering everything in its path.

Crina looked up, first at Crotch and then to Flynn. When she spoke, it was an anguished whisper.

'I wish to confess.'

26

That can't be right, thought Bobbie as soon as she had recovered from the shock of hearing Jason Crane confess to the murder of Smiley Stanton. Something about what he'd said or how he had said it did not ring true. Hardly what an established actor would want to hear from an audience member.

Bobbie turned to Devenish and said, 'Do you believe him?'

Devenish raised a sceptical eyebrow and then nodded towards the stage, 'What I think hardly matters. It looks to me as if our friend, Grimm does.'

Grimm was virtually wagging a tail in delight. He almost skipped over towards the actor while motioning for two patrolmen to go over and take a person he now considered a prisoner into custody.

The reactions from the people sharing the stage were an interesting mixture of emotions. Polly Buckley gasped and stepped backwards from Crane, as he walked onto the stage. Lane Vidal went very quickly to comfort her, which confirmed a suspicion that Bobbie had held since the opening night.

Wickham McNeil, meanwhile, simply said in a loud undertone, which had Bobbie marvelling, 'Rot. Absolute rot.'

Interestingly he had not said "rotter", which Bobbie knew to be a term of abuse used by the island race across the Atlantic. In the ranking of terms of invective by those of a British disposition, the word was probably ahead of "shower" and "bounder", but just behind "cad".

Crane looked a little shell-shocked himself as the two patrolmen took his arm, none too gently it must be said. Wickham McNeill was outraged now and he stepped forward.

'This is outrageous. What are you doing old fellow?' he asked.

Bobbie almost applauded him. She felt she had to say something. Devenish was on his feet and began walking towards the stage.

'Crane, what are you saying?' said Devenish, before the actor could be led away.

'Crane has just confessed,' pointed out Grimm in a voice that made him sound like a Puritan at a children's party. 'This is a police matter now, Mr Devenish.'

Bobbie could no more accept the matter being closed than Devenish.

'Mr McNeill,' shouted Bobbie. She had raised her voice to stop the two patrolmen leading Crane away. 'Why do you not believe him?' This succeeded for a few moments as it captured everyone's attention.

McNeill nodded a thank you to Bobbie. He said, 'I was standing a few feet away from him as you can see. I would have sensed something even in the darkness.'

Even if McNeill's most perceptive sense was where to find his next bottle of gin, there was enough outrage and scepticism in his voice to give everyone a pause for thought. But it was only momentary.

'Take him away,' said Grimm. His voice had turned into a snarl. He was losing patience with any delay to his triumphant moment on the stage.

'Stop,' shouted Bobbie, which worked as the two patrolmen did just that. She ran up onto the stage with, Devenish, and addressed Crane directly.

'Are you confessing to the murder of Felix Stanton?'

'Murder?' muttered Crane in a surprised voice.

Grimm's patience snapped, he strode forward towards the two patrolmen and Crane.

'Enough,' he shouted. 'Take him away, now.'

The two patrolmen had not often seen Grimm angry. It brought to mind a constipated Chihuahua. Or, perhaps, their patience was wearing thin. They led him back across the stage, past Tommy Hart in the wings.

Grimm had regained some of his composure, but he was clearly in no mood to have any further truck with Devenish or even the daughter of a police inspector. He stared at Bobbie and Devenish for a moment before following the two patrolmen across the stage to the wings and disappearing.

Silence descended on the auditorium broken only by the sound of Polly Buckley crying on the shoulder of Lane Vidal.

'Murder you say?' asked McNeill after a few moments. 'So, Smiley died after all from the wound. I thought he was going to make it. How sad.' There was a weariness in the actor's voice. It was low and authentic. Everything that Crane had not been when he confessed.

'He did make it, Mr McNeill,' replied Bobbie, turning to the actor. 'He was murdered this morning at the hospital.'

'Good Lord,' said McNeill. 'Really?'

Bobbie nodded and turned to Devenish. The private investigator looked thoughtful.

'No Bobbie,' he said. 'I don't think Crane had any idea that Smiley was dead.'

'He sounded surprised to me,' agreed Bobbie. 'How come that fathead Grimm can't see it then?'

'You may have answered your own question, Red,' laughed Devenish. 'Don't worry. Your father will soon tear hole in that story and, I suspect, a large one in our friend Grimm, too. You know, I rather miss O'Riordan. He'd never have believed that nonsense despite the fact he never avoided the path of least resistance.'

'What shall we do now?' mused Bobbie in a tone that suggested she was talking to herself rather than asking a man's advice. Devenish wisely assumed it was the latter rather than taking his life in his hands and telling her what he thought they should do.

Up on the stage, it felt like a pin had successfully been put back in a grenade, such was the sense of anticlimax, following the police taking Crane away. McNeill turned to Bobbie and Devenish.

'You don't believe all that then?'

'No,' replied Bobbie. 'Why would he do that?'

'You mean you don't know?' asked McNeill. There was a hint of amusement in his eyes. Bobbie shook her head.

Devenish and the rest of the cast were now all gazing at the English actor, in astonishment. Tommy Hart and Clement Crispin were now on the stage, having witnessed with mute shock, the astonishing events unfold.

'I look forward to you enlightening us, Mr McNeill,' said Devenish.

McNeill was now holding court, a role that he enjoyed immensely, and knew how to milk, like the old ham he was. He puffed his chest out, and surveyed the audience, as he had once done as Falstaff. Then he smiled rather ruefully, 'Old Jason and Crina have been lovers on and off for years. At least as long as I've known them, and that's a bloody long time, I can tell you.'

The cast were surprised to hear the news, as were Bobbie and Devenish.

'I had no idea.' This was Polly Buckley, who was the first to speak, after McNeill dropped this bombshell.

'They kept that rather quiet,' agreed Lane Vidal, who was still clutching Polly and, clearly, no longer worried about keeping their romance a secret, any longer. The irony was rather lost on the young actor, but it earned a wry look from McNeill.

Bobbie was processing the news that McNeill had just shared. While Devenish was happy to give voice to what everyone was thinking, 'This could mean that he wanted to get old Smiley out of the way and leave him a clear run. A bit dramatic for my tastes. Not sure he thought it through very well.'

Bobbie shook her head at this. She could hear the sceptical undertone in what Devenish had said. It didn't ring true for her, either.

'Perhaps he was protecting someone,' said Bobbie.

'Crina?' asked Devenish. 'I mean, perhaps. Although, it does sound a little far-fetched, Red, like something out of a, particularly ingenious, mystery novel.'

'Think about it. They both worked in a circus at one time. Perhaps that's where they met.'

'As knife throwers?' asked Devenish, still dubious.

'It would certainly explain things,' said Bobbie. She turned to McNeill, 'Do you know what Miss Colbeck and Mr Crane did, before they took to the stage?'

McNeill shrugged, in a manner that did not inspire any confidence that the solution to the crime was imminent.

'I knew about the circus, obviously, but I don't know if it was a knife-throwing act. She never denied that she came from a circus family, but more than that I cannot say. I remember Crane said many years ago that he worked in a circus but, again, I don't remember anything about his act. I doubt he said much about it.'

'What was the name of the circus?' asked Bobbie.

'Ravel's European Circus, I believe,' said McNeill. 'I went with Crina to see it once. Actually, this may be useful to you. Her parents were once an act at this circus. They were part of the management by the time I met them.'

'Might be worth paying them a visit,' said Devenish to Bobbie. Then he turned to McNeill, once more, 'Are Miss Colbeck's parents still alive?'

'That I cannot tell you, dear boy.'

Tommy Hart approached Bobbie and Devenish. He seemed a little in shock, at the turn of events. The colour seemed to have left him.

'You don't think that Mr Crane had anything to do with this?'

Bobbie shook her head and said, 'No, but he has confessed and I know Lieutenant Grimm. He'll take that happily and shut the investigation down.'

'They will check into his story?' pressed Tommy.

'I imagine they will. Something about it doesn't stack up for me, though. I can almost touch what it is.'

'I know what you mean,' said Devenish. 'What was it he said? Or, at least, how he said it. He said the word "murder" as if he was asking a question. As if he didn't know that Smiley was dead.'

Bobbie's eyes widened momentarily. She knew what was bothering her.

'When he came on stage. Do you remember what he said, Dick?'

'It was me or something like that.'

'No, just after,' said Bobbie. 'It was something like – "I tried to kill Stanton". That was it. Don't you see?'

Devenish smiled and nodded. He said, 'I really should make a point of listening to what people say more. I might learn something. Highly unlikely, but who knows. I live in hope.'

'Dick,' scolded Bobbie who was in no mood for Devenish playing the fool.

'Yes, I understand, Red,' said Devenish, becoming more serious. 'He said "tried". He was confessing to attacking Stanton. Not killing him.'

'We need to go to Midtown North first and tell my father or Detective Nolan...'

'The handsome Detective Nolan,' said Devenish with a smile which earned a frosty look from Bobbie. Then another thought struck her. She looked around the people on the stage.

'Where is Mr Jeffries. Shouldn't he be here?' asked Bobbie.

'He's not an early riser,' said Tommy. There was just a hint of a sneer in his voice.

There was too much loaded in how Tommy had said this for it not to be clear that he meant something else.

'What do you mean by that?' asked Devenish.

Tommy shrugged and held his hands up. It was clear the young man knew something but he didn't want to seem like a stoolpigeon.

'Look, I don't want to speak, out of turn, about Mr Jeffries. He's a nice guy. He's a bit of a night bird as far as I can see.'

'Meaning?' pressed Devenish. This was an unusually brief approach by the private detective and Bobbie realised that, despite his extravagant volubility, there was a lot more to the man than the dandyish rogue he portrayed himself to be.

Tommy laughed in embarrassment. He really did not want to say much more. And then it was if there was a gun being held to his head. It all came out.

'He offered me something one time. Drugs. I wasn't interested. I saw enough of what they do to people when I was at college. I didn't want to know.'

'What sort of drugs?' asked Devenish.

'You know, Hashish. He took me along to a Tea Pad one time. Everyone was a little strange. I left early. He stays out pretty late at them. I never see him here before one in the afternoon,' explained Tommy, then he rolled his eyes as if he was reluctant to say the next thing. 'He was high a lot of the time.'

Just as Bobbie was about to ask her next question, an ear-splitting scream reverberated around the auditorium.

It was Polly Buckley. She was pointing up into the lights above the stage.

Marv Jeffries had just enjoyed his final high, swinging from a rope attached to the lighting bridge over the stage.

27

Let us pause for a moment in this chronicle of murder, in the city of New York, to consider the paradox of Lieutenant Grimm. He wanted nothing more than to wield an air of authority and command that would inspire both fear and admiration in equal measure. Yet, for poor Grimm, it seemed the universe had other plans. His greatest desire, the yearning that gnawed at his very soul, was to be respected, perhaps even liked. Alas, the more he strove for this elusive affection, the more it slipped through his fingers, like sand.

From his meticulously starched shirt to the razor-sharp creases in his trousers, he treated the men under him with a sternness that could curdle milk. Yet, his demeanour towards his superiors was in marked contrast. The barked command to his subordinates, softened to a honeyed purr when dealing with senior officers. He peppered his speech with flattery, so thick you could spread it on toast. And it was noticed by all.

And Grimm noticed how people reacted to him.

It hurt him that, despite his best efforts, the respect of the men was proving ever elusive. His attempts to bring structure, and military-like precision, to the running of the precinct had been met by these hardened New York policemen with a mixture of indifference and insurrection.

Much of his four months at this new precinct, to him, Midtown North, had been marked more by administrative achievements rather than actual detection.

Until now.

He had a killer in his custody, and he was going to milk it for all he was worth as he entered the rather unhallowed portals of the precinct. Grimm could already envision the headlines: "Lieutenant Grimm Cracks the Case!" His name would be spoken with reverence, respect finally within his well-manicured grasp. This was the dream as he marched up the stairs of the precinct.

However, Grimm should have known that all dreams evaporate with the morning mist.

Or, in this case, with the news that Inspector Flynn was interviewing Crina Colbeck who had just confessed, herself, to the murder of Smiley Stanton.

Grimm stared at Sergeant Harrigan, who had just conveyed the news to him, as he entered the squad room. Before he could speak, his prisoner, Jason Crane spoke forcefully.

'Crina is no more a killer than Santa Claus is. She's lying. I killed Stanton.'

The last few words were said with decidedly less intent than the opening shot. The anger in his voice was certainly convincing to Grimm who had, just at that moment, forgotten he was dealing with actors who can do that sort of thing, convince, that is.

'Perhaps you should see the inspector,' suggested Harrigan, looking mystified at Crane. 'He's in the interview room.'

'Come with me,' snarled Grimm, who was finding his temperature gauge running at an alarmingly high rate. He and Yeats took Crane along the corridor to a room at the end. He could hear voices inside. One was a man he did not recognise who appeared to be having an epileptic fit of anger. Another voice, female, was wailing like a bad actress in an even worse play and the final voice was Inspector Flynn who was obviously in the middle of a brutal fight with himself to keep his composure if the strain in his voice was any guide.

They, obviously, had not heard Grimm's, rather tepid, knock on the door. It was time to take the bull by the horns. Grimm opened the door and marched into the room followed by the handcuffed Crane.

Their arrival was like a belch at a burial service. One moment there is wailing, the next the sort of silence that would have made the sound of a page rustling seem like a yodeller's Alpine echo.

All eyes turned to the new arrivals, first to register the faces and then to see the handcuffs decorating Crane's wrists like metal bracelets. Detective Yeats was rather gratified by the shock on the chiselled features of his friend, Nolan. Their eyes met. The two men raised their eyebrows and suppressed smiles.

'What in the name of Sam Hill is going on here?' bellowed Flynn, his voice echoing through the room like an irate lion that just arrived home to find dinner not ready.

'Crane has just confessed to murdering Smiley Stanton,' replied Grimm, trying not to sound too defensive.

'I see,' murmured Flynn. 'Well, coincidentally, Miss Colbeck, has just said the same thing.'

'Crina,' exclaimed Crane, 'What are you doing?'

'That's what I'd like to know,' said Crotch who was standing in the corner like a naughty schoolchild. 'Look inspector, if Crane here is anteing up to the murder, then I'll take Crina home now. I'll let you know about the lawsuit in the morning after you've charged Crane here.'

'You really are the most deeply unpleasant man it's been my misfortune to meet,' said Crane.

A few other pleasantries were exchanged that your reporter will draw a discreet veil over as they reflected badly on both men and at least one of the suggestions was certainly anatomically challenging, as well as being illegal in thirteen southern states.

Crina, meanwhile, could not bring herself to look at Crane. Instead, she put her head in her hands, and continued to weep quietly.

'Lying is what she is doing Mr Crane. Now, let's see what you are up to,' retorted Flynn. He was a man who had long since come to terms with his own impatience. Why hide from people that he thought were idiots? Let them share the joy, too. 'Sit down Mr Crane. And take those damn handcuffs off him. Notwithstanding his confession, the only danger posed, by any of these people, is overacting.'

That was bound to hurt, thought Nolan. He deliberately kept his eyes away from Yeats because he knew he would only explode into laughter if he caught sight of his friend. Yeats, meanwhile, suddenly found that a coughing fit had descended upon him and he exited the room with an apology.

Grimm led Crane to the seat beside Crina. He sat down and they glanced at one another. Crane's eyes blazed at the actress, but more in irritation than anger. Nothing was said between them.

Flynn slumped down in the seat opposite them.

'Now, I want you to explain to me, Mr Crane, how you killed Smiley Stanton. Please, give as much detail as possible,' said Flynn, in a weary voice, that barely stayed on the right side of patronising.

Crane's experience, in being interrogated for murder, was alarmingly limited, which made it more difficult for him to draw upon anything that would help him in this performance. If the inspector had only been a bit angrier, it might have helped. However, being treated like a lying idiot was really beyond the pale.

'I don't see why you are adopting such a churlish attitude. It's perfectly clear what is going on here. A child could see it Inspector,' said Crane, huffily.

'Oh, they could,' agreed Flynn.

This wasn't quite the response Crane had wanted. The line he'd used had first surfaced in a dramatization of "The Hound of the Baskervilles". His Holmes had received rave notices. In Albuquerque.

This brought an angry glare from Crane. The confession was not being received with quite the due gravity he felt it merited. As a potential murderer this was probably a relief. For an actor, though, it was nothing short of demoralizing. Even his anger was being treated with a disregard that was almost libellous. In this regard, he had some sympathy with that insufferable pig, Crotch and his desire to file a suit against Flynn or the police.

'Unless you have been sleeping rough for a few days, Inspector and have just come back to civilisation, you will surely have heard that Stanton was murdered last night in full view of the theatre.'

'It was dark, apparently. No one saw a thing,' replied Flynn. He was now resting his head on his hand which further irritated the actor. Bad notices are one thing, but when your audience is bored, it's either the script or the actor. In this case he was both writer and performer. 'But tell me, Crane, how did you do it?'

'I threw a knife at him,' exploded Crane, who'd had quite enough of this. 'How do you think I bloody did it.'

'Can Crina go now. You've got your confession.'

'She's going nowhere Crotch. But you are,' snarled Flynn.

'I'm her lawyer, Flynn,' retorted Crotch. 'She's entitled to representation. Hey Crane, for a moderate fee, I'll represent you.'

'Go to blazes,' shouted Crane.

'Go to jail,' sniped Crotch before breaking into a cackle that was as unpleasant to listen to as it was borne of an unhealthy lifestyle.

'Are you two finished?' asked Flynn.

'I don't see why that man should be here while I make my confession,' muttered Crane to Flynn.

'Right now, I don't know why I'm here, listening to your confession. But I am and for the moment, Crane, he's your lawyer,' said Flynn.

'Him?' expostulated Crane.

'As your lawyer, I'd advise you not to say anything. As someone who hates you, Crane, I'd say "spill your guts out", but that's only as Crina's lawyer.'

'How did you kill him?' repeated Flynn, adding a little impact to this question, by slamming the palm of his hand on the table.

That appeared to silence the room sufficiently for the interview to continue. Crane glared at Crotch and then began to speak, 'I positioned myself opposite Stanton and when the lights went out, I took the knife out and hurled it at him.'

'How could you be sure you would hit him?' asked Flynn. There was a weariness in his voice.

'I worked in a circus. I was trained to do this with my eyes shut,' replied Crane, almost affronted that his circus skills could be doubted openly.

'That's what Miss Colbeck said,' replied Flynn. 'You know, of course, we will check this out. My bet is the nearest either of you got to a knife at the circus was when you were eating dinner, but go on... Okay, continue, we've established the means and opportunity. What was your reason for killing Stanton?'

Crotch began to laugh at this, earning a sour look from both detective and suspect.

'However, in all of this, there is one thing, that neither of you have mentioned, that makes me question your story, Crane and yours Miss Colbeck. It's what we might say is an important fact and it's one that leads me to conclude that the only things you are guilty of is wasting police time and interfering with an ongoing murder investigation. It is quite clear to me that you are both covering for someone. Possibly one another, but that is to be determined. In the meantime, I think we will hold you both in a cell until such time as we straighten out your stories and establish who really killed Stanton.'

Crotch was outraged at this.

'You cannot seriously be considering putting my client in a cell.'

'Clients,' pointed out Flynn with a sour smile. 'And I'm not just considering it, I am doing it whether you like it or not. Don't forget, whether I believe them or not and, for the record, I don't, they have confessed to murder. I won't be releasing them any time soon.'

'But you just said that they've not provided you with a correct story of how the murder was committed. Surely that proves they are innocent.'

'Stupid, more like,' said Flynn, and Crotch had to stop himself nodding in agreement at this.

There was a knock at the door and it opened suddenly. Yeats appeared in the entrance. He said to Flynn, 'Sir, your daughter is on the phone. She has some news you'll want to hear.'

'Later,' said Flynn.

'Sorry sir,' said Yeats. 'This really can't wait.'

28

Century Playhouse, New York

    Dick Devenish climbed the steps that led from the wings up to a bridge over the stage where scenery could be hauled up and a basic lighting rig was situated. The unfortunate Jeffries was hanging from the bridge. Following Devenish up the steps were Lane Vidal and Tommy Hart. Wickham McNeill, wisely, decided that such exertions were for younger people, and his duty lay with comforting the ladies, although his observation about Bobbie was that she was not quite the fragrant fainting type.
    Devenish was panting when he reached the top and had to acknowledge two things about his trip. Firstly, he was a little out of condition and, clearly, his weekly game of golf was not quite sufficient to remedy this, and secondly, he also had never been very keen on heights. His 5th Avenue apartment was on the third floor, which was plenty high enough for him. New York's race to build ever higher buildings felt like madness to him, but who was he to stand in the way of progress, as long as he had a Napoleon Brandy in one hand and a beautiful lady… well you get the picture.

'Jolly high, isn't it,' said Devenish to Tommy as they carefully walked across the bridge.

'No more than two people,' said Tommy to Vidal who was the last to arrive at the top of the steps.

Vidal did not seem too concerned about being asked to stay back, noted Devenish. Perhaps, Vidal, sensible chap that he was, was less than thrilled about being so high while standing upon a wooden construction that the term "rickety" might have been coined for.

'Are we going to try and pull him in?' asked Tommy as the two men walked across the bridge.

'Only on the off chance he's alive,' said Devenish. His voice did not seem to hold out any hopes on that prospect. 'Try not to touch anything, Tommy. We don't want to smudge any finger prints that aren't either yours or Crispin's or poor Jeffries. I take it no one else comes up here.'

'No sir,' said Tommy.

'More sense probably,' said Devenish, taking a look down at the people on the stage below them. The bridge was swaying slightly now that there were two men walking on it. There was also a worrying creak, which made Devenish's head turn sharply.

'Don't worry Mr Devenish,' laughed Tommy. 'The bridge is solid enough. It can easily support our weight.'

'I hope the bridge knows this,' said Devenish tersely. He had now reached the point where the props man was attached to the bridge. A rope had been thrown over one of the rafters of the theatre and then tied to the bridge. This suggested that if Jeffries had committed suicide, he had merely jumped from the bridge and let gravity do the rest. If he had been killed by someone then the challenge of carrying a body up the steps was easily worked around by using the rope and the rafters as a lever to pull Jeffries up. The autopsy would determine which of these were the most likely cause of death.

Devenish pulled on the rope to haul Jeffries up to the bridge with some help from Tommy. When they finally recovered the props man, it was immediately clear that he was dead.

'What shall we do with the body?' asked Tommy, unused, as he was, to such scenes.

Devenish said nothing, but began slowly to lower Jeffries down again which, Tommy supposed, probably answered his question.

While Devenish was high up in the theatre dealing with his own vertiginous demons and the dead body of Jeffries, Bobbie was in the stage manager's office with Crispin, calling for an ambulance. She rang Mount Sinai hospital first to request the ambulance and asked for her father. This took a couple of minutes and then she was informed that he had left half an hour earlier. Interestingly, the receptionist mentioned that he had been accompanied by Crina Colbeck.

Bobbie knew of at least two police precincts nearer to the Mount Sinai hospital than Midtown North. She tried both on the off chance that he had gone there. They had not seen him.

She tried Midtown North next. Her call was answered by Sergeant Moran.

'Bam, it's Bobbie. I don't suppose my father is there by any chance.'

'He is, Red. I think he's interviewing someone at the moment. Hold on, Yeatsy is here. He just got back himself with the killer.'

Bobbie doubted whether Crane was really a killer, especially in the light of the discovery they had just made at the theatre. She heard Moran calling out to the big detective.

'Hey Yeatsy. I have Red here. She wants to speak to her father.'

Bobbie heard Yeats say, 'He's with Crane and Miss Colbeck. They've confessed.'

They? Bobbie couldn't quite believe what she was hearing.

'Bam, can you put Detective Yeats on. What's happening?'

There was a muffled conversation and then Bobbie heard Nolan's partner speak. He said, 'Hello Miss Flynn. Inspector Flynn is interviewing Mr Crane and Miss Colbeck. Both have confessed to killing Smiley.'

'They didn't. That's nonsense,' said Bobbie when she heard the news about Crina.

'Your father thinks so too and he's beginning to lose his patience. You know what he's like,' laughed Yeats.

Bobbie grinned at this. She said, 'Oh yes. Listen, there's a new development down at the theatre. Do you remember Mr Jeffries.'

'That strange props manager?' said Yeats.

'That's the one. Well, he'd dead. He's either hanged himself off the lighting rig over the stage or someone did it to him.'

'You're kidding,' exclaimed Yeats in disbelief. 'That'll stir up a hornet's nest.'

'It sure will. It could be suicide which might suggest he was responsible for killing Mr Stanton or maybe he saw something he shouldn't have.'

'I'll tell your father, Miss Flynn. I guess you'll be seeing him soon enough.'

No chance of that, thought Bobbie. She was hardly a suspect and there were plenty of witnesses around to deal with the police when they returned. She had a story to tell.

She and Crispin returned to the stage area where she found Devenish happily on *terra firma* once more.

'The ambulance and the police are on their way, she said to Devenish who seemed a little paler than usual. 'Is Mr Jeffries...'

'Yes,' confirmed Devenish before adding, 'If the rope didn't kill him then it was probably a heart attack from being up there.'

Bobbie tried to hide a grin at this. Then she took Devenish by the arm and led him away from the group of actors.

'You're not going to believe this,' began Bobbie.

'Right now, I'm ready to believe anything. This case is crazy.'

'It's just became crazier. Crina Colbeck has, apparently confessed to killing Smiley.'

'Your father won't believe that.'

'He doesn't apparently. Nor does he believe Mr Crane.'

They both looked up to the heavens and saw the macabre sight of Jeffries still hanging in mid-air. He was swinging slightly in the air and there was an audible creak as he did so, that made the scene all the more ghoulish.

'Should you not have cut him down?' asked Bobbie, shivering slightly.

'Your father would hang me if I did that,' replied Devenish. 'I wonder what happened to Jeffries. He's either just confessed in a rather gruesome manner or we have someone among us who is running amok. You met him. What was he like?'

'Strange,' said Bobbie. 'I felt a little uncomfortable with him. I gather he may have been a user of narcotics.'

'So, I gather, both Vidal and Tommy mentioned this. They think he topped himself and to be fair, it does make some sense. He was the only one we know for certain who was down in the Trap room while the performance was on. Who is to say he didn't sneak through to the orchestra pit and throw a knife at Smiley. Where I start to have my doubts is around him going to the hospital to finish off the deed. That doesn't fit and I'm also struggling with motive.'

'Me too,' admitted Bobbie. 'Why don't we go to the room he used below stage. Perhaps there's something there that can help us. Obviously don't touch anything.'

'Yes, sir,' said Devenish.

They departed from the stage into the wings to a set of stairs that led down to the Trap room. Thomas Jefferson watched them arrive. Curiosity piqued; he took a break from his rat-catching to accompany them.

'That's his room there,' said Bobbie pointing to a door that was on the other side of the Trap Room, directly opposite the orchestra pit. They weaved their way around the various bits of scenery and props, which had been dumped in the room, and over to the door.

It was open.

Devenish pushed it open. The dim lighting made it difficult to see much, aside from the fact that the space was quite small and no tidier than the area below stage. Bobbie found a light switch and flicked it. This threw light into the room from a naked bulb. The room was a mess, but not due to someone searching for something. This had all the hallmarks of the impression they had gained from the props manager.

'Good Lord,' said Bobbie, as her eyes adjusted to the light. 'Look at that.'

'Yes,' murmured Devenish. 'Just noticed that myself. How interesting.'

They were staring at a thick plank of wood. It had a number of painted marks on it. This was less interesting than the other key feature. There were a number of knife marks in the wood as if someone had used it to practice throwing. And there was a large knife sticking out of the wood.

It was just like the one that had been used on Smiley.

'Interesting,' said Devenish, after a long pause.

'Convenient,' added Bobbie.

'Indeed,' replied Devenish. Just as he was about to expound more on this particular insight, he saw Bobbie turn and start to leave the room. 'Where are you going, Red?'

Bobbie glanced back at him and grinned, 'I have a story to write. You can deal with my dad.'

'And the ever-handsome, Detective Nolan,' added Devenish.

'Oh, you're not too bad either, Dick,' replied Bobbie, but she was already out of the door as she said this.

29

Bobbie reached the Tribune building around four thirty in the afternoon. The news room was quiet. Many of the journalists were out for the day. Even Thornton Kent was packing his briefcase readying to leave for the evening. He spied Bobbie's arrival and paused what he was doing. He suspected his office was her destination.

It was.

Bobbie arrived almost breathless with anticipation, her face flushed and with eyes glittering with the lustre of triumph.

Bobbie said, 'You're never going to believe this.'

'Try me.'

'Crina Colbeck has confessed to killing her husband.'

'You're right. I don't believe it.'

'Nor does my dad. However, she's not the only one in the frame. Jason Crane has confessed also.'

'Now you're kidding me.'

'I'm not. For the record, my dad doesn't believe him either. Now we get to the big news,' said Bobbie, trying to contain her excitement.

Kent's eyes widened. This was already a scoop. How could there be anything to top what Bobbie had already told him.

'Go on,' said Kent, sitting down.

'There's been another death at the Playhouse. It might be suicide, but it's just as likely to be murder.'

'Who?'

'Mr Jeffries the property manager.'

This was not quite as exciting as Crina Colbeck confessing to a murder she almost certainly had not committed. But it wasn't bad either. Kent looked at his watch. The he said, 'Get me something now. I'll work on the headline.'

Kent watched as Bobbie quickly typed up the story. He knew, with this young lady, a front-page headline request was never far away and, sure enough, this was the first thing she said as the report was handed over to him. He said nothing, either way, on that topic but they both knew what they would be leading with the next day.

'What next?' asked Kent. His questions were invariably short and right to the point.

'I need to find Perry. I presume he's left for the evening.'

'You presume right,' said Kent. 'You can find him at the Two Hundred Club. Do you know it?'

'I do,' smiled Bobbie.

The Two Hundred club was a speakeasy in the middle of the theatre district. It was a haunt that attracted a colourful mixture of Broadway characters from both sides of the law and from the stage. It was where the Honourable Peregrine Wimslow began most evenings before he went to the theatre. This is to say that he visited the speakeasy almost every night of the week, every week of the year, perhaps, with the exception of Christmas and New Year's Eve when it got a little bit too lively, even for the veteran theatre critic who was not unappreciated for his conviviality. The son of a nobleman had found a natural home in the vibrant underbelly of New York.

It would, perhaps, have dismayed Inspector Flynn to hear that his daughter had been to the Two Hundred Club, on a few occasions herself, both before and after the arrival of the Volstead Act which, nominally, prohibited the club from selling the very reason for its existence.

'Hi Red, long time no see. How's the old man,' said Shoosh, the doorman, as he spied the arrival of Bobbie. Sedgemoor 'Shoosh' McKay had been the doorman of the club since its opening which was one year to the day after the end of the war. Shoosh was a lanky six foot five and had once been a star basketball player, destined for a college scholarship, despite a limited interest in academia, when Uncle Sam thought his abilities would be better suited to fighting Germans. Shoosh was a lot less keen on the idea and, given the size of target he presented, who is to say he was wrong?

In fact, it was due to his size that few people tended to argue with him, which gave him both his nickname and his employment. Shoosh rarely got into fights at the club. It was a situation he invariably nipped in the bud by putting his hand up, palm facing towards the potential trouble maker. This simple act was enough to ensure that said troublemaker was given pause for thought about his next action. Would it be to cause turbulence or tranquillity. Common sense, and good fellowship, usually prevailed. And thus, Sedgemoor McKay earned the name "Shoosh" because he ensured peace, if not quiet.

'Hi Shoosh,' said Bobbie and grinned, 'Dad's doin' just fine. How are your kids?'

'Growing up. The eldest just started school,' said Shoosh, with a roll of his eyes. This turned into a glare as a couple of young men came out of the speakeasy a little too unpleasantly pickled for Shoosh's liking. They were singing a rather bawdy song that might have found favour at some frat party, but was not appropriate, in Shoosh's view, outside a classy establishment, such as the Two Hundred Club. His finger went to his lips and the two young men wisely stopped mid-note and smiled an apology.

'How did you get your name,' laughed Bobbie as she entered through a door that Shoosh held open for her.

She entered a large room, dimly lit by *Art Deco* sconces which cast a warm and intimate glow over the polished mahogany bar and plush velvet booths. The air was thick with the scent of expensive cigars and the faint, intoxicating aroma of forbidden cocktails. Patrons lounged on plush, velvet settees, their conversations a low hum, punctuated by bursts of laughter and the clinking of glasses.

Amid this convivial chaos, Bobbie spotted Perry, in one such booth, opposite the door she had just entered through, holding court with two black jazz musicians and a man she recognised from the previous night, Lucky Luciano. Quite how this disparate group knew one another was a mystery, that Bobbie did not have time to ponder.

Bobbie made her way over to the table. They all rose to their feet as she arrived. Perry greeted her warmly with a kiss to both cheeks before turning to the table and presenting her.

'Gentlemen, may I introduce a colleague of mine, Miss Roberta Flynn, a colleague of mine at the paper. You may call her Bobbie.' Then he glanced wryly at Luciano. 'You may know her father, Lucky.'

Luciano half-smiled at this. He said, 'Inspector Flynn I respect greatly. Miss Flynn, I see at the theatre last night.'

He held his hand out and Bobbie decided that offending a well-known mobster was probably not the best idea, so she shook hands with Luciano. Then she held her hand out to the two men, who were both dressed in dinner suits.

'Roberta, may I introduce Mr Duke Ellington and Mr Billy Strayhorn. They are wonderful musicians.'

Bobbie smiled at them and said, 'I hope to see you play sometime.'

'If you stay, Miss Flynn, you'll hear us imminently.'

At this, the two musicians departed leaving Bobbie with Perry and Luciano. The Italian spoke first.

'Miss Flynn, what news of Mr Stanton's killer.'

Perry shook his head sadly at this. He said, 'Such sad news. Who would want to hurt Smiley?'

Bobbie had news for them, that would shock them both.

'Crina Colbeck and Jason Crane have both confessed, separately, to his murder.'

Luciano's face remained impassive as he processed the news he'd just heard. Perry, however, was not a man to receive any news, good or bad, without honouring the drama within.

'Why this is outrageous. Surely no one believes either are responsible for this dreadful deed,' said an outraged Perry.

Bobbie almost smiled at her friend, but he was clearly either very upset, or good at playing upset. Bobbie had no doubt that he'd had plenty of practice on this score.

'My dad certainly doesn't. We both think they are trying to protect someone, maybe each other. Who knows?'

This stopped Perry in his tracks somewhat. Facts eventually work, even with those whose preference is to live life like it is fiction. Bobbie noticed the change in her friend.

'What's wrong, Perry?'

Perry frowned, as if reluctant to reveal more about what he was thinking. Of course, such noble commitments in an inveterate gossip rarely last as long as it takes to decide how best to communicate what they know.

'They were lovers, long before either became famous, of course. I believe the affair ran its course just as Crina became a star. Yet, I know, for a fact, that she often returned to Jason when her latest romance went up in flames. His was always the shoulder she cried on. Personally, I don't think Jason ever stopped loving her. At the same time, a little of Crina goes a rather long way. I say this as her close friend and someone who is not unaware, shall we say, of how difficult she can be, sometimes. Particularly towards those she loves.'

'When did you first meet Crina?' asked Bobbie.

Perry smiled at this and replied, 'You know, your predecessor came to me about writing her obituary. It's all in there.'

'But there were gaps in it,' pointed out Bobbie. 'For example, what was she at the circus? Then she took a few years off, but there is no detail on what she did until she took to the stage in 1904.'

'I first met her around 1897 and my she was a beautiful girl. All the boys were after her, but she was with Jason Crane then, I believe. I saw her a couple of times in Vaudeville. She was a singer and dancer. Lovely voice, I must say. I wouldn't say I was friendly with her but I told her that she had the talent to go all the way. We bumped into each other a few times after that and then, as you say, she disappeared for a while. I was not so close to her that I gave it any thought. Then she reappeared around 1904 in a play that was going around the country and getting good notices. It came to Broadway and the rest, as they say, is history. Which technically, it is, of course.'

'She never said what she did in those years that she was away from showbusiness?' pressed Bobbie.

'No, and shamefully, I never asked her. It felt like prying,' said Perry.

'You are a journalist,' observed Bobbie with a grin. 'It goes with the territory.'

This brought a guffaw from Luciano who had been listening to everything in fascination. Even Perry had the good grace to laugh.

'What do you need to know?' asked Luciano.

'I would love to find out what she did at the circus and also why she spent five years away from showbusiness.'

'Her mother is still alive,' replied Perry. 'Crina introduced us once.'

'Where does she live?' asked Bobbie.

Perry's eyes widened at this, in mock horror. He said, 'I hope you are not going to propose what I think you are.'

The grin, which greeted this statement, was full of unforgiving mischief.

'You are a sport, Perry,' was all Bobbie could say in response to this.

30

The Honourable Peregrine Wimslow was in a churlish mood, as he and Bobbie tramped along Park Avenue towards an apartment building with a the rather opaque name 'Verities'. It was around six thirty in the evening and not quite dark. Cars drifted along the road at a snail's pace, the rush hour was becoming the rush two hours if traffic was any guide.

'I can't believe you talked me into this,' complained the Englishman. 'If God had meant me to be an investigative journalist, He would have endowed me with the instincts of a bloodhound and the tenacity of a tax collector. The only thing I am persistent at is drinking fine wines and cognacs.'

Bobbie happily ignored her friend as they went up the steps of 'Verities'. The doorman opened the door, for the two of them, and received a quarter for his efforts. He didn't look so pleased at this.

'Do you think she will remember you?' asked Bobbie. This was done, partly, to needle Perry, in revenge for having listened to his complaints in the taxi journey, all the way from the Two Hundred Club.

'I shall not dignify that with a reply,' said Perry, eyeing the list of names on a board at the reception. 'Fourth floor, by the looks of things.'

Moments later they were in the elevator travelling up to the fourth floor.

'Do you think she will be in?' asked Bobbie.

'I imagine she will be. It's a while since I saw her, but she was not a well woman, if you take my meaning.'

Bobbie was not quite sure what he meant by that, so said nothing. The elevator doors opened and they were soon outside the apartment of Mrs R Alexandrescu. Perry decided that, as he was there, he may as well take the lead. He gave the door a solid rap with his silver-topped cane.

'Careful,' said Bobbie. 'We're not trying to burst into the apartment.'

They heard some voices speaking inside and then a few moments later a woman in her fifties opened the door. She eyed Bobbie and Perry suspiciously.

'Hello,' boomed Perry. 'My name is Peregrine Wimslow. I am a friend of Crina and I have met Mrs Alexandrescu, on many occasions. This is my friend, Miss Roberta Flynn. We were in the area and thought we should call in. Crina would so appreciate someone looking in on her mother.'

The woman before them seemed a little unsure that this would ever be the case, however any desire to send them on their way was halted as another voice, with a thick Eastern European accent asked, 'Who is visiting me?'

'A Mr Wimslow and a Miss Flynn. They say they know Miss Colbeck and that they want to call in on you.'

'Well let them in Firth. Don't be rude,' barked Mrs Alexandrescu.

Firth tried to smile at the visitors but gave it up as a bad job. She stood back to let them through. Bobbie and Perry walked into the apartment and it felt like they had been transported back forty years. Unlike the modern minimalism of *Art Deco*, this was very much the parlour of a Victorian house.

The walls were adorned with intricate wallpaper in deep burgundy and gold, accented with stars and acrobats. Heavy velvet drapes framed tall windows, their tassels and fringes adding to the room's opulent feel. Delicate porcelain figurines, and a miniature trapeze, lined the mantlepiece and the furniture.

Seating was provided by overstuffed armchairs and a plush settee, upholstered in rich red brocade fabric. They were arranged around a low mahogany table, holding a mix of Victorian bric-a-brac and circus memorabilia, such as a pair of old juggling clubs, a top ha, and a photograph of a pair of trapeze artists captured mid-leap through a ring of fire. The circus theme continued the walls with framed posters, showing clowns and scantily clad women performing handstands on horseback. The room left the visitor in no doubt as to the profession of the owner.

'Mrs Alexandrescu, how wonderful to see you again. You have not changed one bit. You are as young and beautiful as I remember you when we first met at Crina's opening of Anthony and Cleopatra.'

The lady, to whom this outrageous flattery was directed, was clearly delighted by what had been said, although, one suspected that her memory of Perry, along with many other things, was slowly evaporating with age.

Bobbie could see that she had once been beautiful. She was tiny, certainly under five feet tall and quite slender. Her dress was late Victorian and her hair was almost Regency, pulled back and up to reveal a swan-like neck, which reminded Bobbie of Crina. The eyes, though, were very modern. It was as if Theda Bara's makeup up artist had decided to have a go at creating a clown. Her lips were painted red with little or no attempt to stay within the lines. The eyes were framed in black that highlighted the very dark Eastern European Romany in her. Oddly, it kind of worked, thought Bobbie.

'I am delighted to meet you again,' said Mrs Alexandrescu, grandly. This further confirmed Bobbie's impression she had no idea who she was with. Gesturing with the grace of a ballerina towards a chaise longue which appeared to have been commandeered by a small Pomeranian, she said, 'Please take a seat. Bring some tea, Firth. Now tell me, how is my daughter?'

In jail, after confessing to a murder, was probably not the thing to say here, thought Bobbie. A quick exchange of glances was enough to confirm that deception was, sadly, in the best interests of this lady's peace of mind and their objective.

Perry avoided the dog, and sat across the table from Bobbie, who sat down by the dog. They eyed one another warily.

Mrs Alexandrescu smiled and said, 'He does not bite, do you Vlad?'

Vlad? This did not inspire confidence in Bobbie. He was tiny, but there was a distrustful look in his eye and Bobbie, who loved animals, decided not to make friends with this particular pet.

Perry decided to fill the silence that followed the lady of the house's question with something that was completely true, if not all together a comprehensive picture of the opening night.

'My dear, she was a sensation. One of her great roles. You should have come.'

'I wanted to but my darling Crina did not want me to tire myself out. You know I may not look it but I am sixty years old.'

She was probably closer to eighty that sixty but, in fairness, her beauty, like her daughter's, was undimmed by age. The dark eyes, which had probably once beguiled men, were still as striking but now there was a vagueness there, a slight tilt of uncertainty in the smile. Bobbie felt, intensely, sad for the woman. However, she seemed happy, as Perry spoke about the opening night and Crina's performance. And, at least, Perry did not have to stretch the truth in this regard.

While he was talking, Bobbie's eyes fixed on a picture of the young Rosa Alexandrescu with a man, she presumed, was Crina's father. She picked up the framed photograph. They were dressed formally and posed with that distinctly Victorian seriousness.

'My husband,' said Mrs Alexandrescu. She appeared to want to say more, but it seemed to Bobbie that she could not quite remember his name. She gave up and smiled.

'He's very good looking,' said Bobbie. 'And of course you were quite the beauty.' Mrs Alexandrescu bowed and smiled in response to Bobbie. 'Do you have any photographs of Crina from when she was at the circus.'

This was met with a shake of the head. Mrs Alexandrescu said, 'I don't know. It was all so long ago.'

'You were a trapeze artist?' asked Bobbie, pointing to a picture of the couple dressed in what certainly looked like trapeze artist costumes.

'Yes, my husband,' said Mrs Alexandrescu, before her voice drifted off into a sad murmur. 'So long ago.'

Bobbie felt desperately sorry now, for bringing up the subject. In fact, she was more than sorry. She was beginning to feel a real sense of guilt for being here with the old woman. However, just as she was about to suggest to Perry that they should leave, Mrs Alexandrescu suddenly became livelier.

'I have other photographs. Would you like to see them?' asked the old woman. There was a hopeful look in her eyes and Bobbie immediately felt any guilt fade away. She realised then that this old woman desperately wanted to talk to them. Whether it was loneliness or a desire to follow the river of life back to a time when she was happiest, safest, most fulfilled, Bobbie did not know, but something told her that the key to the murders might be found somewhere in this old woman's memories.

The tea arrived and Firth began to pour it into the China tea cups. She had cut some lemons up to serve with the tea which amused Bobbie. She glanced at Perry whose face curled up into a look of disgust.

'I don't suppose you have milk?' asked Perry, trying not to sound horrified at the prospect of drinking tea with lemon.

Mrs Alexandrescu rose from her seat and went to the sideboard. She took a leather-bound photograph album and brought it over to Bobbie and Perry, who had to move around and sit beside the Pomeranian. The little dog seemed no happier about the new arrival than it had about Bobbie.

The first few pages were devoted to newspaper cuttings about the circus which Mrs Alexandrescu insisted on reading out, word for word. This was going to take longer than they imagined, thought Bobbie.

Finally, they arrived at some old photographs of circus folk including the middle-aged Alexandrescu couple. After about fifteen minutes they encountered the first photograph of Crina.

She had been an acrobat.

'I don't suppose Crina ever did knife-throwing?' asked Perry archly, a sidelong glance at Bobbie.

'Oh no,' said Mrs Alexandrescu with a frown. 'We would never allow that.'

'When did she leave the circus?' asked Bobbie

Mrs Alexandrescu smiled vacantly and shook her head. After a few moments she said, 'She was always singing and dancing. That was what she wanted to do. We did not stop her. Maybe the circus was no life for her.'

Another ten minutes passed. They saw more reviews of the circus. More of them mentioned Crina now. It seemed she was also one of the clowns. The tramp. The photograph reminded Bobbie of Charlie Chaplin, right down to the baggy trousers and the moustache.

More photographs followed. Mostly family and friends. It felt as if they were going nowhere and not very fast either. Finally, the album came to an end, but there was no more about Crina that they could use beyond the certainty that she had not been involved in knife-throwing.

'May I ask you about Jason Crane?' asked Bobbie. 'When did Crina meet him?'

Mrs Alexandrescu seemed confused by the name. Her head shook a little. And then Perry stepped in.

'I think Miss Flynn is referring to Hector. Hector Nilsson, Mrs Alexandrescu,' said Perry gently.

The old woman's eyes widened momentarily and she swung her arm dismissively.

'Ah, Hector. I remember him. Seducer. He almost ruined her life. I never knew why she liked him. Good looking I suppose. She should never have married him.'

'Married?' exclaimed Bobbie, almost spilling her tea. She glanced at Perry, who was just as surprised as she was. 'I didn't realise they were married.'

'I have a photograph somewhere,' said the old woman. She rose once more and went to the same sideboard. Opening one of the drawers she extracted a manilla folder and brought to over to Bobbie and Perry.

It was a wedding photograph and there was no question that Crina and Crane had married. They were standing with a large group of family members. Bobbie turned the photograph over. On the back was a printed inscription.

Wedding of Crina Alexandrescu and Hector Nilsson, 1900. The elder Alexandrescus were standing either side of the couple. Mrs Alexandrescu was holding a baby.

Bobbie pointed to the baby and said, 'What a beautiful child. Who is this?'

A smile radiating love crossed the face of the old woman, but as quickly as it came it faded.

'Crina never wanted to marry when she was carrying the baby. She wanted to wait until she could wear her dress.'

'This is Crina and Jason, sorry, Hector's child?' asked Bobbie, almost incredulous. She glanced at Perry who was equally astonished by the news. This was based less on what it meant for the case than the fact that he had missed out on one of the most delicious pieces of gossip that he could have dined off for years.

'Yes,' said Mrs Alexandrescu. Yet there was no mistaking the sadness in her voice.

'What was the child called?' asked Bobbie.

31

'Do you think this is pertinent to the case?' asked Perry as he and Bobbie climbed into the cab. There was a fuzz of rain in the air, now. Not quite April showers, but they would come soon.

Bobbie was not sure how to answer the question. So much of what she had seen and heard made her doubt her own mind. Could she trust the memory of a woman like Mrs Alexandrescu who was clearly on a journey of her own within the apartment? She felt disconsolate at how even the happiest of lives could end up so lonely, with only memories left to comfort you and the cruellest trick of all, having those memories slowly wiped from your mind until there was nothing.

Finally, realising that Perry deserved a response, she said carefully, 'I think it's clear now who our main suspect is. The question is, how do we prove it? It certainly wasn't poor Mr Jeffries. Whatever problems he may have had, I don't think he was anything other than a victim. Someone who was in the wrong place, at the wrong time, and saw what really happened.'

'What would make someone commit such vile crimes? The cold-bloodedness of it all,' said Perry, clearly horrified.

Bobbie understood what Perry was saying and yet she felt a marbled mix of uncertainty and certainty about who had committed the crime. If it had only been the attempted murder in the theatre then it was feasible. However, the subsequent attack, in the hospital and then the murder of Jeffries, for it was murder, left Bobbie wracked with doubt.

Then there was the look on Mrs Alexandrescu's face as she spoke of the child. It made Bobbie wonder what had happened that should cause her so much evident sadness. As much as she had wanted to press her on this, it was a step too far. Despite her best intentions to be a hard-nosed journalist, the truth was, as ever, morally complex.

Guilt is a cage in which devils play. And she felt an overwhelming sense of shame. Bobbie knew that she and Perry had used the old woman, a woman in the early stages of an illness that would one day claim her life. They had done so because they believed their cause noble. And finding murderers or, in this case, proving someone's innocence, was a just cause.

Perhaps it was her silence, or something in her manner, but after a few moments, she felt Perry take her hand.

'It's not easy, is it?' he said gently.

Bobbie shook her head. It wasn't easy. And why should it be?

'No,' acknowledged Bobbie. 'It's not easy. Maybe this isn't for me. This world.'

'How do you mean?' asked Perry.

Bobbie sighed and thought for a few seconds. Then, along with tears, it came flooding out.

'I tricked her.'

'We tricked her,' pointed out Perry.

Bobbie shook her head quickly. She said, 'I did. I dragged you into this. It was deceitful. We made her remember things that I think she wanted to forget and this is someone who is losing enough of her memory as it is. It felt low.'

'You've all but confirmed that her daughter is unlikely to be the killer. Not that there was ever any doubt. Surely that's a good thing. I would argue that Crane is in the clear too. Everything points in one direction.'

'That still seems implausible to me. I mean a photograph of a child. Can we even be sure it is their child? That dear old lady can hardly be considered a reliable witness,' replied Bobbie.

'She's never going to be in the dock, so to speak. What she's done is given you a path to follow. See where it leads and stop worrying about what it took to get you there.'

Bobbie smiled back at her friend. He was right. It was time to stop worrying about the morality of questioning an old woman, whose memory was failing, and focus on helping the investigation into the murder.

They continued the rest of the journey, in silence, before dropping Perry off at the Two Hundred Club, while Bobbie decided that she had done enough for the day. She gave the cabbie her address in Greenwich Village and they set off towards her brownstone house.

When she arrived back Mrs Garcia was in the kitchen, but there was no sign of her father.

'*¿Qué estás cocinando vieja?* (What are you cooking old woman)' asked Bobbie.

'For you *chile con arsénico añadido (*chilli with added arsenic*).*'

'I hope you'll join me,' laughed Bobbie. 'Do I have time for a bath. It's been one of those days.'

'You have time,' said Mrs Garcia. She looked with some concern at Bobbie. They spent the better part of their conversations insulting one another, but Bobbie was like a daughter to the elderly housekeeper. She could see the tiredness in her eyes. The sadness was still there. She wondered what was wrong with Bobbie. Perhaps she missed her mother.

These years, when you are just beginning to negotiate adulthood, and its responsibilities, were difficult enough as it was. Without having someone to talk to, like Nancy Flynn, then Mrs Garcia could see that Bobbie might be caught in the doldrums, a sailboat without wind. Flynn was as decent a man that the housekeeper had ever met, smart too, by the, admittedly not high, standards of men. But he was only a man.

He would never understand, really. How could he?

Patience is a virtue that neither Bobbie nor her father possessed in great quantity. After this exchange with Mrs Garcia, Bobbie felt a pressing need to speak to her father. Although it was now almost seven, in all likelihood he was still at Midtown North. If she could reach him there then she would be able to tell him what she'd learned with Mrs Alexandrescu. She knew it was important, something had changed in the case.

She picked up the telephone and asked to be put through to the precinct. The next voice was one she did not know.

'Hello, this is Inspector Flynn's daughter, Bobbie. I desperately need to speak to him. Is he still in the precinct.'

'I'll check Miss Flynn. I've only just arrived on duty. I'll put you through to the squad room.'

Moments later another voice came on the line. It was Detective Nolan.

'Miss Flynn. It's Nolan. I'm afraid your father just left five minutes ago. He's off to City Hall. The Mayor and the Commissioner requested an emergency meeting with him. He didn't seem too pleased.'

Bobbie resisted the temptation to say something purported to be unladylike. Luckily, her frustration at not finding her father somewhat blunted her shock at speaking with Nolan. However, it was but a temporary respite. There followed a short and quite awkward silence.

'Miss Flynn, are you still there?' asked Nolan when it lasted longer than he was comfortable with.

'Yes, I'm sorry. I was just thinking,' admitted Bobbie. This was understating it. Her mind was in a whirlwind. There was so much she wanted to say. Was this the time to say it? Hardly. This is a detective story, not a love story, she thought.

'Look Detective Nolan, I have something on the case that you and my father need to know. Are Miss Colbeck and Mr Crane still being held?'

'No,' replied Nolan. 'Your father threw them out a couple of hours ago. Said he would arrest them for wasting police time before he arrested them for murder.'

Bobbie burst out into laughter at this, but there was also a moment when tears stung her eyes. She said, 'Sounds like my father.' The laughter had an anguished tinge, however. The thought of her father facing Mayor Hylan and Commissioner Enright and having to explain the circumstances that had led to the murder of Smiley Stanton were almost too much for her to bear.

Nolan sensed the sadness at the other end of the line. He wanted desperately to say something that would provide solace. Then he remembered something about what had happened earlier.

'Look, Miss Flynn. I know you're worried, but there's one thing you should know. There was a lawyer called Crotch, would you believe, representing Miss Colbeck. At the start he was threatening to sue Inspector Flynn, but by the end the two of them were in an office smoking a cigar. I don't think he had much love for Mr Stanton. It may not be so bad.'

'Dad shouldn't be doing that,' said Bobbie smiling at the thought of her father smoking with the lawyer.

'I'll let him know Miss Flynn.'

Bobbie took a deep breath. She had to say something. This could not go on. It was intolerable. She closed her eyes and then opened them again hoping her voice would not betray her nervousness.

'Look, Detective Nolan. I think perhaps you can call me Bobbie. Or Red. Anything but Miss Flynn. I sound like an old maid.'

This was met with silence. Bobbie decided that Nolan probably needed a moment to process what he'd just heard. In fact, he was probably more in need of smelling salts than anything else. Women were unfathomable to him. His sister aside, their moods were as changeable as the weather. In Ireland. What was happening?

'Uhhh,' said Nolan by way of response. This probably was not quite nailing what he should say, but it was a fairly accurate reflection of what he was thinking. However, it was probably not quite what was needed at that moment, if the silence that greeted it was any guide, so he pressed on, 'You said you had something new on the case Miss, uhhh, Bobbie.'

This was going to be a lot harder than she had imagined, realised Bobbie.

'Yes. Look, you may have to do some checking while my father is on his way back here. I'll send him straight back to you, Detective Nolan.' Then she paused a moment, took her life in her hands and then added, 'Sean.'

Thankfully, Nolan was sitting when he heard his name being said for who knows what accident might have befallen him? He wasn't sure whether to be shocked or just enjoy the feeling of happiness that was enveloping him.

Bobbie decided to press on. The poor man was clearly in a state of shock. Get used to it, my boy, thought Bobbie, a smile crossing her lips.

'Look, my father won't be happy, but what's done is done. I went to see Miss Colbeck's mother. She's still alive and lives in an apartment near Park Avenue. She's not quite with us these days but she did tell us a couple of things which may explain what happened today with the two confessions. Miss Colbeck and Mr Crane were once married. I think they would have married and presumably divorced, under their old names. She was Crina Alexandrescu. He was Hector Nilsson. Now we come to the important part. They had a child. That child is twenty-one now.

'What was the name of the child?'

'The name he was born with was Sorin Nilsson. Can you check on him? He was born in 1900. But that's not the key thing. Miss Colbeck and Jason Crane separated. I presume they divorced. Anyway, as Miss Colbeck became a big star, Mrs Alexandrescu and her husband were the ones to bring up the child. In fact, his existence was kept a big secret, as was the marriage. Mrs Alexandrescu showed me photographs of the boy as he grew older. And I can tell you, he has a new name now.'

32

It was hardly atypical for Inspector Flynn to come home from a day dealing with criminals, politicians and journalists with more than a hint of cantankerousness in his rarely ebullient manner. It was bad enough dealing with suspects who, invariably, were not as clever as they thought they were, hence the fact they were suspects. To deal with people who were plainly innocent, but pretending to be suspects, was altogether another level of vexation for Flynn.

He arrived in through the door and flopped onto the sofa with a nod to Bobbie who was in her usual armchair. Just as he was about to take off his shoes, Bobbie cleared her throat. This caused Flynn to glance up at her wearily. His face showed that he suspected the worst.

'I wouldn't if I were you,' said Bobbie.

'I dread to ask.'

'I just missed you when I called the precinct an hour ago. I had something to tell you,' said Bobbie.

'Which was.'

There was something rather disconcerting about the way her father could look at you. Bobbie instantly appreciated why so many suspects broke down when he interrogated them. She was on the receiving end of just such a look at that moment.

'I'll tell you on the way to the theatre,' replied Bobbie.

'Why on earth are we going there?'

'Because that's where Detective Nolan and the suspects will be. We know who the murderer is and I think I know how he did it.'

Around eight thirty, Bobbie and Flynn walked through the stage door, which was manned by Lewis, the patrolman that Bobbie had met last when dealing with a case of murder at the Metropolitan Museum. He nodded and smiled to her.

'Good evening, Miss Flynn.'

'Hello Mr Lewis,' replied Bobbie.

Flynn and Lewis merely nodded to one another which made Bobbie smile inwardly. Women used words as weapons, as solace, as revelatory insights to mood, feelings and thoughts. Men had not yet evolved that far. Instead, the male side of the equation had to rely on semaphore signals and grunts. Still, she acknowledged, it seemed to work for them.

They walked along the corridor that led past the dressing rooms and the green room towards the stage. They passed Clement Crispin on the way.

'Who else is here?' asked Bobbie.

'Everyone,' replied Crispin. He was sweating profusely and looked as if he might pass out with worry. Too many policemen around. The murders had confused matters somewhat, but once they were cleared up, perhaps the police would investigate the little matter of the craps game he'd been part of.

A minute later Bobbie and her father stepped out onto the stage where they could see all the principal actors as well as Lieutenant Grimm, Detective Nolan and Detective Yeats with a few patrolmen that Bobbie was not familiar with. Crispin followed Bobbie and Flynn onto the stage while Tommy Hart, Frida Haynes the make-up lady and a couple of patrolmen were sitting in the front row used by Arnold Rothstein and Luciano while Crotch sat in the seat occupied by Smiley. He was looking on with his arms folded puffing contentedly on a large cigar.

The last person to arrive, as ever, was Dick Devenish. He was dressed in white tie and tails. He came walking down the aisle with a wide grin on his face.

'I say Bobbie, do make this quick, old girl, I have a dinner to attend. Where do you want me?'

Bobbie's eyes narrowed in amusement at this. Then she pointed to the seats where they had been sitting on the opening night.

'Inspector Flynn, I really must insist this charade end.'

This was Jason Crane. His eyes were bulging, and a vein throbbed on his temple. As if not to be outdone, Crina burst into tears. This brought a roll of the eyes from Flynn.

'I've had quite enough of you two to do me a lifetime,' snapped the Inspector. Grimm was, for once when in Flynn's presence, looking just like his name. Gone was the unsuppressed unctuous manner and perhaps the real policeman peeped out, tired, cynical and a little angry.

Meanwhile, Polly Buckley and Lane Vidal held hands fearfully. The other member of the troupe, Wickham McNeill had brought a seat onto the stage and had made himself comfortable while everyone else remained standing. He was openly taking a swig from a hip flask and smiled shamelessly at Grimm who scowled at him for such flagrant disregard of Congressional folly.

'I'll be honest with you,' began Flynn, addressing the people on the stage, 'I've had as much as I can take from this case. It seems to me I would happily hurl a few of you in jail and throw the darn key away.'

Flynn fixed his eyes on the leading man and lady; the latter did not notice as her head was buried in Crane's shoulder. Crispin flinched a little too, noted Bobbie, in amusement.

'I'm not going to say much now. I'll let my daughter and Detective Nolan take over from here. I gather we are going to stage a reconstruction of what happened.'

'Oh, for the love of...' began Crane before he was swiftly silenced by an angry glare from Flynn.

'Can you take your places on the stage,' said Nolan, stepping forward. 'Just the performers on the stage, in the positions that you were, approximately, before the lights went out.'

Wickham McNeill rose wearily or was that unsteadily from his seat.

'I hope this won't take long,' he said in a low Shakesperean rumble of a voice.

The policemen exited one side of the stage while Crispin retired to the other, joined by Flynn and Grimm.

The performers, with all the shimmering enthusiasm of a child requested to tidy their room, took up their positions, while Bobbie and Nolan remained on stage with them.

What would happen now was a reconstruction that Bobbie and Nolan had planned out over a couple of phone calls earlier in the evening while they waited for Flynn to return from Mayor Hylan's office.

When the grumbling had ceased, the actors had moved to their positions. Bobbie had moved stage left and was at the edge of the stage now standing just over the orchestra pit. She took over the thread of the narrative from here.

'As we established earlier, with Lieutenant Grimm's help, the attempt on Mr Stanton's life could not really have been done from the stage. Quite simply, you are either too far away, or in the wrong position, to throw a knife. It would have been impossible for any of you to move without the others being aware of this.'

'What about the people in the audience. I gather there were some mobsters around him. Friends of his no doubt,' sneered Crane. 'It's perfectly obvious that they had the best opportunity to kill Stanton and probably good reason too.' This comment was made with some sorrow in his voice. He looked at Crina. 'I'm sorry my dear. You must face facts about Felix. He was mixed up with some very dangerous people and it's cost him his life.'

'Here, here,' said Crotch, still sitting in Smiley's seat. 'About the only thing you and I will every agree on Crane.'

This earned a frosty look from his client, and her former husband. Tears began to fall freely from Crina, once more and, for once, this was not a performance.

'It's true that Mr Stanton was involved in illegal activities,' conceded Bobbie, 'but this is not what cost him his life. Although I suppose it's difficult to know where gambling ends and greed begins.'

'Detective Nolan, you have the gun the that was used on stage that night. Detective Yeats is manning the lights. Now I won't ask you to redo the dramatic ending to the play, but I will ask Detective Yeats and Detective Nolan to help with the key aspects of this.' At this point, Bobbie extracted from her pocket, a tennis ball. 'I don't have a knife, but this should suffice for our purposes.'

Bobbie held the ball up and walked over to the side of the stage. She nodded to Yeats. Moments later the lights went out. Seconds later there was a gunshot, courtesy of Detective Nolan. It took a few more seconds and then the lights came back on. Bobbie was standing at the side of the stage where she had been when the lights went out. She was holding her hands up. They were empty.

'Over here,' said Devenish. He held up the tennis ball.

It took a few seconds for everyone to understand what had been done. And the answer to that, was not very much, in one person's view. Jason Crane exploded.

'Now look,' he roared at Flynn. 'I've had just about enough of this charade.'

To be fair, Flynn was not too far away from the actor either geographically or emotionally on this point. He had no idea what exactly Bobbie had proved. However, to say as much would have smacked of disloyalty to his daughter who had assured him that the reconstruction would have to be done twice as they had travelled over from their house.

'Mr Crane, you are in no position to lecture anyone on the subject of having your time wasted. I believe my daughter is going to repeat what she did a few moments ago, this time with the lights on so that we can all see.'

Unable to resist the opportunity for mischief, Dick Devenish began to clap Flynn and shouted 'Bravo. Encore.' This earned him glares from the two men who were both the subject of his praise as well as his sarcasm.

'Thank you, Dick,' said Bobbie, in a dry tone. 'As they say in theatre, we'll do this again, "from the top". Dick, may I have my tennis ball back?'

The ball was thrown up onto the stage and Bobbie, rather impressively, caught it one-handed which earned another "Bravo" from Devenish.

'I want you to imagine that the lights go out,' said Bobbie, pausing dramatically before adding in a slightly louder voice, 'now.'

There followed a silence and then Bobbie, from her position on the stage suddenly jumped down into the orchestra pit, landing just as Nolan fired another blank from the gun. She had removed her shoes which enabled her to land on the floor of the pit without anyone hearing her

Bobbie stepped forward, and lobbed the tennis ball to Dick Devenish from a position that allowed her a full view of her friend, from between Tommy Hart and Frida. 'No one would have heard the landing because of the gunshot.'

Then, moving swiftly, she ran up the steps and back onto the stage. Then she said, 'The shot caused a few screams in the audience, if you remember. This enabled the person to return to their position. And then the lights came back on.'

Silence greeted the demonstration. Then Crane spoke once more.

'Fine you know how I did it. I admit it.'

'Hogwash,' replied Flynn. 'If I hear another word from you Crane, I will arrest you.'

This silenced Crane, but he not only looked far from happy, but his face also seemed genuinely to have turned pale.

'No Mr Crane said Bobbie. It wasn't you. You know as well as I do, who tried to kill Mr Stanton here. And who then succeeded to do so in the hospital. It was the only person who could conceivably have done what I just did.'

'Stop,' said Crane. 'I beg you.' Everyone ignored him. Their eyes were transfixed by the sight of Detective Yeats, who had now appeared, and was moving down the steps that led to the audience seats. On the other side, two policemen were walking down the aisle, between the orchestra pit and the front row.

Crina Colbeck screamed as she saw what was about to happen.

'Stop them,' she shouted.

Tommy Hart jumped to his feet, eyes wide with fear. He took one look at Yeats and decided his chances were better with the two policemen. He ran towards them, but just before he reached them, he leapt over the first row into the second. And then the third row, but the patrolmen and Yeats were hunting him down remorselessly.

There was no escape. They had him trapped. He stopped on the fourth row, as he saw the patrolmen walking down both that aisle and the one in front, while Yeats was also walking towards him.

Suddenly he pulled out a knife. It gleamed malevolently in the theatre spotlight.

Yeats and the two patrolmen stopped for a moment.

'Put the knife down,' said Jason Crane. His voice was almost a sob of anguish. Tommy looked up onto the stage. He shook his head wildly. They could hear him gasping for air like a rabid animal trying desperately to escape a trap.

'I can't. I can't let them take me,' came the agonized reply.

'Enough,' replied Crane. 'It's over. It's over...son.'

33

The worst period of Bobbie's life was when she was losing her mother, Nancy. Knowing that nothing could be done and sitting by as she slowly passed away was a prolonged agony. The pain would never truly leave her or Flynn. The death of someone close does that to you – innocence is lost. Everything changes. The gap that Bobbie's mother had left in their lives was simply too large to fill. Nothing would ever seem so bad after that day, because nothing could be worse than losing your mother. Except perhaps... but Bobbie never thought about that.

The morning after the arrest of Tommy Hart / Sorin Nilsson was perhaps the second worst she could remember, yet the day ended a little bit better than she could ever have hoped it would. It was a day that reminded her that impermanence is the only permanent thing we can be sure about.

The day after she had helped catch Tommy Hart was the day she walked out of her job.

The morning began early with her father who was in a talkative mood and Mrs Garcia, who was unusually silent as Flynn held court. Normally, her father tended to be rather spare when it came to providing the details of cases that he was working on. This had been a frustration for Nancy and, even more so for Bobbie, especially since she had become a reporter.

But Flynn owed Bobbie, and he was a man who paid his debts.

The previous night had ended with the arrest of Tommy Hart. Flynn and the other policemen had taken Tommy to Midtown North. Her father hadn't returned home until after midnight. By then Bobbie was already in bed, mentally writing the story which would adorn the front page.

'Good work from you and Nolan,' admitted Flynn, a little grumpily as he bit into toast, prepared by Mrs Garcia.

'Your acclaim is duly noted,' said Bobbie, dryly, which earned a scowl from her father. 'Now, tell me, what happened last night?'

'He's not admitting anything, which is no surprise, but the evidence is mounting. His original alibi for the attempted murder was no better or worse than anyone else's on the stage, but you showed how he could have done it. He has no alibi for either the murder in the hospital or for Jeffries. He claims that he was alone in his apartment, which is bought and paid for by Miss Colbeck. Yet, the doorman at the apartments claims he saw Hart leave yesterday morning around five. He didn't return until after seven thirty. We have left a photograph of him with cab drivers in the area. Someone may have picked him up. If we can connect him to the hospital, then the case will be as good as over.'

'He may have taken the subway.'

'True, but I'm sure we'll find a cab driver who saw him. Anyway, there's still a few other things that we can prove and some we can find out. The fact that he was expelled from three schools for violent episodes using knives, that he spent six months in a circus in a knife act, the fact that there were several knives in his apartment and a wooden figure that had been used to practice throwing a knife against. It's an open and shut case now. Miss Colbeck wanted Crotch to help him, but he's having nothing to do with it. That tells me something too.'

Bobbie nodded as she listened to her father. The previous evening, before Flynn had returned, Nolan had been able to find out more about Tommy's troubled past. It included a number of arrests for violent conduct, but all charges had been dropped thanks to the influence of Smiley and Crina. From this they had learned how Tommy had been expelled from various private schools. It explained, in Bobbie's mind, why Crina had been absent from the theatre for the last few years. Many had assumed it was grief at losing her husband. Bobbie was convinced it was due to the wayward behaviour of her son.

'Have you established motive yet?'

'That is something that we will have to work out. Personally, I think the kid might be a psychopath. Even if this is not the case, he's violent. Dangerous. Jealous of Smiley. Any number of things.' Flynn fell silent for a few moments and then he fixed his disquieting gaze on his daughter. 'Tell me, Bobbie, did you interview him at any point? Alone?'

Flynn was no longer a detective. This was the father speaking. The tone was subdued, not angry. Full of regret. Full of concern. Full of love. Bobbie, who normally bristled at this line of questioning, did not do so on this occasion.

'Yes…briefly after the first attempt on Mr Stanton's life,' admitted Bobbie, looking away from her father. Sometimes his stare was just too much.

Flynn exhaled audibly but said nothing to this. Everything that could be said at that moment had been said many times before. Nothing had changed. Nothing would change, he realised.

He was wrong.

Bobbie knew something was wrong, long before she set foot in the Tribune building. It was barely seven thirty on Park Row. The air was crisp and fresh, carrying the scent of blooming flowers, from the nearby park, mingled with the aroma of freshly brewed coffee. A couple of street vendors were setting up their stalls and Eric the newsboy was carrying what looked like two tons of newspapers under each arm.

He was putting the batches of papers down as Bobbie stepped out of her cab. As she paid the driver, she heard the newsboy call out something that chilled her.

'Smiley Stanton murderer in jail. Read all about it.'

She spun around and walked rapidly over to the young boy. He could not have been more than twelve years old. Underneath his baker boy cap, he wore a smile that never left his face from early morning until night.

Bobbie handed him two cents and asked for the New York American.

'Here you are Red, and thanks.'

Bobbie always gave him a generous tip. He watched Bobbie set off and once more began to call out the headline.

And the headline was from her story, or at least, some of it. She looked at the headline. Its big black letters seemed to taunt her.

SON OF CRINA COLBECK HELD FOR MURDER

Bobbie looked at the name on the byline. There were two words guaranteed to send her temperature gauge skyrocketing: Ade Barton. She quickly scanned through the article. It was clear he knew some of what had happened the previous evening, but not the story of the arrest in the theatre and how Bobbie had uncovered how the attempted murder had taken place. He did know about Tommy Hart though. At least, everything that had been revealed by Mrs Alexandrescu. How could Barton have found all of this out?

There seemed only one likely answer to this, and her heart seemed to shatter into pieces.

As quickly as she felt the anguish, it disappeared, replaced by anger. Barton had acted duplicitously, of that she had no doubt, and she was going to let Thornton Kent know.

The first person she met when she reached the top of the stairs in the Tribune building, leading to the newspaper's offices was someone who rarely arrived before ten in the morning.

'Roberta,' said a distraught Peregrine Wimslow. 'I've been a rather silly boy.'

Bobbie went over and hugged him.

'It's not your fault, Perry. Barton knew what he was doing and that was stealing my story. He's not even got the full story right. Tell me what happened.' They sat down on a bench on the first-floor landing.

'It was after you dropped me off. I went to the Two Hundred Club as you know. I didn't see Barton at first, as I was telling people that I might have cracked the Smiley Stanton murder and that they would read about it the next day. They asked me who and I said that it was rather close to home but left it there.' Perry paused for a second.

'But you didn't quite leave it there, did you?' murmured Bobbie.

Perry shook his head. He was weeping disconsolately on Bobbie's shoulder. There was no question that he was feeling wretched even when you factored in a certain amount of artistic license, an ever-present dimension of the Englishman's personality.

'Barton was at the table now and buying drinks. He said he was celebrating. I'm not sure he really said why that was, but I think I know now, Roberta. Oh, I'm such an old fool. I really have messed things up for you.'

'Really, Perry. I'm not angry.' She was, of course, just not at the Englishman. There were other people with targets on their back at that moment. 'Now Perry, it's obviously been a late night and a rather early morning for you. I suggest you go back home and rest up. I'll deal with this.'

'I have a gun if you want to kill Barton,' said Perry, peeling a Derringer out of his pocket and showing it to Bobbie, hopefully.

'Tempting, but I think I have another idea that might hit him where it hurts,' agreed Bobbie, a glint in her eyes that no novelist worth their salt would pass up the opportunity to describe as "steely".

'Don't do anything rash, Roberta, urged Perry. Given that he'd just offered her his gun with the suggestion that she use it on Ade Barton, it did rather beg the question as to what constituted "rash" in an Englishman's world.

Bobbie left Perry and marched into the newsroom. There were two other people there. A political sketch writer called Lester Lovell, a man who always emphasised the second syllable of his surname.

The other man was Thornton Kent.

They were chatting outside his office. The arrival of Bobbie, a little earlier than normal for her, caused both men to stop chatting and the newspaper editor to frown.

Normally the sight of Kent frowning was enough to reduce most men to a quivering wreck and even Bobbie would admit to a hint of disquiet when his eyes were fixed on you. Not this time.

She marched over to the editor and said, 'We need to talk.'

Kent was no one's pushover. He snapped back at Bobbie, 'I'm talking to Lovell.' He emphasised the second syllable which brought a half smile from the sketch writer.

Bobbie fixed her stare on Lovell and said, 'I need to speak to Mr Kent now. Would you mind?'

Lovell didn't mind, but he was certainly going to sit nearby and enjoy the floor show.

'In my office, now,' snarled Kent, eyes flaring and starting to turn away from Bobbie.

'No,' said Bobbie. Her voice was far from a honeyed lover's whisper either. 'She knew part of Kent's power emanated from the feeling that everyone had when they entered his office. It was his kingdom. His domain. That said, he was pretty impressive outside it too.

'What did you say?'

Bobbie was in no mood to answer questions from Kent or anyone else. Her response was a low, threatening whisper.

'I said "no". You'll listen to what I have to say right here. Ade Barton has stolen that story. I found all this out last night. Take Ade Barton's name off that story. Ask Perry, he was with me.'

'No. He wrote it, you didn't,' retorted Kent, moving towards her. It was a threatening move, but Bobbie was too angry to back down now.

This was undeniable. So, Bobbie tried a different tack.

'Put my name on the story. First.'

'No,' replied Kent. 'Next time stay late and write the story yourself.'

This was the plan. It was the last resort, but Kent had shown her no support. She would make him regret that.

'Very well,' said Bobbie. 'I shall write the true story.' She said this in a calm voice which Kent should really have had suspicions about. He stopped in his tracks and stared at Bobbie as if trying to figure out his next response. This, after a few seconds, was to shake his head before turning and returning to his office.

Bobbie began typing her story:

```
Last night I showed the police how
Tommy Hart tried to kill Smiley Stanton.
```

The story took twenty minutes to write. Then she ripped the final page from the typewriter. Her next action was to scribble two words on a piece of paper then she walked over to Kent's office and looked through the large window which allowed Kent to survey his kingdom. There were now three other people in the office. All of them from the print department. He waved for her to come in. Bobbie shook her head. She held up the piece of paper on which she had scribbled the two words. It read:

I QUIT

Then she pointed as if to the heavens but, in reality, Kent interpreted it as the offices of The New York Tribune which was a newspaper they shared the building with. Much to Bobbie's great satisfaction, Kent's eyes widened. He realised what she was going to do. The great scoop that Bobbie was holding was now bound for the front page of one of their rivals along with one of his best reporters.

Before Kent had time to react any further, Bobbie turned away from him and strode out towards the doors of the newsroom. She ignored the sound of Kent's office door opening and him demanding that she come back.

She could hear footsteps behind her. Kent was obviously chasing her. But he was too late. She paused briefly and stared at the office door. It read 'Obituaries'.

The first, and only, moment of doubt she had was when she reached the corridor and saw her old office. It was where she had started her career in newspapers. It was where she had worked with Buckner Fanley. Oddly, she felt a little guilty about leaving Fanley. He'd never treated her warmly. This had never mattered to her very much because he gave her something so much more important. Respect. Yet she had to go. Trust had been broken.

The footsteps were louder now. Kent was walking not running and she could hear the angry echo of his shoes on the parquet floor.

'Come back here now, Flynn.'

She could not return now. Like much of what was in that room, something had died for her. She thought of her father. Would this make him happy? She would have more time for Violet. And right at that moment, as she went up the steps towards the New York Tribune offices with her story, the sound of Kent's voice fading behind her, she could think of nothing she wanted more

Epilogue

Hotel Claridge, 1500 Broadway, New York: early April

The evening after Bobbie posted her story with the New York Tribune, before exiting the building to begin a new life as who knew what, a group of men met in a hotel on Broadway called the Hotel Claridge. The hotel had become a favoured hang out for members of the Broadway mob.

Arnold Rothstein surveyed the men in the room with a feeling of fatherly pride. Most were younger than him, raw and violently ambitious. Yet, all looked upon him as something of a mentor. He had taught them so much and they appreciated this. Because of Rothstein, people like Lucky Luciano, Bugsy Segal and Meyer Lansky knew how to dress and conduct themselves like businessmen. He gave them a veneer of respectability in a business that was brutally terrifying.

One member of the group was not from the Broadway mob. This was Giuseppe "Joe the Boss" Masseria. Like Luciano, he was a native of Sicily, but had spent the last twenty years in New York. A heavyset man in his mid-thirties, his business interests were very much in the same line as those around the table. His empire took in Harlem and Little Italy.

There were two other men in the room, aside from these criminal luminaries, two men who certainly would not have been mistaken for mobsters. The first was a man with a few tufts of hair peeping out over his ears and a pair of half-moon spectacles.

Clement Crispin was by no means completely without fear being amongst such men. However, he trusted Mr Rothstein and, more importantly, Mr Rothstein trusted him. Crispin had always rather hoped that he could retire from his old trade, yet his desire to be part of a theatre had somewhat undermined his good intentions.

And it was the future of the theatre that was under discussion just at that moment. Arnold Rothstein was chairing the meeting.

'Gentlemen, this meeting is called to order. As you see, we have an old friend who does us the honour of joining our get-together.'

All eyes turned to a burly man, dressed in a tailor-made suit and chomping on a cigar. If Reed Crotch III was afraid of being in such company, then he certainly was hiding it well. As alluded to earlier in this chronicle, being lumbered with a surname like his had given him a hide as thick as the New York phone directory. Crotch caught the eye of each man and nodded to them. A thick hide was one thing, but he was no fool either. These were men that demanded respect, whether they had earned it or not. It cost him nothing to show them something.

'With the sad passing of Felix and the capture of our friend, Captain Frank O'Riordan, we are, once again, without a safe place where our clients can enjoy themselves without interference. Thank you to Lucky and Joe for their suggestions on this important matter. They are, duly, noted. The sudden end to the game the other night has, somewhat, put our business venture with the theatre under a spotlight, if you will excuse the pun, that we can do without. The time has come, sadly, for us to consider the future of the Century Playhouse.'

Joe Masseria leaned forward and looked as if he might ask a question. Rothstein paused, fixing his eyes upon them. However, it was Meyer Lansky who stepped in first.

Lansky was very much a lieutenant to Rothstein. Like his boss, he was more businessman than mobster despite his relative youth. At twenty years old, Lansky, a Russian by birth, had risen through Rothstein's organisation because of his intellect, rather than any predisposition towards violence.

'I believe, Mr Rothstein, the time has come to sell,' said Lansky with an accent as thick as borscht, which had been crafted in the icy winters of Russia, before escaping to the civilised world of New York crime.

Rothstein noted that Luciano was nodding at this. Of all the men here, Luciano was the one who Rothstein both admired and, perhaps, feared. He combined the business acumen of Lansky and, dare he say it, himself, but was also capable of meting out the kind of violence that was certainly more Masseria's domain. This made him an increasingly influential figure in their world.

Joe Masseria spoke up now. He was not as polished as the others who were by no means polished themselves. There was a determined expression on his face, which suggested either anger or trapped wind.

'I think that this unfortunate event is regretful, and I think it something that I speak about many times. I think I make a big mistake, in investing in this enterprise.'

Rothstein frowned at this. It was not as if he had not forewarned the Sicilian.

'Mr Crotch has a suggestion that our friend Mr Crispin believes merits attention.'

Despite his innocuous appearance, Crispin did hold some sway with one and all as a "numbers" man.

'What is this proposal?' asked Masseria.

All eyes fell on Crispin and Crotch, who looked and sounded like a firm of successful undertakers.

Crotch held his hand out to Crispin to begin.

'Mr Crotch has proposed that he and his client take the Century Playhouse off our hands.'

This was greeted with a few heads nodding around the table. None of them had really understood the rationale for having it. It was cheaper to buy policemen than worry about such inconvenient matters like tax.

'My client, Miss Colbeck, would like to raise her stake in the theatre from thirty three percent to one hundred percent,' said Crotch.

'What does that mean for us?' asked Masseria, which was the question on all their minds except, Rothstein, who already knew what the offer was.

Crotch named his price. To say it was met with a rather ominous and stony silence would be understating it. Luciano's mouth curled slightly downward, and his eyes flicked towards Rothstein, who was as impassive as ever. Lansky blew his cheeks out and said, 'That is daylight robbery Crotch. You're a bigger criminal than we are.'

Crispin stepped in at this point, to nip any potential opposition in the bud. Personally, he was in line to receive a five-thousand-dollar bonus from Crotch if he convinced these men to sell. This was his moment.

'Gentlemen, the sale of the theatre will represent a seventy-five-thousand-dollar loss on our original investment. However, I think I can manage to make this loss appear on your tax returns as a one hundred percent loss to each of you from which you can offset many times this amount in mitigation of your taxes.' For another five minutes, Crispin went into a detail that was reassuringly dull about how such sleight of hand with the books would see that the gentlemen around the table were not out of pocket on the transaction.

'You mean we make money while we lose it?' said Luciano.

'If you remember, Lucky, this is always the point,' said Rothstein with a shrug.

'You are happy with this?' asked Masseria. He sounded sceptical.

'No,' admitted Rothstein. 'I am greatly disappointed. The theatre, the game and most of all for our dear friend Felix. But I see that we cannot continue, the game is up, gentlemen. I vote we sell to Mr Crotch. He is giving us a fair price and he is not a man who will ask too many questions when we agree contracts. We must, Giuseppe, be seen to make a loss on this. Enough of a loss that we can write it off as Mr Crispin has so kindly outlined. I suggest we take a vote.'

The vote passed with only one dissenter, who abstained, Joe Masseria.

'I hope that this will not prevent us working together again, Giuseppe,' said Rothstein who genuinely had no desire for conflict. There was no profit in gang warfare.

'I am interested in a few things,' said Masseria, 'but, no, there is no trouble from me.'

'What are you interested to know, Giuseppe?'

'Are we going after the people who ruined this operation for us?'

'Who do you mean, Giuseppe?' asked Rothstein. His voice was quiet, almost chillingly so.

'The cops, Flynn and Nolan? Nolan sold us down the river.'

Rothstein was not happy to hear this and made no attempt to hide his displeasure.

'This is dangerous territory Giuseppe. We want the New York Police Department on our side. We cannot go around killing their hard-working members. It's bad for business, bad for recruitment, bad for everyone.'

Masseria was not happy with this response but was old enough to know that undermining Rothstein in front of so many young and impressionable mobsters was not in his interest. Yet.

'Was that all, Giuseppe?' asked Rothstein, one eyebrow raised in a manner that communicates a desire to move on.

'There was one other thing. This kid. Crina Colbeck's son,' began Masseria. 'He makes lots of problems for us, a lot of problems. He has cost us a craps game, one police captain and now we sell the theatre at a loss. What happens to him?'

Rothstein turned to Crotch at this point. The lawyer was smiling.

'I doubt my client is particularly worried what happens to Mr Hart. Let me correct a misapprehension on your part. Mr Hart and my client are no more related than we are.'

This brought a smile from Rothstein and a few looks of surprise from others around the table.

'But I read the paper yesterday,' said Masseria, utterly baffled by this revelation.

This brought a ripple of laughter in the room, partly because it was news that Masseria could even read and partly because Rothstein gave voice to a moment later.

'You shouldn't believe everything you read in the papers.'

Even Masseria had the grace to smile at this and he shrugged good-naturedly.

'My client adopts the boy when he is three years old,' explained Crotch. 'He is trouble from the start, I understand. My client, sadly, cannot have children. You know how it is, but she wants to have a child. So, she adopts this boy from someone in a circus. A knife thrower who accidentally kills his wife with a knife, but maybe it was not so accidental as all that. The police do not think so and he goes to Sing Sing. My client feels sorry for the boy and then, when she sees what he is like, not so much. But it is too late then. The boy is nothing but trouble whatever my client does. He costs her a few years of her career. He costs her marriage to the only man she truly loves. I think she gives up on him. She puts him in a circus. He is thrown out because he likes to hurt people. He is put in prison, but still, he comes back to my client. She gives him a job at the Playhouse. He tries to kill Felix. What am I saying? He kills Felix. This is a bad boy, gentlemen.'

'She must be angry at him for killing Felix,' pointed out Masseria.

'You know, this makes no impression on my client, maybe he does his adoptive mother a good turn for once. Who knows? Every cloud has a silver lining.'

'Why do you say that?' asked Lansky, now very curious.

'Well, look at it this way. My client no longer has a husband who is involved in things she disapproves of, but she has her own theatre now. I think she will recover from her grief quite quickly.'

The End

If you enjoyed Opening Night Knives, please consider leaving a review – this helps improve my sales and it means I will be able to write more in this series!!

Research Notes

This is a work of fiction. However, it references real-life individuals. Gore Vidal, in his introduction to Lincoln, writes that placing history in fiction or fiction in history has been unfashionable since Tolstoy and that the result can be accused of being neither. He defends the practice, pointing out that writers from Aeschylus to Shakespeare to Tolstoy have done so with, not inconsiderable, success and merit.

I have mentioned several key real-life individuals and events in this novel. My intention, in the following section, is to explain a little more about their connection to this period and this story.

John Hylan (1868 – 1936)

John Hylan was elected as Mayor of New York in 1918 and served two terms before quitting in 1925. After his term as mayor, Hylan spent much time attacking the "interests," arguing that industrial concentration gave great power to individuals to influence politics and impoverished the poor. In this regard, Hylan was very much ahead of his time. The absence of social media probably limited his ability both to 'prove' his theories as well as to spread them.

Lucky Luciano (1897 – 1962)

Charles "Lucky" Luciano was born Salvatore Lucania in Sicily. He started his criminal career in the Five Points Gang and was instrumental in the development of the National Crime Syndicate. Luciano was a protégé of Jewish mobster, Arnold Rothstein who was famed for bringing a business-like edge to criminal activity in New York. He was convicted in 1936 on vice charges and sentenced to 30 to 50 years in prison. Legend has it that during World War II an agreement was struck with the Department of the Navy to support the Allied war effort in Italy. In 1946, for his alleged wartime cooperation, his sentence was commuted on the condition that he be deported to Italy where he lived under tight surveillance.

Giuseppe (Joe) Masseria (1886 - 1931)

Joe Masseria was born in Sicily before his family moved to the US in 1902. He was involved in crime from an early age, convicted of burglary in 1913 and serving a period of time in prison. He joined the Morello crime family and was the first to recruit Lucky Luciano. He eventually took over the gang with Morello becoming a *consigliere* (a mentor). The next few years of Prohibition saw Morello ramp up the family's aggressive activities across various areas of crime. This brought them not only into conflict with the forces of law and order but also other crime families.

Masseria's death is popularly attributed to his one-time protégé - Lucky Luciano. The story goes that he was lured to a meeting in Coney Island where he was murdered by a man who would then take over many of the rackets that had been headed up by his victim.

Meyer Lansky (1902 - 1983)

Meyer Lansky (born Maier Suchowljansky) was born in Grodno, Russia in what is now called Belarus. He moved to the US in 1911. For over fifty years he was a senior figure in the Mob, outlasting many of his contemporaries who were either caught by the police or did not survive a particularly brutal part of American history.

Lansky was a protégé of Arnold Rothstein and a senior lieutenant in the Jewish Mafia in New York. He played an instrumental role following Rothstein's death in consolidating the actives of the Italian American Mafia. He supported the war effort which may have allowed him to escape prison and certainly allowed him to spend a few years in Cuba before the revolution where, once more, he became heavily involved in gambling operations in the country, just as he had in the US and beyond.

After the revolution he returned to the US and ended up in Israel to escape tax evasion charges. Israel did not extradite citizens at that point. Then it did. Lansky returned to the US and had to testify against former colleagues. He spent the last few years of his life in relative poverty in Miami.

About the Author

Jack Murray was born in Northern Ireland but has spent over half his life living just outside London, except for some periods spent in Australia, Monte Carlo, and the US.

An artist, as well as a writer, Jack's work features in collections around the world and he has exhibited in Britain, Ireland, and Monte Carlo.

A spin off series from the Kit Aston novels was published in 2020 featuring Aunt Agatha as a young woman solving mysterious murders.

Another spin off series features Inspector Jellicoe. It is set in the late 1950's/early 1960's.

Jack finished work on a World War II trilogy in 2022. The three books look at the war from both the British and the German side. They have been published through Lume Books and are available on Amazon.

Acknowledgements

It is not possible to write a book on your own. There are contributions from so many people either directly or indirectly over many years. Listing them all would be an impossible task.

Special mention therefore should be made to my wife and family who have been patient and put up with my occasional grumpiness when working on this project.

My brother, Edward, has helped in proofing and made supportive comments that helped me tremendously. Thank you, too, Dave Robertson, Debra Cox, David Sinclair, Anna Wietrzychowska and Patricia Goulden who have been a wonderful help in reducing the number of irritating errors that have affected my earlier novels. A word of thanks to Charles Gray and Brian Rice who have provided legal and accounting support.

My late father and mother both loved books. They encouraged a love of reading in me. In particular, they liked detective books, so I must tip my hat to the two greatest writers of this genre, Sir Arthur and Dame Agatha.

Following writing, comes the business of marketing. My thanks to Mark Hodgson and Sophia Kyriacou for their advice on this important area. Additionally, a shout out to the wonderful folk on 20Booksto50k.

Finally, my thanks to the teachers who taught and nurtured a love of writing.

Printed in Great Britain
by Amazon